THE IMPOSTOR

And Other Dark Tales

MARLENA FRANK

Edited by: Vicki Greer

http://vickiedits.com/

Cover Art by: Shivana Brhamadat

https://sinsvalentine.com/

Cover Lettering by: Kelley M. Frank

http://morbidsmile.com

ISBN EB: 978-1-955854-00-9

ISBN PB: 978-1-955854-01-6

For those fascinated by monsters

Preface

I was a scaredy-cat as a child. Everything frightened me. Being a shy, scrawny kid, the world was a big, scary place, and my imagination was in overdrive. I lived in my head, playing out stories with fantasy characters in fictional situations, but when the lights went out, that spark of creativity meant the monsters felt real.

That shy, frightened little girl came to my mind a lot while writing these stories. I thought of what terrified her years ago. Those dark woods hid all sorts of creatures, and that movement in the corner of my eye wasn't a mere shadow.

What lies ahead may have been spawned by my childish nightmares, but these tales are far more disturbing. From fantasy stories full of love and discovery, to dark humor and identity, to exploring the darkest corners of the human psyche, these might keep you up at night.

Enjoy, but leave the lights on. Just in case.

Marlena
5/31/2021

PART I
THE BEAUTIFUL

Almost

WE STAND IN LINE WAITING OUR TURN. THERE ARE ONLY A few people in front of me, with a long snaking trail still behind me. The woman passing out tickets only has a sliver of them left and I worry I won't get one in time. One, two, three, the tickets disappear, and the sliver grows smaller. When I reach the table, and the final blue ticket is placed in my hand, I'm giddy with relief.

I step aside and hear cries of pain and outrage behind me, but I clutch the ticket to my chest and don't turn back. With one hand on my suitcase, I head to the tunnel. I hear a child crying on the floor, a woman shouting, and two armored guards raise their guns in warning. I don't turn back. I don't want to see the ones left behind or their desperation.

When I exit the tunnel, I gasp. The ship nearly fills the sky. Families cry and hug one another here in the fenced-in yard, in stark contrast to the tension outside. When the ground trembles beneath my feet, a frightened hush falls over everyone. I might be safe soon, but the others won't be. I allow myself to turn and see the long line of people winding down the hill until they're out of sight. From here I can't see the fear and hatred in their eyes, but I know it's there. I can't blame them.

As another tremor shakes the ground, I know none of those people will make it off this ruined planet in time. Regardless of what ships are scheduled to come, regardless of the promises that were made, this will be the final ship to leave.

I almost return my ticket and let someone else take my place.

Almost.

The Strangers

Everything was so very different now. The snow
went on and on as far out as the light from the torches went,
making the forest floor look like a giant sloping pillow that
fell into distant shadows. Kayla liked watching it – she was
always curious to see what kinds of animals were brave
enough or desperate enough to venture out into the frozen
wasteland. In the back room she could hear Mama screaming,
and Kayla pursed her lips, wishing she could drown out the
noise. Outside it was completely peaceful, silent, even serene.

She pulled her layered sweaters down over her fingers and
wiped away the fog on the window that threatened her view
outside. It wasn't as if she would have minded a little brother,
but they all knew the chances were slim that he would
survive. It was an unspoken truth that no one had the
courage to mutter. This was her third potential sibling, but
Kayla was sick of them. The last two had passed away before
ever reaching their first birthday. The self-proclaimed leaders
had been bickering late into the night, trying to decide the
fate of that little boy – was there enough food for another
mouth? Would Mama be healthy enough to nurse him? These

were all questions that they didn't have answers to, and Kayla now found herself hating her little brother before he had even entered the world.

As a child she had wished there were more kids to play with and wondered what might lay beyond the thick blanket of snow. Now she understood. Snow was always on the ground and temperatures dipped beyond freezing every day. Their food supply was always near depletion. Mama said it hadn't always been this way. Eighteen years ago, these skeletal pines had once been surrounded by giant oaks and flowery cherry trees. That field of snow outside was what she called a 'parking lot' and their building had once been the home of multiple families called an 'apartment'. Some families left to search for help, but they were never seen again. Kayla was young at the time, but she watched the woods for days waiting for them to return.

"You over here moping again?"

Jason was the only other kid near her age she knew, a year older than her but also a good half foot shorter. He had a mop of black hair and pale skin. He probably wanted to escape the noise as much as she did.

"No, just... thinking."

He pulled a chair over. "Your mom seems to be doing okay."

Kayla shrugged. She wished she felt as apathetic as she was trying to appear. "What about *him*?"

He sighed. "You mean your brother? So far he's doing fine."

"Good." That wasn't kind to say, she knew that, but she couldn't put words to her confused feelings. Part of her wished she was in the back room with them, helping some-how, but she was also afraid of seeing her baby brother be born, knowing that he was likely going to ultimately die like the others. She couldn't allow herself to get attached again, so she sat and stared at the snow instead.

Another wail of pain from the back room and Dad rushed through with a mess of bloody rags clutched between his hands. Kayla gave the rags a long look before turning to stare out the window again.

Jason leaned in close. "You know, we don't have to stay here. I was going to go take a look at the rabbit hole again and see what I could find. Want to come?"

There wouldn't be anything, she knew that already. There hadn't been rabbits in that hole for weeks. But she jumped at the chance of escaping the screams and her thoughts about her little brother and Mama. No, just Mama. She didn't need to think about her little brother. She sprang to her feet and donned her thick clothes for the outdoors.

Jason smiled as he followed. "I take it that's a yes."

***

JASON LIKED TO THINK THAT EVEN IF THEY WEREN'T betrothed, he would've asked for Kayla's hand. He'd read plenty of books on the subject: boy meets girl, boy woos girl, boy and girl marry.

Sometimes he longed for the place Mr. Burgins called 'The South' before the entire planet had dipped into a deep freeze. There hadn't been any warning that the great freeze was coming. One day it was hot and sunny with temperatures boiling in the summer heat, and the next it was fifty below with folks dying in the snow. Over the next few years, everyone who hadn't died from exposure had to deal with starvation. The animals were taken off guard too, and it took about two years for the deer to die off. After that came the birds, who migrated to whatever warmer climate they could find. Hundreds of people in their apartment complex died off – most went mad.

Then the families – including his and Kayla's parents – decided that to survive they needed to start their own families. There would be no rescuers, and there would certainly be no escaping. Squirrels and rabbits were the common meal – they made up the few animals that were somehow capable of surviving. Occasionally they would see birds high overhead, but there was no way they could kill them.

There was a time in Jason's youth when he remembered oil lamps – smooth flames with a knob that turned the heat up or down, but apparently what short supply of oil they had at the time hadn't lasted long. These days torches were a rule of thumb.

Kayla was gearing up, and Jason joined her, keeping silent until she'd donned her mask and goggles.

"You ready?" His voice was muffled behind the scarves and knitted mask. He hooked the knife onto his belt and shouldered one of the bows and a quiver of arrows. They never knew what to expect as they ventured out into the freezing wilderness.

KAYLA WAS TRUDGING ON AHEAD OF HIM, HER BOOTS leaving bucket-pail holes in the snow with each step. Jason had to trot to catch up.

"Wait up!"

She didn't turn around but at least she paused, leaning against one of the enormous pines. The snow fell heavily and the flakes of white clung to her sweater and what little of her blonde hair was poking out under her sock hat.

His breath came out in foggy mists as he caught up to her. "You're really pissed about all this, aren't you?"

She sighed and glanced around the woods as if to make sure they were truly alone, as if anyone would be out here other than them. "Would you think terribly of me if I said that I didn't want to have a brother?"

Jason dug his hands into the pockets of his coat. "I think you're just upset. Everybody's been upset over this."

"He's such trouble already. Another person to feed – as if we're not already starving."

Jason sighed. He understood her position. A single animal was being stretched to feed all of them for a week at a time, and only in the form of a thin soup. Having to share that with another person was worrying, especially as squirrels and rabbits were becoming harder and harder to find. "Did you ever think that maybe they had the same questions about us when we were little?"

Kayla laughed, turning to look out into the deep shadows of the woods. "They didn't have any other kids when you and I came around, remember? They were probably thrilled."

"I'd like to think so, but my old man gets to talking sometimes when he's been out walking a long time by himself. He gets dark thoughts, and sometimes he's pretty bitter about the whole thing."

"The whole thing? You mean having you as a son?"

Jason shrugged but he could tell that she understood exactly what he meant. Everybody had their problems, and in their tight-knit group everybody knew about them. Kayla's frustration wasn't a secret, but she needed to get it under control.

A cold wind came up, whipping through the sentry trees, and showers of snow fell from the treetops. A shiver went up his spine, a familiar warning. The temperature was dropping. Sometimes it would be a slight change, other times it would plummet. "We should head back in, Kayla. Feels like we're getting a drop. We can check out the rabbit hole later once it's passed."

She held up a hand to him. "Shh! Did you hear that?"

He turned toward the woods and strained his ears for any sound: clumps of snow falling, the rustling of the pines in the wind, and... something else. "What is that?"

She shook her head. "That can't be a bear."

Mr. Burgins swore up and down that he'd seen one while out on hunting duty last year. It was one of the reasons any group outside was required to carry a weapon with them. Jason pulled out his bow and pulled back an arrow. He aimed it into the darkness past the edge of light provided by the torches. They were a good fifty feet from the entrance to the complex, and running was a decidedly bad option if it was a wild animal. If it were big enough, though, it might be enough to feed them for weeks.

"Get behind me, Kayla," he whispered, biting off his outer glove so he could hold the arrow straighter.

She backed up slowly. "That can't be a bear, Jason. That sounds... mechanical."

It was true, the noise was whirring like the battery powered shaver Martin sometimes pulled out to demonstrate electric current. Jason wasn't sure what to do, and the temperature kept falling. He began to shiver. His fingers felt numb.

"It's too cold out here," Kayla said as she folded her arms in. Slowly they started backing up to the complex, even as the whirring became louder and the wind picked up. The snow was coming down heavily as they let themselves into the building.

Kayla pulled off her face mask and goggles in a single motion, moving over to the window to get a better view of the creature. "Dad, come quick!"

Something was making its way out of the woods. It had

four legs, but 'legs' weren't quite the right word for it. They moved in strange angles as the thing narrowly avoided walking into a tree. It was making a straight line toward the fire of one of the torches, and as it turned, Jason realized it was pulling a large, black, covered pod behind it.

Kayla's father, Martin, was suddenly by her side. "Whatever it is, that thing is man-made. Quick, we need to bring it in!"

"We can't," Jason said. "There's a bad drop going on. It's too dangerous."

"Then we'll have to move quickly. Who's coming with me?"

Kayla grabbed his arm. "I will, Dad."

He turned to Jason. "And you?"

Jason looked to the floor. He couldn't do it. Not in a cold snap like this. He'd already had one brush with hypothermia before and was missing a pinky toe on his left foot because of it. He couldn't face that level of cold again. "I'll keep an eye out for you inside."

JASON HADN'T BEEN LYING WHEN HE SAID THE temperature was plummeting. Kayla could immediately tell it was at least twenty degrees colder than it had been earlier, and she was grateful for the extra pair of gloves she had pulled on, as well as the second head mask. Still, the wind seeped cold through to her cheeks and she clung to her father's jacket as they moved through the sheets of falling snow.

She took hold of the red lifeline they kept tied at the entrance and tied the loose end tight around her waist. Dad did the same with a second line.

She took his hand in hers as they moved out toward the

whirring sound. It was still audible but got drowned out when the wind howled. Only a few feet out and the house disappeared behind them along with the start of the red line. All was hidden behind the gray blanket of wind and snow. There was no telling if they were headed in the right direction, and they could only trust their ears in brief gaps of wind as they searched for the creature with groping arms. When a black, gleaming head came into view, Dad grabbed onto it with both hands, nodding to the other side for Kayla to do the same. Now that she could get a better look at it, she saw that it was indeed made of metal, with black rubber covers on each of its legs. Over the whirring she thought she could hear the faint sound of a human voice. "Hello, my nam... ited States Milit...," but whatever message it was trying to say was lost in static.

She grabbed hold on the opposite side, putting her hands on its neck while Dad grabbed its body, and they directed it away from the torch and toward the entrance. It wobbled and resisted as it fumbled in the snow, and they had to work to force it to go where they wanted. The wind blew harder, and Kayla couldn't feel her fingers through the layers of gloves she wore.

"A little further!" Dad called to her, trying to be heard over the wind and the broken electronic message from the mechanical beast.

The red lines they were tied to disappeared into the gray cold. Dad was wrapping the line around his arm as they walked, one hand on the side of the metal beast. Kayla's teeth started chattering. Where was the door? How far had they walked out?

Her eyes watered and each step through the thick snow felt harder as the wind thrashed against them. The world had turned into cold gray snow. What if the red line got cut? They would get to the end of the red line and see it lying in the snow, lost like their home. Nothing but cold and gray in every direction.

Were they lost? Were they going in circles, like the time Jason got frostbite on his foot? Isolated in the blizzard, it felt as if the world had disappeared and they would be walking forever.

But then the vague shadow of the house emerged as though Kayla willed it. And she shed tears again, only this time for joy.

The door was opened only moments before they reached it, so that they were able to lead the four-legged animal directly inside — including the long black pod behind it. Jason closed the door behind them, and as Kayla pulled off her masks, goggles, and gloves, still shivering violently, Jason pressed a mug of hot water into her hands.

"Warm up," he demanded. "And there's plenty more snow to melt if you need more."

She managed a small smile, unable to speak from the chattering of her teeth. Jason could be sweet sometimes.

She rushed for the fireplace while her father stood in the entrance, covered from head to toe in white powder, explaining what had happened. A small crowd gathered close around the mechanical creature.

Dad pulled off his goggles and gear while Jason handed him his own mug of hot water. Mr. Burgins approached cautiously from the back rooms, anxious about getting too close. Kayla sipped at her hot water and tried to get warm again. The fireplace helped.

"What a noise," Mr. Burgins muttered. "Are you sure it's safe?"

"What is it?" Jason asked.

"I'm not sure what it is, to be honest," Dad said through chattering teeth. He was examining the sled pod the creature had been dragging. It appeared to have a glass cover, but the case was too foggy to see much. Two dark shapes were barely discernible inside, but there didn't seem to be a way to open it. He couldn't find a switch or lever of any kind. Jason even tried to pull up the lid with his fingers, but it was sealed tight.

"Hello, my nam... ited States Milit... Hello, my nam... ited States Milit..."

The robot continued its static-filled voice for several moments before a hiss of steam erupted from its rear. The entire room went silent and backed away. Slowly it lowered itself to the ground.

Jason stayed close to it, still trying to open the pod. His fingers trailed over the words that were emblazoned in steel on the creature's rump: Big Dog. "Martin, do you think it's U.S. Military?"

Then the pod popped open with a loud click. Mr. Burgins gasped, and Martin put a hand on Jason's shoulder. "Be careful," he said.

Jason gave a nod before opening the pod the rest of the way.

Inside were a man and a woman, neither of them breathing or moving. They honestly looked dead. Kayla put a hand against the woman's cheek and pulled her hand back from the chill.

"They're so cold," Kayla whispered.

Dad turned to Jason. "Get your father. We'll need his help."

Jason ran off. His father, Peter, was the only person around with real medical experience, having been an intern in the local hospital for two years before the world turned into an icy mess. He'd been present for every birth, illness, injury, and death they encountered. His skills had been a bit clumsy at first, but after 18 years of practice, they considered him an expert.

Peter was shorter than his son, with shoulder-length black

hair he kept in a ponytail, with streaks of gray around his temples. He looked weary from delivering her little brother, but he wasn't wearing the apron spattered with blood she had gotten used to seeing during a childbirth. His eyes went wide when he saw the squatting mechanical dog and its contents. He checked for a pulse, but Kayla spotted something on the woman's chest.

She reached down and pulled a card out of the woman's hand. She had to pull hard because ice had formed between her fingers and the paper.

"What does it say?" Jason whispered.

Kayla swallowed before reading it loud enough for everyone to hear. "It says: Warm me slowly. I am merely sleeping."

For a moment, the room was so silent, all you could hear was the crackling of fire from the hearth. Then all at once the entire room fell into chaos. Dad and Peter lifted the strangers out of the pod, one by one. Dad was barking orders the entire way.

"Kayla, get some pillows! Jason, grab some blankets!"

Kayla ran off and returned with a pair of lumpy pillows under her arms. Peter took the pillows from her and gently lifted their heads to place the pillows beneath them.

"Kayla?" Peter asked, "I have a special task for you." He pushed a blanket into her hands. "I want you to hold this up in front of the fire, dear. They can't be exposed to the direct heat. It might hurt them."

Kayla nodded and held the blanket in front of the hearth, feeling the fabric get hot almost immediately. She understood what Peter meant, and Jason hurried over to help her hold it up as the others moved the second person over closer to the hearth. The man and woman lay still on the ground, their bodies stiff and lifeless.

A few offered to get warm drinks for the strangers, but

Peter shook his head. "It's too risky. You might drown them while they're unconscious. It's not worth the risk. No, we'll simply have to wait. Martin, why don't you and I see if we can find something to put up in front of the hearth? That way those two can give their arms a break."

He nodded and the two went hunting through the apartment complex. So many strange belongings had been left behind at the freezing that surely there would be something of use lying around. They came back with a flowery pink room divider. Kayla and Jason covered it with their blanket to add another barrier, and then took up their previous seats in front of the window. Outside, they could no longer see the trees; the snow obscured everything. It felt as though they had been transferred to another world. This must have been what it was like for Dorothy when she was traveling to Oz from inside the tornado: lost in a sea of wind and simply trusting that she would land safely.

"Do you think they're still alive?" Jason whispered.

"I don't know," Kayla said with a smirk. "You're the one that's gotten medical training. Do you think they're dead?"

He sighed. "I'm not saying my Dad's wrong or anything, but there's no way they could have survived out there like that. Look at them, they're not even wearing warm clothes! There was ice on her fingers when you pulled that paper out. They would have died from exposure in half an hour. I looked at the pod, Kayla. There's no heating inside it. Who would send two dead bodies like that? I mean the machine – that's valuable! Why would they part with it?"

Kayla looked again at the mechanical dog. "Where do you think it came from? I mean, how far away would it have had to come?"

"I don't know, but Martin's looking it over." He shook his head. "I don't like this at all. It's way too dangerous. I think your Dad was wrong to bring it in to begin with."

She smiled. "That's pretty harsh coming from you. I thought you were the optimistic one."

"Yeah well," he replied, shifting. "I just don't think it's a good idea to try and warm up corpses. There's no telling if the cold is what killed them, or if they were diseased..."

All eyes were fixed on the man and woman bundled in blankets in front of the fireplace, the large divider looking like some giant tombstone next to them. Kayla couldn't even see their chests rising and falling. Peter kept readjusting their heads on the pillows. Dad was pacing in the corner near the pod, and Mr. Burgins was seated in front of them, staring down at their faces. If they were diseased, then all of them would get exposed. Kayla shuddered.

"I wish you wouldn't say that," she whispered, rubbing her arm.

"Medical training, remember?" Jason shrugged.

Mr. Burgins got to his feet – it was a formal tendency he blamed on a Catholic upbringing to stand when he gave an announcement. He wiped half of his spectacles on the front of his shirt, having long ago resigned himself to having only one usable lens. The other was cracked almost entirely through, and when he was reading, he often had to turn his head in different directions like a bird to make out the words. "I know that we're all eager to believe these people are somehow saviors, but I'd like to make a somewhat distasteful proposal: they could have been sent as a trap."

He readjusted his glasses on the bridge of his nose as calmly as he could, despite the hushed voices that filled the room. Lauren had come out from seeing to Mama, apparently having heard the details already. She was wiping blood from her hands with a damp towel, and her auburn hair had fallen about her face, but her eyes were clear despite the circles beneath. "And what kind of threat can two dead people be?"

"It is entirely possible that there are patches of survivors out there that want our resources," Mr. Burgins said. "In fact, Martin, I believe you mentioned a few months back that you found the remains of travelers in the area."

"That's right." Dad had pulled a stool over next to the mechanical dog, keeping watch over the strangers and getting warm at the same time. He pushed his blonde bangs out of his worried eyes. "But only traces of where they'd been. It looked as though they had a dog sled team they were using. We weren't able to follow them. The snow was coming down too quickly and the tracks didn't stay but for half an hour at best."

"We know that the area has been scoped out by someone," Mr. Burgins added. "But the question remains, and Lauren, I think you posed it best. What kind of threat can two corpses be?"

"Disease carriers," Jason said. Kayla shuddered again. "They could be carrying some sort of infection and they're hoping to clear us out." The room went quiet. Almost all of them had come into contact with the bodies.

"I'll not be putting them out in that cold again." Lauren balled the bloody rag in her hands, giving Jason, her son, a long stare. "Diseased or not, if they're alive then they're welcome here."

"Honestly − what if they're carrying a plague or something?" Mr. Burgins said. "For all we know, we could already be infected."

"If they were trying to get rid of them," Kayla said, "why would they send that along?" She pointed at the mechanical dog. "I mean, that thing looks expensive."

"Money used to be important," Mr. Burgins said, "but isn't anymore. If someone has dozens of these robots lying about, why not use them? I'm sure plenty of hapless people like us would fall prey to them."

Peter rubbed his eyes with exhaustion. "If the strangers

really are alive like the note said, then I can't in good conscience turn them away. You all are welcome to lock me up somewhere with them if that's what you think is best, but I can't leave them unattended." He yawned into the back of his hand.

Peter, Dad, and Lauren were considered the unofficial leaders of their small community, with the doctor typically serving as the tiebreaker amid conflicts. This appeared to be no exception. Peter was also the glue that kept the entire community together as the group's doctor. If he was locked up, quarantined away with the two bodies, they might well be signing their own death warrants. Even the slightest injury could spell death in these icy days, and without the doctor's care they could all soon meet their end.

"I guess that settles it," Dad added with a chuckle. "The bodies stay where they are. No one is to harm them or move them without Peter's permission. Any questions?"

A few sidelong glances were made, and Peter gave a hearty yawn, but other than that the dissenters were silent. Kayla was glad. If the strangers did wake up, she wanted to know what they had seen, where they had been, and, most importantly, what they wanted. She had never felt so excited.

DAYS WENT BY. THE FIRE WAS KEPT UP AND SHIFTS WERE assigned to keep watch over the pair. They didn't start breathing, they didn't move a limb, and on the third day Peter was doing more tests to determine if they were in fact dead. Jason helped as best he could; he was still in training after all. Peter was still the foremost expert, and Jason still merely the aide. He watched silently as Peter applied pressure on the toes, poked a sewing needle under a thumbnail, and even shot a squirt of icy cold water into an ear. Neither man nor woman squirmed. Oddly enough, there were no signs of decomposition. Jason took notes as Peter listed out all the gory details.

"The limbs are indeed warm now, but when we slice into the skin the blood is still coagulated." He took a sterile scalpel and sliced it gently over the tip of the woman's finger. Immediately a wet goblet of blood puckered out of the wound, and the finger twitched ever so slightly.

Jason gasped. "Did you see that?"

"Oh wow!" Kayla cried, bolting from her seat to see the blood puddle out of the wound. It was so strange, since only a few days ago those same fingers were covered in ice.

Peter smiled. "It's working. It's really working!"

Jason crouched down to look closer. "If they're coming back to life, why is it taking so long?"

Peter patted him on the shoulder and let Jason begin cleaning the wound and bandaging it. "It takes a long time to come back from the dead, my boy. It will be quite an achievement. I imagine few doctors such as ourselves are privy to such a miracle."

Jason offered himself and Kayla up for the first nighttime watch. She offered to read Mr. Burgins' beat up copy of The Wizard of Oz aloud, but Jason wasn't in the mood. Instead, he paced. He wanted to be wide awake when and if the strangers did wake tonight.

Four hours later, the excitement had worn off and Kayla had almost finished the book. Jason checked his watch, winding it a few times to keep it on track. The evening was turning out to be uneventful. He had given up pacing a long time ago and had slumped into the chair, staring into the flames in silence. Kayla had thought he had fallen asleep until he stood, stretched, and popped his back.

"It's getting to be that time," he said with a yawn. "We'd better wake the others."

Kayla nodded, flipping a page. "I'm almost finished."

Jason fetched a mug of hot water from the kitchen and checked the timber and water levels. The fire was hardly ever put out except for managing the ashes, and the water was always kept fresh. New snow would just be dropped into the tub again whenever the water got low, and ever since they started using bins to collect freshly fallen snow outside, there was hardly any cleaning of the snow that had to be done. When he came back, he froze.

"Kayla," he hissed.

"I told you, I'm almost done," she huffed.

He pushed the book into her lap and pointed to the woman on the floor.

The frozen stranger lifted her arm into the air, flexing it slowly as if the limb had fallen asleep for a long time. Kayla's eyes went wide. "What do we do?"

Jason stared at her blankly for a few moments. Surely there were some medical procedures, something that his father had mentioned to him earlier, but he stared at her in absolute confusion. All that pacing hadn't done him any good.

Kayla got to her feet and crept over to the woman. She hoped she knew English. "How are you feeling?"

The woman was still sluggish, but she could speak. "Better," she said, putting a hand to her head as if the reverberation of speaking surprised her. "I'm feeling better."

"You were brought here by something called Big Dog. Does that name mean anything to you?"

"Yes," she nodded, clarity slowly returning to her eyes. Good, if she knew about Big Dog, maybe she could tell them more about where she came from.

Suddenly Jason sprang into action again.

"Kayla, I'm—I'm going to go get Dad."

"Sure." She nodded as he ran up to the bedrooms, his footsteps echoing throughout the building.

The woman took hold of her arm and pulled herself up

into a sitting position. Kayla had to catch her balance to keep from being dragged down. "Whoa, not so fast. Take it easy, you were... I mean, you nearly died there."

She swallowed hard, blinking a few times before speaking. "We're here to rescue you," she whispered, her voice hoarse.

Kayla crouched down next to her so that she could hear her better. "I think we're the ones rescuing you, actually."

Jason ran in with Peter, who was still in his nightgown. "You two did very well." He got to work quickly, urging the woman to lie down as he examined her. "Ma'am, can you tell me your name?"

"Dr. Johansson," she whispered before falling into a coughing fit.

Jason was about to go fetch the woman a warm mug of water, but Peter stopped him. "Best to put a bit of snow in it first to cool it down. Make sure it's lukewarm. Anything hot might do more harm than good."

As Jason ran off to fill Peter's orders, Kayla glanced over to the man beside their newly awakened patient. He was still unconscious, though occasionally she could see the rise and fall of his chest. "She said they were here to rescue us."

Peter's mouth opened as though he wanted to answer but then thought better of it. "Let's just get her back together again first. She's been through a very traumatic event, and we shouldn't push her too hard for information. Let her tell us when she's ready."

Dr. Johansson smiled weakly, taking long sips from the water Jason brought. It was hard to believe this woman had appeared completely dead just a few days ago, but Kayla didn't see anything even resembling supplies in what they had with them. She wasn't entirely sure how they were planning to rescue anyone. Maybe the cold had made her delirious.

It took about half a week for Dr. Johansson to completely recover from her long, chilled slumber. In fact, her friend, Dr. Bronsky, woke up the next night, though he was in far worse shape. After a bit of examining, Peter found out he'd contracted the flu somehow during his sleep, perhaps a disease which he'd been carrying before they began their voyage. When Bronsky had been warmed again, the virus came back to life as well. As for how long they'd been travelling, well, that was perhaps the most shocking revelation.

"Three months," Dr. Johansson said, smiling as Peter's jaw dropped. "Yes, you heard me right. Three months in hibernation."

"Hibernation?" Lauren asked. She was holding Kayla's little brother, a quiet, wrapped bundle, in her arms. Kayla's mother was in the room, though she was still very weak. She'd been confined to the couch on the opposite side of the room from where Johansson was sitting.

"How is that even possible?" Jason asked.

She reached into a pouch on her waist and retrieved a vial. "Two drops of this into a drink and your body temperature plummets, putting you into a state of perpetual hibernation until you're warmed up."

"Isn't that dangerous?" Kayla asked.

"Very. Bronsky and I went through quite a bit of training before being allowed to send out a rescue mission. Your group is the first."

"You went through training." Peter narrowed his eyes. "Where are you all from?"

"Atlanta, believe it or not. We've made a kind of city within the buildings, enclosing whatever green space we could find and using it to grow our own food."

"Incredible," Mr. Burgins sighed. "I always hoped we weren't the only ones left. When can we get to see this city?"

"Just a moment." Johansson smiled before pocketing the

vial. "Before you all start jumping to travel back, there are a few things you must know. Travel by this means is very dangerous. While you are in this state you are pretty much a sitting duck. Raiders, bears, and mountain lions can all get to you if they're determined enough. That pod you see over there is mostly made to keep the inner cabin from getting too cold. Once I fetch the path out of Big Dog's memory banks, you'll have a straighter shot to Atlanta, but it still won't be easy. We estimate there's about a 20% chance something could go wrong, and not just due to attacks. I'm talking about people not waking up from the serum for whatever reason, or contracting a disease along the way like Bronsky. With that in mind, though, which of you would be willing to travel back?" She folded her arms over her chest and surveyed the room. Her eyes fell on Kayla. "What about you, dear?"

"Me?" Kayla was speechless. "I would love – "

"Now, wait just a moment here," Lauren said. "Why should Kayla go? What I mean to say here is why should any of us go if the odds are that high that something bad might happen?"

"If Bronsky and I were the ones to return, assuming of course that he recovers completely, we would have to wait about six months before attempting it. That's a long time for you all to wait. And might I add that the sooner that baby gets into a more stable environment, the better off he'll be."

"But won't we all have to do this eventually? I mean, the only way we're going to get there is via this hibernation process, right?" Jason's eyes glanced over to Kayla's little brother. "I mean, not to be rude or anything, but the odds of him even surviving the hibernation are pretty slim, I'd imagine."

"Not quite," Johansson replied. "Once Big Dog gets back, my people back home will be able to see a straight path here and plan a bigger trip to pick the rest of you up with a larger crew, a bigger heated vehicle, and an overall much less dangerous trip."

"So these two people who go now, they're pretty much a reconnaissance mission," Kayla added.

"Not exactly, I mean, you won't be gathering much information. You'll report information about yourselves to headquarters, then go through a vaccination process to make sure you're ready to be incorporated into the group, and Big Dog will enable them to send a rescue vehicle straight here."

"It sounds exciting!" Kayla grinned.

"That's not exciting, Kayla, that's dangerous," Dad said with a frown.

Jason took a step forward. "I'd like to join her."

Lauren shook her head. "I don't think it's a very good idea to send our only kids out into such a dangerous area. I mean, Jason's our doctor in training here, he needs to be here where he can assist us, not slumbering away in a metal pod for who knows how long."

"But I want to go."

Mr. Burgins waved a hand. "If the kids want to go, Martin, I don't see why you should stop them. I think we've been pretty clear about the fact that we don't want to control anybody here. We don't try to stop you when you want to rush out and risk your life hunting."

"But that's different, I'm just outside," Martin said.

"I think there's just as much danger in that as it is for them to make this journey."

"I still don't like the idea of having only one doctor on hand," Lauren said as she stared down at the newborn in her arms.

"And why not? You were fine with that when we first started out," Peter said indignantly. "I mean, no offense, Jason, but you're still a long way off from being a true doctor. Hell, so am I in a lot of ways. And personally, I think it's a good idea to send these two ahead. They're younger and probably more likely to survive the ordeal than we are." He went over and put a hand on Jason's shoulder, giving it a squeeze. "And if those two did run into trouble, I think they'd be smart enough to handle it."

Jason blushed. Kayla had never seen his father openly brag about him like that.

***

DR. JOHANSSON FINALIZED BIG DOG'S PROGRAMMING AS Kayla and Jason got ready. It was going to be difficult leaving the place they'd known as home for so long, but they both knew that spending their entire lives in the apartment complex without ever knowing the rest of the world would be far worse. Peter watched his son with tears in his eyes.

"Do you think I'm missing anything, Dad?"

"No, I think you're good. Have I ever told you how proud I am of you?"

Jason smiled. "No, not lately. Though that speech you gave about me yesterday doesn't count, does it?"

Peter hugged his son tighter than he ever had before. "I'm proud of you, you know that?"

Jason blinked. "Thanks, Dad." He pushed his father away gently, trying not to show how shocked he was to see tears in his eyes. "Don't worry about us. Kayla and I will be seeing you soon anyway, right? It's only a few months."

His father wiped his eyes on his sleeve and nodded. "I hope so."

Kayla sat on the couch next to her Mama, staring at her baby brother in her mother's arms as though he were from a different planet. Mama's long brown hair was a little frazzled, but she looked satisfied, and not at all shocked that Kayla wanted to go. Her mother was giving her a list of things to watch out for. "... and if Jason tries to be fresh with you while you're in that pod, just tell him to keep his pants on until you get to civilization again."

Kayla blinked. "I don't think Jason's going to be that stupid."

"Oh, trust me honey, we all can be stupid. Nobody is logical all the time. Despite what people say, logic eventually always loses out." Fishing a hand under the couch she pulled out a dusty brown belt with some kind of harnessed compartment on the side.

"What's this for?"

"Open it." Her mom gave a devilish smile.

Hesitantly Kayla unsnapped the satchel and pulled out the handle of a large hunting knife. "Mama, what the hell..."

"That's from when I used to go hunting with Martin. We used to catch us piles of rabbits so big we had to shove the extras into the backyard to keep them fresh until we could eat them. I want you to take it with you. Keep the two of you safe, alright?"

Kayla stood up and wrapped the holster around her waist, amazed at how perfectly it fit. "Thanks, Mama."

"Now, before you run off to go do this crazy thing, you have to do just a few more things for your mother first."

Kayla nodded reluctantly. She should have known her mom couldn't give her such an amazing gift without some kind of compensation.

"First of all, I want you to give me a big fat hug."

Kayla smirked as she leaned over the couch to awkwardly embrace her. Mama felt so fragile compared to how she normally felt. The thread of doubt pulled at her that she might not ever see her again, or her Dad, or her little brother. It was one of those realizations that she had never really thought about or considered. Kayla hugged her even harder.

As she stood up again, she saw her mother grinning.

Kayla rolled her eyes with a smile. "Do I even want to know the next one?"

"A name."

"What?"

"For your little brother. I need a name. Then you can run along and not have to worry about your mother's foolishness again."

Kayla glanced over at her little brother and his pudgy features. He looked like a tiny alien in her mother's arms. Mama knew how much she was trying not to get attached to him, yet she still asked her for a name. She always was tricky. Kayla couldn't leave him with something silly, and she knew it.

"What about Hugo?"

She laughed. "Hugo? Really?"

"Yeah, why not?"

"So why Hugo?"

"If I remember right, I think it means something about being smart, and I hope he's smarter than I've been, Mama. Cause if he has a little brother or sister, he should totally love them to death instead of being a jerk like I've been."

"Oh Kayla, honey, I didn't mean –"

"I know, it's okay. Tell him that I love him. Just in case I don't get to see him again. Don't tell him I hated his guts."

Her eyes went misty. "You can tell him that yourself when we see you again, honey."

"I hope so."

THE CUP OF LUKEWARM WATER WITH THE TWO DROPS FROM Johansson's vial didn't feel like much at first. Then she started to feel cold – all the heat seeped out her fingertips like a squeezed lemon. It started in her limbs at the tips of her fingers and toes, then moved inwards until it reached her chest and stomach. It felt like someone slowly dropped her body into a pit of ice cubes, but Kayla tried to relax inside the black walls of the pod. She felt Jason's fingers entwine with hers, but he felt just as icy as she did. As the lid closed down and Big Dog was led outside into the snow-covered forest, she could hear his now repaired recording drone.

Hello, my name is BIG DOG. I work for the United States Military Rediscovery Mission. I'm travelling back to the ATLANTA BASE. Hello, my name is...

It didn't seem real. She watched as the snowflakes fell from the sky and gathered on the glass lid. Slowly she was drifting off to sleep as the cold set in. There was no telling how long she'd sleep or even if she would ever wake. She thought of Mama, Dad, Jason's parents, Mr. Burgins, and even little Hugo at home. She squeezed Jason's hand once more as consciousness left her completely and she drifted off to someplace near death, tossing her body to the whims of chance.

"KAYLA? KAYLA, WAKE UP."

She opened her eyes to bleary glass towers and a blur of faces and voices, all looking down at her and talking at once. Then her eyes met his and she felt the warmth return to her chest again.

"Jason. We made it."

"That was terrible." He grinned. "Let's never volunteer for that again, okay?"

She laughed.

Little Bird

MANY FIGHTERS HAD ANSWERED THE QUEEN'S SUMMONS. There were retirees from the royal military, bounty hunters with specialized weapons, bands of mercenaries, and Medulla hunters from across the sea, with their painted skin and pierced faces. Salma frowned as she surveyed them, knowing how great the odds were against her. She was one of the smallest people there, and even though she was confident in her skills, never before had she felt so insignificant.

The odds against her were enormous. Why would the queen pick a petite loner like her instead of the bands of experienced fighters that milled about the streets? Part of her considered going home to forget this mad mission, but unlike the others, she knew what they were up against. Anyone else would go in blind, and she couldn't allow that. She couldn't risk waiting any longer to fix what she had caused. She needed to draw their attention somehow.

A scruffy man with an enormous mustache sat in front of the main castle gate with a scroll. Beside him sat a small round table with a cheap goblet that was probably filled with wine. He raised his eyebrows as she approached. "You here to register?"

"Yes," she said, wishing she had more steel in her voice.

He looked her up and down as though assessing whether or not this was a joke. His gaze fell on the two daggers on her hips. "Prefer your blades, do you?"

"I like them fine, but I prefer this." She removed the quarterstaff from her back. At nearly eight feet in length, it was easily taller than her. Keeping it on her back beneath her pack made it look like it was a tool instead of a weapon.

"My, my! That's a big weapon for such a small woman." The scruffy man chuckled and put his hand out to examine it, but with a whirl she put it away instead. He frowned and narrowed his eyes. Good, at least he was paying attention.

"Is there anything else you need to know?" she asked, ignoring his scowl.

He looked down at his scroll. "Your name."

"Salma."

He narrowed his eyes. "What's your full name, girl?"

"Salma the mercenary."

He gave a sigh and shook his head, mumbling to himself, but wrote the name down regardless. "And why should the queen choose you, Salma?"

Salma doubted any of the others had been given such lip. She considered pulling out her quarterstaff and demonstrating in more detail, but four guards posted nearby watched her closely. Salma leaned in close, placing a hand on the table as the man leaned back in his chair. "Unlike most of them, I know what we're up against. I used to be... friends with her, the Dark Sorceress. She's the target, am I right?"

He gaped at her with wide eyes. "That information hasn't been released to the public! How did you learn about that?"

She gave a small smile. "I follow the patterns. This is the third time she's attacked the kingdom, right? And now the queen's own grandson has been kidnapped. Now it's personal, and I'm certain she's involved. " She pushed off the table and the goblet of wine teetered slightly. The guards in the distance relaxed their posture. It was all a careful game.

"Is that all you need of me?"

"Yes, that's everything." He pulled out a handkerchief and dabbed at his brow.

Salma turned and headed back into the crowd, moving past a few drunken mercenaries and a rowdy group of Medulla hunters. She spotted a few of them with skin as dark as hers. Sometimes they met her gaze, but she knew better than to speak with them. Saying the wrong words to a Medulla hunter could mean death, or at the very least becoming a few limbs lighter.

She was glad she had decided to bring the daggers. Even if she didn't draw them, the sight was enough to dissuade most. Knife wounds could get bloody and debilitating, which meant potentially being knocked out of the competition.

There wasn't enough money in the kingdom to pay every person who answered the summons to retrieve the queen's kidnapped grandson, so she assumed there must be a competition. The queen must have some way of trimming down the options. It was a desperate move to summon so many, and it wasted time. The Dark Sorceress was impatient, and the clock was ticking.

A voice hissed behind her. "Now why would the Dark Sorceress be interested in a little bird like you?"

Salma spun around, her braids flying out around her. In an instant she drew her dagger and placed it against the man's throat. He was wiry and only a little taller than her. He had a scraggly beard and a bitter smile that put her on edge.

His laughter caught her off guard. "You're quick, aren't you?" He didn't move away from the blade she held to his throat. "Please now, I'm merely curious."

"Curiosity is dangerous." She looked him up and down. His legs and forearms were wrapped tight with cloth. Even with a blade to his throat, his movements were calm and leisurely. His exposed fingers were scarred in a way unlike those of a typical swordsman. Most importantly, his hands were wrapped to hide the backs of his hands. People who got caught stealing from the wrong person typically wore a brand there to warn others. "You're a thief, aren't you?"

His smile faltered. "That has such a foul ring to it, but yes, some might call me that."

"Do you have a name?"

"Nadim to my friends, death to my enemies." He nodded, as much as her blade would allow.

"Assumed I would be easy to steal from, is that it?"

His smile flickered and he blinked, betraying his nerves. "Of course not. You have nothing I desire."

"What then?"

He swallowed, wincing as the delicate skin of his throat scraped against the blade. "The queen wants a word with you."

"What?"

"If you would be so kind, little bird, I'll tell you more."

Reluctantly, Salma removed the dagger.

"Thank you." Nadim rubbed his throat, chuckling. "Come, she's waiting just outside of town."

It felt like a trap. Why should the queen send this rat to fetch her when she could send any of her guards instead? Nadim turned back to her. "Come along. It is wise not to keep Her Majesty waiting."

"How can I trust you?"

Nadim smiled and unwrapped his left wrist. Instead of the branding of the thief like she expected, there was a different mark. Dark against the bronze skin of his arm was the queen's emblem, a tattoo inked with flakes of gold that caught the light. "Believe it or not," he cooed, "I am part of the Queen's Inner Circle."

IT DIDN'T TAKE LONG TO REACH THE LARGE TENT ON THE outside of town, but Salma was surprised at how few guards were present. There were also at least two magicians that she could identify. At first glance they looked like priests in their black robes, but instead of crosses they wore pentagram medallions about their necks. She had to assume they were in the queen's company since they were deep in talks with several of the guards. Perhaps the queen had a better understanding of her foe than she expected.

They walked past several pairs of guards who eyed Salma with more suspicion than Nadim and entered the large tent. It was modestly decorated with merely a few tables and chairs. Tapestries were pinned up to the walls and a rug was laid out for the queen's throne, but the queen herself was nowhere to be seen. What Salma had assumed was a single tent from the outside was really a connection of tents, with edges pinned up and green curtains dividing each section. Nadim left Salma in the center of the room, then clasped his hands behind him as he approached the curtains.

"My Queen, I have brought the final member."

There was laughter from behind. Salma turned to see an enormous woman with pale skin lounging in a chair in the corner. Her great sword was leaning against a table and her face was painted in overlapping blue and yellow swirls. She was one of the Medulla warriors. "Nadim, you simplistic fool, please tell me you're joking!"

"She is quick," he said with a smile. "She'll be invaluable to us."

The great woman shook her head. "I would rather take

one of those shamans outside. It seems foolish not to bring magic to fight magic."

The green curtains were pulled back and a woman with an aura of authority entered the room. She was dressed in a plain brown robe, and although she wore no crown, Salma knew that she had to be the queen. Nadim didn't kneel and neither did the Medulla warrior, but Salma bent a knee without a second thought. The queen barely seemed to notice and sat down with a glum expression.

"What can she do for us?" the queen asked.

Salma opened her mouth to reply, but Nadim was rattling off information faster than she could keep up.

"She's an unknown fighter, but she's small and quick. Although she doesn't look like much, she caught me off guard, and I consider that a bonus in her favor."

"Nonsense," said the Medulla warrior. "A mouse could take you off guard, and you don't see us bringing vermin with us."

The queen propped her head on her fist. "Yutu makes a good point. I have nearly a hundred at my choosing; how is she the fastest?"

Nadim smirked. "I never said she was the fastest, my Queen; merely that she is fast."

Yutu got to her feet, easily towering over everyone in the room. "Why don't we bring one of your shamans out there? It's foolish to fight a witch without one."

The queen rubbed at her temple. "We can't. I already tried sending three. They were burned alive before they even got near the old monastery." She turned to Nadim. "Tell me what good the girl is or else I'll send you both away this instant. I don't have time to play your silly games."

Nadim's smile widened as he leaned in closer. "She knows the Dark Sorceress personally, My Queen. They used to be friends." The tent went silent. "If my methods fail you and if

Yutu's steel isn't enough, then diplomacy may be our best option."

The queen sat up, now eying Salma with renewed curiosity. "How did you know this Dark Sorceress? They say her name used to be Nyah."

Salma's mouth went dry. "We were friends," she said. "We used to be rather close." Salma felt her cheeks burn.

The queen watched her for a long moment with hard eyes. "You will negotiate my grandson's freedom," she said. "If the three of you bring him back alive and well, I will grant you each land, a title, and a thousand gold pieces." Salma's jaw dropped and Yutu whistled over her shoulder, but the queen wasn't finished. "Know however that this could mean death for all of you. You might catch aflame just as the shamans did."

Salma nodded. "I understand."

The queen nodded, then turned to Nadim and Yutu. "You two keep this girl alive, whatever the cost. I fear she is our best chance at bringing my grandson home alive and ensuring the continuity of the kingdom."

A chill went down her spine.

TOGETHER THEY LEFT THE SAFETY OF THE QUEEN'S LAND, away from the shops, homes, and farmland, and into the wild lands to the west. Nadim led them along the well-worn path as the trees grew denser and the brambles more treacherous. When Nadim came to a stop, Salma knew they had reached the edge of the Dark Sorceress' realm.

The trees here were the same old, familiar hardwoods she knew, sprawling high into the sky. She thought of the shamans attempting to enter the land before and catching fire. Was

Nyah aware they were here? Was she watching? A shiver went down her spine.

She understood the urgency, but it was ridiculous approaching at night. All they had was starlight and a few measly torches to see by. The moon was nearly full, but that would do little once they entered and the canopy of trees closed overhead.

"Is this it?" Yutu brandished her sword.

Nadim's voice was low. "This is as far as the shamans could go. The oak grove marks the edge of her territory. They were caught aflame just past this tree, I believe."

Salma turned to him. "That quickly? We're so far out still."

Nadim caught her gaze. "Yes, she was aware of their presence even this far out. You knew her before. Tell us: what can we expect?"

Yutu smiled. "Yes, please contribute something, oh great negotiator. Perhaps you helped her set up a few death traps?"

Salma sighed. She should have known Yutu's snide comments would escalate once they reached the grove. "I can't say what she has planned, but—"

"Of course, you can't." Yutu strode forward, her sword lifted just to the height of Salma's belly. "Be honest now, you don't know anything about her, do you? That was all a lie to get chosen by Nadim here."

"That's not true." Salma dropped a hand to the hilt of her dagger. She would have to be fast to avoid the Medulla warrior's blade when they were so close.

Nadim pushed Yutu's blade aside. "Please," he sighed. "We're working together, remember?" He turned to Yutu. "The queen ordered us to protect her, not slay her."

"She's useless," Yutu spat. "A child would be more helpful."

"She had several alligators when last I saw her," Salma said. Both Nadim and Yutu went silent.

"Gators." Yutu laughed. "What in the world does a Dark Sorceress need with a bunch of ugly reptiles? Isn't magic good enough for her?"

"Nyah raised them as pets. They once were tiny enough to fit in the palm of her hand. They're devoted to her. I imagine she has far more now than she used to."

Yutu was quiet.

Nadim approached, his eyes glowing in the firelight. "So she has pets, something she values. She is protective of her land, which means she wants to be left alone. This is useful information."

"Yes, she wants to be left alone to kill a prince. Useful indeed. You two are both fools." Yutu stepped over one of the enormous roots of the oak tree and moved into the grove.

Salma moved to follow her, but Nadim took her shoulder. He withdrew his hand quickly, as though remembering the blade at his throat from before. "Don't let Yutu's attitude dissuade you from speaking your mind," he said. "She is a skilled fighter even if she doesn't understand the nuances of stealth and strategy."

"Don't worry about me. If I think we're doing something stupid, I'll let you know. Besides," Salma said, looking into the grove where Yutu was slicing her way through the vines that hung from the oak branches. "I've met plenty of mercenaries like Yutu. A few cuts ought to put her in her place when it comes to it."

"That's what worries me." Nadim grumbled. "We need her. Keep that in mind when you're tempted to attack."

Salma nodded. Nadim was right, Yutu was valuable to the group. So Yutu's fighting arm was off limits. Fair enough.

THE CANOPY HID MUCH OF THE STARLIGHT, SO TORCHES were a necessity as they carved a path through the grove. Yutu had given Salma the task of torch bearer. It was child's work, but Salma held her tongue. Yutu's enormous blade made quick work of the vines, but the foliage only got thicker as they delved deeper.

Yutu put her blade down to catch her breath. Her blue and yellow war paint was smeared from the sweat. "It's difficult to breathe here." She took a drink from her water skin.

"The air is humid," Nadim said.

"Most of this land is swampland," Salma said.

Yutu sat down on one of the roots. "This woman is a nuisance. Anybody who enjoys living in this heat is mad."

A crow cawed overhead. It was the loudest sound they had heard since they entered the grove and they all looked upwards. Then Yutu screamed. Salma thought she was sitting at an odd angle on the ground, and for a moment believed Yutu had merely fallen off the root she sat on. Then she realized that Yutu's left leg was *in the ground*. It had been pulled into the earth, her right leg splayed out in front of her, and her sword fallen out of reach.

"The trees!" Salma yelled and lunged for Yutu. She could see a root still sticking up out of the dirt, wrapped tight around Yutu's leg and squeezing slowly. Yutu screamed again. Salma pulled out her dagger and started stabbing at the root. It unwrapped from the leg and descended into the earth. Together Salma and Nadim pulled Yutu to her feet even as the ground beneath them trembled.

"What is it?" Nadim asked.

"I think we made it angry," Salma said.

More roots emerged, hovering in the air like cobras before striking. Salma gritted her teeth and pulled out her second dagger. She glanced to either side; there must have been twenty or more of them. Her daggers alone wouldn't be up for the task.

"You coward!" Yutu cried. Salma turned to see Nadim sprinting away from them, but Yutu's cry spurred the roots into action. They descended like the legs of a spider, and Salma ducked as one went for her neck. Another tried to grab at her leg. She sliced at it, tearing it in half, but another one was already trying to wrap around her other arm. There were too many of them. Suddenly something cold and dry wrapped around her mouth, and she breathed in the heavy scent of wet earth. She tried cutting at it, but with her left arm captured as well, it was difficult to cut without slicing open her own face.

Yutu's weapon, on the other hand, seemed made for slicing through the roots. But her leg was still injured, and the roots sensed it. She was having trouble keeping her balance, which was necessary to wield her great sword. One root whipped around, striking her in the stomach and slamming her against a tree trunk. From above her an enormous limb fell, torn free by another root. Yutu saw it and leaned forward, but her foot was pinned to the ground by smaller roots. The branch landed on her back, knocking her flat on her face and knocking the wind out of her. Slowly the roots wrapped around her body, just like they did to Salma. Only instead of holding her in place, they were going to drag her down into the earth.

The pressure around Salma's head loosened. The root that had wrapped around her mouth and most of her upper body fell limp to the ground. The ones that were wrapping around Yutu fell still as well. Salma spat dirt and looked around in confusion. Nadim was standing at the base of one of the biggest oak trees. In one hand he held his scimitar. A zig-zagging cut circled the trunk of the tree; the oak was bleeding out.

"Are you alright?" he asked.

She nodded.

"Yutu..."

Yutu didn't move when the roots fell still. Nadim tried to push her over but needed Salma's help. Yutu's face was a bloody mess. Her mouth was opening and closing like a fish pulled from water. Together they pushed her into a sitting position and Nadim had to rub her back until Yutu could breathe on her own.

"Even the trees are hers," she said in a hoarse voice.

"We're lucky," Nadim whispered. "We've made it farther than anyone else." He examined Yutu's leg. She had a bloody gash that coiled around it, but her bones were thankfully not broken. He moved to her chest. "I'm surprised you're able to breathe at all. You don't seem to have any broken ribs at least, just bruising."

She smiled, her face a mixture of blood, dirt, and the spattered remnants of her facial paint. "I've always been tough. That Dark Sorceress is going to have to try harder than that to get rid of me."

Salma shifted uneasily. "You shouldn't talk like that. She can hear you here."

Yutu's smile faded. Earlier she might have scoffed at Salma's words, but after almost being dragged underground by one of the many oak trees that surrounded them, she didn't argue. Nadim came over to check Salma for injuries.

"I'm fine," she said.

He smiled. "I'll decide that, little bird." He felt along the back of her skull.

"Why do you call me that?"

"Because that is what you are." The amusement in his voice didn't sit well with her.

"You chose me for this team. Why do you mock me?"

He caught her eye as he checked her arm. "Mock you?

Birds are some of the most vicious creatures in this world. They are also quite clever. How would that be a mockery?"

She narrowed her eyes. "I'm not a fool. Don't talk to me as though I am one."

He chuckled as he checked her jaw and throat for damage. "You don't have a scratch on you."

"Of course not," Yutu said. "She's under the witch's protection."

THEIR TREK WAS SLOW AND CAUTIOUS NOW THAT THE VERY trees had been marked as villains. Nadim offered to carve rings around every tree they passed, but Yutu cautioned against it. The sorceress' eyes were on them now, and an act like that could lead to more attacks. They came to a creek that meandered through the land. The recent rains had over-flowed it many times, and the ground around it was soft under their feet.

The earthy perfume brought back a flood of memories that Salma had long wanted to forget. Bare feet sinking into the banks of the creek, long talks about their future, stolen kisses and questions that were never answered. Nyah had been a different person back then, filled with a vibrance that was infectious. A longing filled her heart that she hadn't felt in years, and for a moment it took her breath away.

Yutu lowered herself onto a large rock. Despite Nadim's attentions to her leg, she was still clearly in pain. "This place is enormous. How far away are we?"

At Salma's silence, she pressed. "Salma?"

She blinked, pulled from her memories. "Halfway, I think." She crouched down to the edge of the creek and looked down into the water, her torch illuminating her brown skin and her bright, fearful eyes. She remembered when another pair of eyes used to look down with her. "This land belonged to the monks of the monastery before she came here. They cared for the trees and the land. I don't know how this place got so sick."

Yutu shook her head. "Perhaps your friend spoiled the place, made it fester."

Salma said nothing but avoided Yutu's gaze.

Nadim rinsed his hands in the creek and climbed to his feet. "Some say the Dark Sorceress had to wrestle this land away from the spirits of those monks. They say she banished them to a horrible fate so she could live here."

Salma couldn't hold back the retort that blurted out. "That's not true. This place was abandoned."

"Oh?" Yutu grinned. "What makes you such an expert? Did you help her curse these lands?"

Salma paced along the creek, curling her hand into a fist and swinging the torch with her as the words flowed from her lips. "I helped her move here. The land is the problem, not the dead. This place was cursed before we came here. Nyah owns it now, but the curse holds sway over her."

Yutu shook her head but Nadim asked, "Is that why she captured the prince? I admit, I know little of curses or how they work."

She turned to look at Yutu, the torch crackling in the darkness. "I don't know. She fell in love with this place when we came. She felt like it sat here waiting for her to come here, but I think it drew her in. I think it ensnared her and wouldn't let her leave. I'm afraid..." she said, her voice breaking as she tried to gather herself. "I think she is lost to this place."

A crow cawed overhead. She looked up to see the flapping of black wings as it landed in a giant limb of an oak. Her gaze drifted to the side, spotting more and more movement. Black wings fluttered and dozens of black eyes stared down at them. The tree was so full of birds that she could barely see the swaying branches.

Her foot slid in the dirt as she took a step back, unable to speak as she looked up at them. Yutu made a small noise as she pulled herself to her feet and backed away. Soon they both stood with Nadim, and just as they began to carefully pick their way across the creek, a bird gave an angry screech. It sounded like a battle cry.

The tree shifted in the darkness, all the limbs moved at once, and there was a sound of rattling leaves and flapping wings. The crows took to the sky.

"Run!" Nadim screamed.

Salma bolted. She leapt through the creek, her heart pounding as beating wings blocked out any light that might have been visible through the canopy. After several yards, she realized she held the only torch in the group. Nadim and Yutu were running blind in the darkness. In her terror, she had abandoned them.

She came to a halt, intent on turning around to find her team, when the flock of birds hit her like an ocean wave. Claws ripped across her cheeks, up her arms, and along her scalp; those were the ones that missed her. The others slammed straight into her chest, knocking the air out of her lungs, as she landed hard on her back. She couldn't breathe and could barely move as her body reeled from the impact. Her torch fell from her fingers and the swarm of birds quickly blocked out the light.

All she could see were black feathers and black eyes, sharp beaks and scrambling claws; all she could hear was the beating of wings. She shut her eyes against them, unable to hold off panic any longer. Bloody streaks ripped across her skin. The mounting pain was what broke her free from the shock. She pulled out her daggers and began cutting wildly.

Blood splattered her face, wings flailed, feathers threatened to suffocate her, but Salma kept slicing.

"Stop!" She heard Nadim's voice and froze. She couldn't see, her breath was coming in pants, but she forced herself to be still. A scimitar sliced cleanly through at least ten birds, decapitating several and cutting off the legs of others. Yutu beat back several more and Salma took in a deep, painful breath; her entire body was shaking.

Yutu grabbed hold of her hand. Nadim picked up the torch she had dropped, and together they ran. Salma stumbled to keep up with Yutu's strides. She glanced back over her shoulder. Of the remaining birds, a few were tending to their wounds, but the others were watching them. No, not them, *Salma*.

"Nyah..." Salma whispered.

Had she heard her? Had she been insulted? Was that why she attacked them? Her chest grew tight at the thought. A deep pain took hold of her that had nothing to do with her bloody wounds. Salma had come to prevent her from digging her own grave, but now she understood. This land had consumed her, and Nyah had lost herself completely.

ONCE THEY WERE CERTAIN THE FLOCK OF BIRDS WERE NO longer in pursuit, they stopped in a clearing. "Are you okay?" Yutu asked her.

"Yes," Salma said, breathless. "Thank you both."

Salma was still shaking. Her body didn't want to obey her any longer and she couldn't tell if it was from the attack or if it was more than that. She tried to act like she was fine, but Yutu frowned at her, disapproval in her eyes.

"Those birds acted as though Yutu and I weren't even there," Nadim said. "They were focused solely on you."

Yutu shook her head. "I thought you were her precious pet, but that's not true, is it?"

Salma shook her head, rubbing the stray feathers and dirt off of her arms. "I honestly don't know what we are... what I am to her anymore," she whispered.

Nadim studied her in the torchlight. "You weren't just friends, were you?"

Salma let out a shaky breath. It was difficult enough to admit the truth without being here in this cursed place again, knowing Nyah could probably hear them. Her body wouldn't stop shaking. Nadim put a hand on her shoulder and Salma found the courage to speak.

"We were lovers before we came here. She had heard of the monastery, how it was burned down, and how it was supposed to be haunted. She thought it would be a good place to practice her magic, away from the rest of the world." Salma looked up through the trees, up to where the stars were still visible through the canopy. "I helped her rebuild it. It took us nearly a year." She shook her head; memories of their laughter and their joy tried to interfere with her explanation, but she pushed them away. This was no time to lose herself. "I should have known better. I should never have let her come here. Nyah didn't just love the place, she became obsessed with it."

"The *place* drove her mad?" Yutu asked in disbelief.

"I think so...I don't know," she admitted, wrapping her arms around herself. "All I know is that she changed. She would stay in the woods for days, wanting to commune with the land like the monks did, but it drained her. Sometimes she would come back and sleep for days. The trees needed her life force, she told me, but I thought she was being metaphorical." She put a hand to her neck at the thought of those long, worrying days when Nyah went missing, the haunted look in her eyes when she returned, and the way her voice didn't seem like hers. "She was sick and tired all the time. I told myself she was resting, recuperating, but I knew deep down that wasn't it. I knew it was worse than that."

Salma took a deep breath and both Nadim and Yutu waited for her to collect herself. ""One day she wanted me to go with her into the woods, to give them *my* life force, but I refused. I was so scared seeing what was happening to her that I was terrified of becoming the same. No magical power is worth a life, I told her. She came back and slept for three days, and when she woke, she was too ill to get out of bed. That was when I left for good."

She hung her head. She had forgotten how heavy that weight was when she carried it, but now that she had shared that load, she felt lighter, calmer.

"You feared her," Nadim whispered.

"Of course I did. Every time she came out to these woods, she became more powerful. You see how her magic is. She wasn't this powerful when I left. I was hoping I could come and maybe change her mind, try to talk her out of this. I thought she still had some affection for me." Salma took a deep breath. "I didn't want to see her slaughtered."

Nadim got to his feet and gave a heavy sigh. "I hate to say it, but you're perhaps the worst negotiator we could have."

"I realize that now," she admitted.

"However," he added, "there might still be a way to resolve this without any death. Let me think on it."

"Can we think while we walk, then?" Yutu asked. "We shouldn't stay still. It gives her time to surround us."

Nadim looked around at the trees. "Yes, let's do that."

Salma followed. The guilt she had denied for so many years filled her. She might have been able to prevent Nyah from getting to this point if she hadn't been a coward. She could have maybe convinced her of the danger back then.

This time there was no telling if Nyah would even listen. She was still angry, and in all honesty, she had every right to be.

SALMA DIDN'T RECALL THE MOAT AROUND THE MONASTERY, but she knew what was likely lurking beneath the black water. Nyah must have built it as a home for her alligators; it also served to further isolate her from the outside world. The moat, however, was only one obstacle that stood between them and the monastery.

Enormous dead oaks grew around the building like pale dead hands reaching up for the night sky. The moonlight shone down upon the limbs, and nearly every one of them was covered with birds. At least this time they could see the birds; but there was no telling how many alligators awaited them.

Yutu emerged from the underbrush in a crouch. "There's a dirt path on the opposite side with an enormous bell. It's the only way in without swimming, but the water comes right up to the edge of the path."

"We would be easy targets for her pets," Nadim said, groaning. "And plainly visible to the birds."

Yutu looked up into the vines that hung from the trees. "I could try to tie together some kind of raft. We could float our way across."

"How long would that take?"

"A few hours, I think."

Nadim frowned. "We don't have the time. She has too many spies. Salma, where are you going?"

Salma moved through the trees until she reached the bell that Yutu mentioned. It was nearly twice the height of Yutu and was badly rusted. There used to be a bell tower when the monastery had been active. The bell was used to call the monks in for prayer, but it had fallen during the fire. It crashed through two floors before slamming into the tile on the first floor. Despite their attempts, neither she nor Nyah could move it, so they used it as decoration and grew ivy up its sides. That was nearly a decade ago.

Somehow Nyah had found a way to move it on her own. It stood as a testament to how powerful she had become, and how dangerous. It was also a warning that only Salma would understand. If Nyah could move something as heavy as a church bell, what chance did they have of survival? It was her way of telling them to turn back now or die trying.

Nadim appeared at her side. "Don't run off like that! We need to work as a team, remember?"

"We can't fight her," Salma said. "It won't do any good to try."

Yutu gave a nervous laugh. "She's lost her mind. We haven't come all this way just to—"

Salma pointed to the bell. "Do you see this? Nyah moved it herself, with her own magic. She made the roots come out of the ground to attack you, Yutu. She can make the birds flock as she wishes. This is her final warning. We leave or she kills us."

Nadmin gaped at her, glancing to the bell and then to the monastery. "A warning."

"Or a promise," Yutu snarled. "As intimidating as this place is to us, there's a kid inside who is even more frightened. We chose to be here. He did not. I'm not going anywhere." She looked between them. "What about you two? If you're too scared, this is the time to turn around."

Nadim closed his eyes briefly. "I'm not leaving. I told the queen I would save her grandson or die trying, and I will not return a liar."

Salma pulled out her quarterstaff and approached the bell. "Alright, then."

"What are you doing?" Nadim asked.

"I was brought here to be a negotiator, wasn't I? Let me do my job."

She struck the bell as hard as she could. The church bell rang out through the forest for the first time in probably years. Flocks of birds flew up like black clouds from the trees. Something scurried away into the underbrush.

"Think that was loud enough?" Yutu spat, pulling free her great sword.

"That definitely got her attention," Nadim added.

Salma ignored them. She stared at the monastery door and watched the candlelight flicker in the windows. A black shadow moved, and the door was pulled open.

Nyah stood before them, a smile on her lips. With the candlelight behind her she was a shadow in the doorway. "I'm glad one of you had the decency to ring first. You're welcome inside. I believe I have something you're searching for."

Nadim grabbed Salma's arm. "Remember: the prince is our priority, regardless of what happens to the rest of us."

"I'm aware of that." She pulled her arm away and started down the thin, dirt path that crossed the moat. Black water lapped at the edges, inches away from her feet. She had only made it a quarter of the way toward the house when she saw the first scaly backside surface from the water. The size of the creature made her mouth go dry. More and more alligators emerged, and one giant beast crawled ahead of them, blocking the path and still having length left to leave his tail submerged.

"Your little pets don't seem keen to let us visit," Yutu called out.

Nyah shrugged and gave a wide smile. "What can I say? My little babies have a mind of their own."

"Your little *babies*," Yutu said, positioning her great sword, "are going to taste my steel."

Nyah's voice dropped to a growl. "If you harm one scale, your beloved prince will be sent back to your queen in pieces."

Nadim cursed and put a shaky hand on Yutu's forearm. "No weapons."

"*What?*" Yutu asked. Salma had to agree with her. Nadim was mad if he thought they could get past any of these creatures without force.

"You heard me," he muttered. His eyes were wide and his face moist with sweat. He knew what he was asking, and he didn't reach for his scimitar. "With our weapons out, she could easily say we harmed them somehow. No, we have to move quickly. Avoid them."

Yutu looked from Nadim to the giant beast that stood waiting in front of them, her eyes wide. "How do we avoid that? You do see how big that gator is, don't you?" Yutu stepped forward, brandishing her great sword.

"Don't do it," Nadim warned. "Don't make me stop you."

"Then stand back!" Yutu growled.

"Wait, wait a moment." Salma said, watching the sky. The flock of birds flocked toward them, more of Nyah's pets. "Aim for the birds!" She pulled out her staff and readied her stance.

Crows swarmed across them and they attacked without mercy. Nadim sliced across several with his sickle and Yutu tore through three with one slice. Salma used her staff to knock the injured and dead birds into the water. The alligators were quick to take the bait.

"To the door!" Salma screamed. They moved as a group, slicing through birds, leaping over lunging gators, and somehow keeping their feet out of the water. Many more gators had come to join the feast. The footbridge was surrounded with them.

They had nearly reached the door when a tiny alligator,

barely more than a baby, latched onto Yutu's injured leg. She screamed and on reflex swung her great sword to chop off its head, but Nadim's sickle stopped her.

"No!" he cried. "You can't hurt it!"

"It's got my leg!" she cried and punched at it instead. The largest alligator of the group took notice, the same one that had blocked their path earlier. Salma tried to drag both Nadim and Yutu toward the door, but it was impossible. Nadim couldn't back up without Yutu trying to slice the baby gator's head off. Blood was pooling around Yutu's leg as she punched at the baby alligator's face. Then the giant alligator attacked. It lunged up out of the water and fitted its enormous jaws around Yutu's waist. With a sickening crunch she took Yutu and Nadim's sickle into the water. Yutu's scream was cut short. Soon the other gators were lunging in after Yutu and the water turned a deep red.

Nadim froze. "Yutu... Oh, I'm so sorry." His voice was a hoarse whisper.

Salma took his arm and dragged him into the monastery, slamming the door behind them. She slid to the floor, cold and numb. Nyah stood before them, barefoot and smiling, looking just as beautiful as Salma remembered.

***

"My babies haven't eaten that well in a while," Nyah said.

"Nyah..." Salma whispered. She thought she would be able to handle seeing her ex-lover after ten years. She thought she could convince her to give up her hostage. She thought that if anyone could convince her to step down, she could. However, her heart had other plans. Nyah radiated a powerful, magnetic presence, and Salma was powerless against it. Her heart was still just as snared as the day she first laid eyes on her.

The sight of Nyah must have brought Nadim to his senses. He was breathless as he spoke. "We came... to negotiate the release of the young prince..."

Together he and Salma got to their feet, staying close together for fear of more surprises.

"I know that," Nyah said, her voice tinged with disdain. "The prince and I have had fun together." She looked over her shoulder toward a black cage that was more suited for wild animals than princes. Instead of a beast within, there was a small boy sitting in a makeshift crib. He could not have been older than two. "He's the kindest noble I've ever met, though I'm sure that'll change over the years."

Salma couldn't believe her eyes. "You kidnapped a baby? Why?"

Nyah gave a small smile and walked toward the boy, her cloak swirling behind her. "Because the queen didn't give a rat's ass about the others I kidnapped. She left them to rot; it didn't matter who I captured: captains, soldiers, even members of the council. None of them even garnered a response. Steal away her grandchild, though, and every person with a weapon is summoned." Nyah glanced towards her. "Even you, dear."

"Name your terms, madam," Nadim said. "What do you want in exchange for the boy?"

"Hmm, my terms." Nyah's face was empty, unreadable. "I think you know them already." She nodded to Salma. "You brought her, didn't you?"

Salma turned to him. "Me? What...?"

Nadim pursed his lips and gave a short nod.

She gripped his arm. "You brought me as a bargaining chip?"

He pulled away from her. "My apologies for the deception. You might not have come otherwise. The queen put out the call hoping you would appear or make yourself known. And you did. Why do you think I was listening to your conversation?"

"Come now, Salma. You wouldn't have this child killed out of pride, would you?" Nyah asked.

"My pride?" Salma snapped. "If anyone is prideful, Nyah, it's you. I left this ugly place because it has warped your mind. You've been killing people just to get me back here, even kidnapping a baby! You want me to live in this madness with you, but I won't. This land has poisoned your mind!"

Nyah's gaze went dark. "So... you're saying you refuse."

There was fear and fury in Nadim's gaze. "Be reasonable! You can't sacrifice the prince's life over your squabble."

"Why not? Yutu sacrificed hers." Salma backed away. "We came here expecting to sacrifice ourselves. You were going to sacrifice me. What's another life on the line?"

"Yutu knew the risks. We all did."

"Death was the risk!" Salma cried. "To die in combat is an honorable end. To be exchanged like some trinket, to be turned into a hostage... that is far worse than death." Salma brought up her staff and Nadim reached for his remaining sickle.

"Please," he whispered. "I don't want to hurt you."

Nyah's laughter echoed throughout the chamber, surprising them both. "You won't have to, dear." A thunder of wings was the only warning they had before a swarm of black shadowy birds slammed into Nadim's chest. Salma gasped. She hadn't even known they were coming, hadn't heard them take flight. Nadim's eyes went wide, then his entire body was covered in black wings and pointed beaks. The birds engulfed him.

In an instant, the birds were gone, departed back into the rafters. They left behind Nadim's broken body. They had punctured a hole right through him like a pane of glass. A gaping, bloody wound was left in the center of his chest. His eyes fluttered in shock as he tried to breathe, but his lungs were no longer whole. The crows were not real birds, merely magic—Nyah's magic.

"The fool." Nyah laughed. "As though I'd let him kill you."

Salma felt cold. It took an effort to wrench her gaze away from Nadim at her feet. "Why are you doing this?"

"For you, of course! How else was I supposed to bring you back? I have to get the entire kingdom in an uproar to catch your attention." She laughed and held out a hand. "Come here. I've missed you so much! This place hasn't been the same without you."

Salma blinked. "You've killed so many... just to get my attention?"

Nyah nodded. "Remember back when we first met, I said I'd do anything for you? I really did mean that." She tittered a laugh and then shook her head. She had clearly seen Salma's distress. "No, don't be frightened. I've just missed you, dear. That's all. The world isn't right without us together, don't you know that?"

Salma remembered when they first met, apprentices in training, wanting so badly to become the best. Nyah of course had said she would do anything, but she bragged a lot back then. They both did, making ridiculous promises as they pored through thick tomes and sat through boring lectures together.

Nyah gestured for her. "Come back to me. We can forget about... all this mess."

It would be easier to pretend she was right. Salma stepped forward and put a hand out, intent on taking Nyah's hand just as she had back in training, just as she had out at the creek, just as she had when they first came to these lands.

From behind her, Nadim gave a final rattled gasp. His last breath. Salma paused and dropped her hand away from Nyah's. Her gaze was drawn to the black cage and the pair of curious eyes that watched them.

"What about the boy?" she asked.

"What about him?" Nyah grunted, her voice filled with frustration. "Who cares? He doesn't matter."

"What will happen to him? Will you throw him to your alligators? Tear him to pieces with your birds?"

Nyah didn't like the question. Her eyes darted to the cage as though having forgotten it was even there. Salma backed away from her.

"You don't know, do you? You pieced this together as you went. You just expected me to come back to you with open arms."

"Salma, don't..." Nyah warned.

"You thought you could lure me back with your promises and our times together, and somehow I would be unable to resist." Salma's heart thundered in her chest. She could see the waters shifting in Nyah, the cracks just beneath the surface beginning to show.

Salma took both of Nyah's hands in hers, marveling at the tears in her eyes. "We're done. Whatever we once had is over. We've both changed, and I don't belong to you anymore. I'll be your friend perhaps, if you would let me, but not your lover. At least... not in this place. Not here."

Nyah gave a sad smile. "A friend? You mean like that rubbish over there?" She nodded toward Nadim's corpse, tears in her eyes. "Or perhaps that oaf outside feeding my pets? How dare you compare me to them." She tore her shaking hands away. "I have no need of friendship. I have my pets, my trees, my sky and earth, and they're all far more faithful."

"You can't mean that—"

"I do!" Nyah screamed. "They don't betray me, they don't lie to me, and they certainly don't leave me."

"Calm down." Salma tried to put her hands on Nyah's shoulders, but the sorceress spun away with a shriek.

"Don't touch me! Don't come near me." She backed away, hunched forward like a defensive animal. She flung a hand out to her side and the cage door fell open.

"Don't do it." Salma glanced to the boy. Nyah was an unpredictable wreck and the prince was a vulnerable target.

"Don't do what?" Nyah grinned, a mad laughter bubbling up.

"Please." Salma brought up her staff in a defensive stance. "I'll stop you."

"Oh really? You'll stop me with that little stick of yours? You are an insect to me now. This land has gifted me with its secrets. My power is far greater than either of us ever imagined."

Was the room growing darker? Salma was having trouble seeing her. "Don't, Nyah!" Salma was desperate. "I still love you!"

There was venom in Nyah's voice. "Liar! How dare you speak to me of love." The darkness seemed to be coming from the rafters and was beginning to coalesce into a solid black mass between them. The shadow birds were coming for her. They moved like a serpent through the air, coiled back, ready to strike through her like they had Nadim. Salma ran straight for the prince's cage. If she could grab him, they might be able to escape. She put her arms out for the crying child. A few steps more and she would have had him, but the birds engulfed her first. They tore her staff from her grip as she was carried up into the rafters.

Nyah's mad laughter echoed throughout the chamber. "Now you'll suffer like I suffered, you treacherous liar!" Salma was flying through the air. She had no sense of direction, only that she had no control over where she was going. Her left leg slammed into a wooden beam and she cried out in pain. Then she was flying in the opposite direction. Her stomach lurched as her left arm smacked into a wall. Something broke with a wet snap. Salma spat onto the floor as pain reverberated through her body. Nyah's laughter had quieted as Salma hovered in pain.

"How dare you speak of love," Nyah whispered, moving her closer. "You abandoned me here. You didn't even say goodbye! Why did you leave me? We could have been happy together here." Despite the venom in her voice, Nyah began to cry over her, her fingers curling up at the horrible angle of Salma's arm, the bleeding of her leg. It was one thing to talk about what she wanted to do, but very different to actually do it.

Salma hissed, "This land is sick. You're sick. Can't you see that?"

"You had me," Nyah whispered. "We were happy. Wasn't that enough?" She put a hand to her hair as tears rolled down her cheeks.

"No."

Salma's words hung in the air. She expected more bitter words or more pain, but she didn't expect to be lowered to the ground.

Nyah wrapped her arms around herself. "Why not?" she asked with petulance. "Why can't I alone be enough for you?"

Salma managed a small smile despite the pain. "I love you, not this place, not this land, just you. You've been twisted by it. I've always loved you, Nyah."

Nyah put a hand to her lips and fell to the ground, sobbing uncontrollably. ""I didn't mean to change! I didn't mean to hurt people, I just wanted to be happy again.""

"I know," Salma said with a small smile, wishing she could put her hand out to stroke Nyah's hair, wishing she could hold her in her arms. But she was running out of energy, running out of time. "You know," she said, feeling a trickle of blood trail out of her mouth. "Our fights were never this bad before."

Nyah reached an arm around her and hugged her. "I get..." She swallowed. "So angry! I can't help myself. I never meant for this to get so out of hand."

Salma draped her good hand on her head, stroking her hair despite the energy it took. "Shh, I know. It's okay, I know."

"I don't know what to do," Nyah sobbed. "You'll never love me again. If I let you go and give you the boy, I'll have nothing left."

"Come with us. They don't know what you look like. I'll bring the prince back, and you can wait for me. Come live with me, Nyah."

She pulled back, her face scrunched up with tears and desperation in her eyes. "Do you think I could? Would you really want me to?"

"Why not?" Salma smiled as her arm dropped to her side.

Nyah looked around as though watched, hunted. "I don't know if I can. This place... it's part of me. It gives me my power. If I leave, I may not be able to wield magic anymore."

"That's the madness talking, not you."

Nyah stared at her for a long moment, then held out her hand. "Brace yourself, this is going to hurt."

A loud snap sent pain reverberating up and down Salma's arm and shoulder, and then a flare of pain erupted from her leg.

"Hang on, almost—there, done!"

Salma took a deep breath, realizing that not only did she no longer want to pass out, but she wasn't in pain either. She sat up, looking at her leg and arm in disbelief.

Nyah pulled her to her feet. "How do you feel?"

"Amazing. You can heal people? I thought this power only led to destruction."

"It can heal when I want it to, but it can do more than that too." She walked over to Nadim's body and put her hands out over him. A few moments later he gasped in pain. Salma ran over to see the wound in his stomach slowly stitch closed.

"What?" He asked, blinking in confusion.

"Nyah, wait, you can bring people back from the—"

"I'm busy, dear, ask me later," Nyah said with a smile before stepping outside onto the footpath.

Salma shook her head. She hadn't even considered that was possible, let alone that Nyah had that kind of power. For the first time she understood the lure of this land, the temptation that that power had on her.

"What just happened?" Nadim asked in alarm.

Salma smiled and helped him to his feet. "How are you feeling?"

"I—I don't know. I think I was dead." He looked horrified by his own words. "Salma, what—"

"Wow, those gators really did a number on me!"

They turned to see Yutu walk inside, dripping wet and her armor in tatters. "Yutu?" Nadim sounded like he was about to cry.

"Why are you two just standing there? Let's get the prince and get out of here!"

Salma ran to the door, looking for Nyah, but she was gone. "Where did she go?"

"Who, the witch?" Yutu asked, shaking the water off of her scimitar. "Look, I don't know, and I don't care. We need to get the prince and get out of here—fast."

Nadim rushed to the cage and took the prince into his arms. "Shh, it's okay. Nobody is going to hurt you now."

"Great, now let's make tracks before she comes back." Yutu hurried out the door.

Nadim stopped at the doorway before meeting Salma's gaze. "Look, about what just happened..."

"Don't worry about it. We'll talk about it later; for now, let's just follow Yutu."

He paused as though he knew that she had no intention of explaining anything later, but followed Yutu regardless.

They crossed the footpath without any incident and just before they headed deeper into the woods, Salma caught sight of Nyah standing by the enormous bell. She wanted to run over and hug her, but Nyah held up her hand.

Salma nodded. This wouldn't be the last she saw of her.

Together the team made their way back to the queen and her encampment without incident.

———

THE QUEEN WAS THRILLED TO HAVE HER GRANDSON returned, and was even more amazed that all three of them had come back in one piece. Nadim didn't indicate his or Yutu's death, and Salma appreciated his secrecy. They had an unspoken arrangement: she forgave him for his betrayal as long as he kept silent about what really happened. He couldn't complain much; he was given the same fame, land, and wealth that she was granted.

The three of them became known as the Sorceress Slayers, even though no sorceresses were in fact killed. That detail didn't seem to make a difference.

A week later, Salma went back to the woods, back to the edge of the land that belonged to the Dark Sorceress. The trees stood the same as before, still and solemn. She waited several minutes before deciding that she should probably head to the monastery instead. There was no way Nyah had helped her and just vanished.

As soon as she stepped past the great oak tree, a voice called out to her. "I wouldn't go that way, the land is sick, you know."

Salma spun around to see Nyah leaning against the oak, when she knew for a fact she hadn't been there a moment ago.

Nyah smiled at her. "Who knows what that place could do to you."

"Nyah!" Salma cried, running over and crashing into a tight hug. "You came back!"

They hugged for a long time, listening to the wind in the branches, and in the distance a hawk called. Nyah pulled away with tears in her eyes.

"So, Slayer, I hear you have a lovely piece of land that you own now."

Salma smiled. "I do, in fact. It would be great to get some help cleaning it up." She bumped into her. "Think you could help me with that?"

Nyah smiled, and it was more beautiful than any Salma could remember. "I would love that."

Curse of Beauty

SHE KNEW SHE WAS BEAUTIFUL. IN FACT, SHE FOUND IT painfully obvious. Catharine owned no mirrors and her windows had no glass. There was not a scrap of reflective metal in her house, and even her image in the river was a wave of motion. No, Catharine had come to rely on the opinions of the others who came looking for her. And they always came.

She would travel out into the forest, a tune swimming from her lips and up towards the bright blue summer sky. She sang while on the hunt, while fetching water, while bathing. It simply was impossible to resist when the only sounds were the chirping of birds and the whispering wind. She never thought of it as a skill worth much merit, but her throat never tired and she never became winded. It was as natural to her as the rising sun was to the blue jay. It simply happened.

Mother had always warned her of the dangers. Singing in the woods would only bring heartache. The louder you sang, the more dangerous. So of course, Catharine had sung her hardest when she was little. Belting out tunes along the jagged riverbank or while skipping along the deer paths. Yet somehow Mother knew, and she'd lock Catharine up in the cellar for a night without supper, with only the gleam of moonlight seeping through the cracks and the scurrying of mice to keep her company. A place like that didn't inspire song, only silence and guilt, but perhaps that was what Mother wanted all along for her beautiful daughter. Catharine would never know. Mother disappeared when she was a child, when Catharine's hair was so long she could almost sweep the floor with a dance. Mother, her ruby eyes darting back and forth, warned her to stay put, that danger was coming towards them and she needed to keep silent. That was the last she saw of her mother, stalking into the woods with her bow in hand.

Catharine had been so frightened she didn't make a sound for a week. She stayed hidden in the tiny wooden house in the woods, with its chimney leaning against one of the tallest oaks. The rains had come and gone that week, and Mother never returned. Since that day the little girl chopped her hair short and learned to live on her own. She learned to keep to herself, and never, ever, would she sing at the top of her lungs as she had as a child.

These days Catharine was grown up, independent. She knew the forests like the back of her hand and could even point out the busiest bird nests and rabbit holes. It was a sunny day and the sky was a brilliant blue, with stripes of clouds darting across. Catharine gathered up her quiver and bow, a hum already on her lips. The wooden door was old and creaked heavily on its hinges, but it still kept the wind and rains at bay. She avoided the splinters in the handle as she pulled it closed. The scent of the morning dew was fresh upon the breeze. It was a tad bit chilly, but not so much that she needed a cloak. Her three cats stretched and purred as they woke from slumber. Eyes was the black one. She had a striking emerald gaze that watched everything with an equal helping of suspicion. Pies was a tubby orange tabby that always wanted her belly scratched before her head, and tiny white Cries used her most pitiful high-pitched yowl whenever she wanted something, just like she was doing now.

"If you're so very hungry, you could just catch your food instead of begging for mine."

Cries seemed to take that into consideration for a moment, but it was probably easier to make a fuss. Catharine was convinced they were the laziest cats in the land. Every day they begged for food, and every day she gave in. They were her only friends though, and at times it could get quite lonely.

"I'm all out of rabbit," she explained to Pies, whose orange eyes watched from over her belly as Catharine adjusted her quiver. "So I'll have to go out and find something for the four of us." She smiled at the trio before heading into the woods, the leaves alight with red and orange light from the rising sun.

Her feet knew the path well, and already a song was on her lips. It had no lyrics, only the dogmatic rhythm she carried with her on the hunt. It had been difficult at first, figuring out how to use Mother's spare bow and arrows, but she'd caught on after a few failures. Mother had practiced quite often, and although Catharine had accompanied her numerous times, she'd never imagined she would one day be on her own.

The trees were more spaced apart the farther she went. The canopy was owned by the giant oaks and maples that had called this forest home for hundreds of years. This was where she would find game, but it was also the easiest place to be seen. She pushed her song down to a hum, like a flicker of flame lowered to a tiny ember. She found an oak whose trunk had split in three places, and hunkered down to wait. The minutes passed quite slowly here, the wind rustling the leaves overhead and her legs already protesting the position. Catharine knew patience though and waited.

Leaves crunched with an unsteady gait, and she spotted a shadow in the distance. Something stood behind a thick elm surrounded by saplings and brambles, but she could just make out something brown moving on the other side. She lifted her bow. A deer would give them more food than a rabbit ever could. It would mean the four would eat quite heartily for several weeks instead of several days. She aimed through the split of the oak, waited for the deer to emerge around the tree, then let the arrow fly with a great burst of song.

Only just as she let go, the deer turned its head, a very human head topped with a leather cap. She must have shifted the limb of her bow ever so slightly, because the arrow missed its target and instead shattered against the elm's trunk. Wood splintered, bark scattered, and all of it flew straight into the man's face.

<hr>

SHE RACED ACROSS THE FOREST FLOOR, KICKING THROUGH mounds of leaves. The man had fallen to the ground and was turned away from her, but at least he was breathing.

"Are you alright?" she asked.

"Oh, my sweet lady." The man shuddered. "I have travelled so far to hear your lovely voice!" He crawled to his feet. Bits of wood and bark were stuck to his face, from both the sap and the blood. His cap and cloak had been made from deer hide, she realized. The arrow had missed his skull at least, but his eyes were covered with red welts, and blood dripped over his beard and clothes.

"You're hurt," she said. "You must come back with me. I don't know how you managed it, but that could strike you blind if we don't hurry."

"I heard your song and I looked up, wanting to see you." He smiled as though he was immune to the pain. "I should have known better, sweet lady. Please," he pleaded as he reached out and took hold of her wrist. "I must tell you this first! Damn these eyes, I must tell you my feelings!"

Catharine shook her head and tried to drag him with her, but he wouldn't budge.

"Long have I lived in the valley below, and for years I've heard your voice waft down as if the gods were taunting me. I told myself that I would find you and that you would one day be mine. The beautiful lady of the woods!" A thin smile came across his lips and despite his haggard, bloodied face, he looked remarkably jovial. "And here you are. It's as if Cupid himself struck me blind at your beauty!"

She was growing impatient. He needed rest and instead he was rambling. "Have you a name?"

His head tilted to the side and a dumb grin fell across his lips as she spoke, then he pulled himself out of his stupor once more. "I'm sorry?"

"A name, sir. A name!"

He brought her hand close and patted it gently. "Telis, dear lady." He acted as though this was quite normal, being struck blind in the woods.

"Sir Telis, I must impart grave news upon you, and I hope you shall listen closely. I am not yours, nor do I belong to anyone. I am cursed, much like my mother, and I would appreciate being left alone in my woods. I will bring you back with me, but only to heal your wounds for which I am responsible. Nothing more, foolish Telis."

His bushy eyebrows slanted. "But I have traveled so far!"

She pulled her hand free from his. "Then you have done

so in vain." The air was still as though the entire forest held its breath. Catharine had not known anger often, but when it did visit, it was a most cruel thing.

Telis was quiet a moment, wringing his hands with worry even as his eyes continued to bleed. "Please, I meant you no harm, fair lady. Pay no heed of me, for I am nothing more than a poor fool of a man, as you so aptly called me. Lead and I shall follow."

She took his hand and began walking back to the house. Telis was far shorter than she, and far more rotund as well, but there was an air of kindness about him that was genuine, if perhaps naïve. He was peculiar and unlike any of the villagers she had come across before. Men from the village often wanted to hunt her down. They came with spears and swords, and sometimes even pistols, but upon seeing Catharine they would drop their weapons, their devices of violence, and proclaim their love to her. Catharine was not sure what to make of it when it first happened. She had thought the first man had gone mad from prolonged time in the forest, but it happened again and again. She often wondered if these men were the danger to which Mother had referred.

Telis, though, was very different from the others. Usually once they were injured, they snapped out of their stupor as though they'd been bitten by flame. He had never wanted to slay her. Instead he came unarmed and professed his love without once laying eyes on her. Perhaps he was in fact mad, and the others had been sane after all. Either way, by the time she reached the clearing of her tiny home, she felt rather horrible for treating him the way she had.

Sleek Eyes arched her back and bushed out her black tail as Catharine brought Telis closer to the house. Pies took a moment to get to her feet and nearly tumbled over Cries as they scurried under the porch. Only after Catharine reassured her friends that their guest was truly welcome did they calm.

"I'm sorry, they aren't used to guests."

"It's alright." Telis smiled as Catharine set him down on one of the rickety stools inside. His head lolled about. "Is this where you live? It smells like earth."

Catharine arched an eyebrow at him. "Yes, and I think it smells of rotting wood. You are a funny one, Telis. It is a wonder you made it so far on your own." She mixed a broth of warm water and herbs, and soaked a cloth within.

"Hearing your voice kept me going, sweet lady. It sounded fairer than a flock of nightingales." Even though she was tending to his wounds, and the pain must have been sharp, he still smiled.

She frowned a moment before replying, "You are the first man who has not wanted to kill me, Telis. And you are likely the first and only to fall in love with me before you could even see me."

Telis was trembling. "There are many who fear you, lady. Many who say you lure men to their deaths in these woods."

Catharine laughed outright at that. "Lure men to their deaths? How ridiculous! They come hunting my death, and I am forced to defend myself. You are the first to actually speak to me as though I am human and not some silly beast."

He seemed surprised. "You are human then? They say you are a siren with a voice of beauty and a face so hideous that men are driven mad by it."

"A siren? Is that what they call my people? I'm not sure, Mother never mentioned that."

"Your mother... she came to the village once, didn't she?" Catharine's eyes went wide, but Telis could not see her surprise. "She was brought in by a group of hunters, her mouth gagged and her head covered with a black cloth so no one could see her face. They were afraid she would bewitch them. I — I recall seeing it happen when I was very young..."

Catharine felt tears welling up, but she wiped them away quickly. It was the fate she had always feared. "She didn't deserve that."

Telis put a hand on her arm. "I am sorry, I hadn't realized... To hear it from such a bumbling fool too — oh forgive me, beautiful lady!"

She dried her eyes with a scoff. "You know not what you speak, Telis. How do you know I am beautiful? I could be a hideous hag with a face reminiscent of a frog's behind!"

"Because," he whispered, his hands trailing up her face to wipe at her tears. "Your voice, your kindness — how could you be hideous with such a kind heart and beautiful voice?"

She backed away from his touch; something about the way he spoke — it disturbed her. He wasn't one of the regular hunters, and he had no intention of trying to kill her. She had seen what her appearance had done to the others, how their composure had flown away upon gazing at her. Yet this man was not afraid. If anything, he was drawn in despite the danger.

"I — I must hunt." Catharine was surprised at the difficulty it took to speak. "We have no food left, and you must build your strength if you are to heal."

Telis nodded, his face brightening even with his eyes bandaged. "I will wait here for you then, lady. Thank you again."

She took up her bow and headed out the door, nearly tripping over the trio of curious cats at her feet.

"Honestly, ladies! Show a bit of respect, won't you?" She pushed through them and out into the wilderness. She was uncertain how she felt about keeping the man alone with her, but to turn him away might mean killing him, and she couldn't bring herself to that level. Not when the man was innocent and obviously a fool.

THE DAYS PASSED QUITE PLEASANTLY FOR THE TWO uncertain companions, and Telis was slowly gaining strength as his eyes healed. Catharine never found another deer, but a couple of hares were a nice compensation for a few days. Later in the week the storms rolled in, and she and Telis were forced to stay indoors in the small shack as the rain came down in sheets. Catharine lit the fireplace and checked Telis' eyes once again, unwrapping the bandage with cautious fingers.

Eyes was perched on top of the dining table, watching them through half-lidded eyes. The thunder and lightning shook the shack so forcefully that even Cries had grown quiet and was hiding underneath the covers in Catharine's bed. Pies, on the other hand, couldn't care less for the noise and commotion. She'd taken up the evening in the makeshift hammock Catharine had put up for Telis to sleep in, and weighed it down so that underneath all you could see was a round, heavy bump where she lay.

"How does it feel?" Catharine had to raise her voice slightly to be heard over the rain.

"It is painful still, but I find it helps immensely when I hear you sing. It's as though the wound is no longer even there." She probed her fingers along the red, scarred tissue. His eyes were swollen shut still, but each day the improvement was obvious, especially with the herbs she applied daily. "It appears to be coming along nicely. Just a few more days and you should have your sight back."

His chilly, coarse hands took hers and brought them to his lips. His beard felt prickly against the back of her hand, and her cheeks went crimson as she pulled her fingers loose from his. "Telis, what are you doing?"

He smiled, and though his eyes were still red and swollen, he looked quite handsome as he faced her. "Wooing a beautiful woman."

She shook her head, leaning up against the tiny table. "No, you have it wrong, my friend. I am a siren if you recall, and do not have the pleasure of calling myself a true woman."

"Very well then," he sighed, the firelight flickering off his worn face, and a sly grin on his lips. "Perhaps I am wooing a beautiful siren, then?"

Catharine folded her arms. "What if the rumors they say are true? What if I do lure men to their deaths with the sound of my voice? What will you do if you see me, and you lose all reason? What then?"

He was quiet a moment, his brow furrowed with thought. Eyes looked between the two of them, curiosity twitching her tail. "Then perhaps it is best if I never see you, lady."

She laughed. "That is a high price to pay simply to be in my company, foolish Telis. Are you sure it is worth it?"

"I would give a thousand eyes to stay by your side. You have made me the happiest I have ever been. Being near you feels like a dream, one that I would never wish to leave. Why should I not keep it that way?"

"But Telis, surely you don't intend to –"

"Can you sing something for me?"

She blinked. "I suppose."

"Then sing something. Sing something to drive away this rain, to blow away this lightning. Sing something so beautiful that the very clouds divide for you."

"I dare not!" she gasped. "The last time I did that, Mother was captured by those hunters. They heard me in the village and took their vengeance out on her." Her voice trembled more than she liked.

"Damn the villagers," he spat. "Sing for me. Sing for your woods and the ugly rain outside. I will handle them if they come for you. You cannot live in fear of your voice, sweet lady. For it is as much a part of you as... as my heart is."

She didn't know what to say. She was utterly speechless, and yet already a tune had come to her lips. She started out with a low hum that built into a torrent that shook the walls of the shack. The rain outside could no longer be heard. Telis and the three cats stared at her with amazement and wonder. She allowed the song to spill out of her: the anguish, the sorrow, the love, and the laughter. Her voice danced amid green, leafy trees after a summer rain, it soared over the white snowy hills of winter, and drifted in a cloudless blue sky. She sang as a guide, as a storyteller, and as a translator, speaking in a language of emotions instead of words. When the tune came to an end, the torrent of rain had fallen to a sprinkle. The three cats were all together on the dining table, watching her and purring. Tears were streaming down Telis' face.

"That was the most beautiful song I have ever heard, fair lady."

She smiled at him and leaned forward to wipe his tears aside. "Please, Telis. Call me Catharine."

THE NEXT MORNING CATHARINE FOUND THAT SHE COULD not keep her voice silent. Telis had shown her a part of herself that she had never known, a bit of courage that was sturdier than the oldest oak. As she hunted, her song was joined by the birds and crickets and frogs; she felt a connection with them that she hadn't known for ages. This was where she belonged. She was wanted. She was loved. For the first time in her life, she wasn't afraid of her gift.

With two wild turkeys in hand, she headed back to the

house before midday. That was when she saw something most unusual. Eyes was bounding toward her with a speed Catharine had seen only when she was hunting mice. She leapt up into Catharine's arms, shaking from snout to tail. There was trouble, and it was so terrible even brave Eyes had been forced to flee.

Catharine hid the turkeys and pulled out her bow as she crept back to the house. She swallowed down the fearful tune that wanted to take her tongue, and went uphill to see if she could get a better vantage. That was when she smelled smoke, not just of fire but gunpowder. With a gasp she sprinted to the peak of the hill to look over the edge at her house below. There were men there now, villagers by their dress, and not just one. There must have been at least ten of them. At the foot of the doorway was Telis, lying in a pool of his own blood, his eyes still freshly bandaged from that morning. In one hand he held a large kitchen knife, dipped in blood. She couldn't look away from him any more than she could stop the growl rising in her throat.

They had heard her last night, she realized as she stared down at his motionless body. They had heard her song and come with their guns and their hatred. Telis hadn't had a chance. Now he was dead before she had even gotten to know him, before he had even been able to recover his sight. Just as the first tendrils of affection began to burn through her cold defenses, built from years of terror and isolation, just as she began to feel that she belonged, it was all destroyed in a single morning. These killers from the village came and stomped out her one chance for happiness before it had barely begun to sprout. As fire rose up from her small wooden home and encompassed the tall, powerful oak tree it leaned against, a heat filled her. A new song came to her lips, and it was a far cry from the cheerful, whimsical love of last night. This was a song of vengeance.

She shrieked into the sky and the killers turned toward her, terror filling their faces. Never before had Catharine felt such rage. Was this what Mother had feared when those hunters dragged her to the village? She would have hated to see their home destroyed. Catharine's shriek rose to a higher pitch and she rushed down the side of the cliff at such a speed that her feet barely touched the ground. Guns were fired, but fear disrupted their aim.

As she drew near, many fell to their knees, clutching their ears and crying out for mercy, but Catharine would show them none. Mercy was a luxury only one man had shown her, and his blood stained the dirt beneath their feet. She picked up a short sword from where the closest had dropped it, and cut the man's head from his shoulders in a single slice. Without allowing her shriek to falter, she stepped over another who was rolling on the ground, blood seeping out from between his fingers as he tried to cover his ears. Another approached, somehow managing to stand, and held out a dagger as curses fell from his lips. She sliced him vertically and watched as he crumpled to the ground.

She tore through them without care, until finally she stood above Telis. They had shot him through the chest, and he still had a hand covering the gaping wound. The rage fled as quickly as it had come; then her voice gave out. She crouched down by Telis, trembling and trying to catch her breath. She held him close and dragged her fingers along the prickling whiskers of his beard, along those lips that felt cold despite the raging fire nearby.

A sob broke through and she cried for foolish Telis, for her shattered dreams, and for their lost happiness. She cried knowing that she truly was the monster they so feared, but mostly she cried for the inescapable loneliness that draped over her like a familiar cloak.

La Femme en Rouge

FROSTED PINK LIPSTICK, SWEET SUMMER SUNSET eyeshadow, and blushing rose rouge: my hands trembled so badly that the eyeliner went on crooked.

"Shit," I muttered under my breath, arching my face up to the light and dabbing at my eye with my pinky finger, trying to smooth out the line, trying to make it perfect. The false lashes were next, and I swallowed down the dryness in my throat. The lash glue squeezed out slow and smooth, a white strip on the back of the lash. Then the door to the bathroom opened with a loud clacking of heels and I nearly dropped the lash onto the grimy floor.

I turned to look, blowing lightly on the lash, waiting for the white to go clear. A woman with dark hair and spray-tanned skin slipped into one of the stalls. Hopefully she didn't notice me. No questions, no comments, no wondering why I had a whole makeup bag dumped out on the counter-top. I leaned forward over the sink and tried to place the lash on my eyelid, shaking so badly I was afraid I was going to poke myself in the eye.

The toilet flushed and I froze, breathing so close to the

mirror that it fogged up. I tried to avoid her gaze as she walked up beside me to wash her hands.

Sidelong glances. Unreadable features. I tried to focus on the lash instead.

"I always hate those things," the woman said in a thick southern accent as she soaped only her fingers and patted her hands dry with a daintiness that was lost on me.

I smiled, feeling the tension fade just a tad. "It's a pain," I replied, feeling my chest tighten as my voice, clearly a falsetto, echoed throughout the tile bathroom.

Her eyes roamed over my body, lingering on my chest, my too-wide shoulders. My face went hot as I applied glue to the second lash. I blew on it, waiting for the white stripe to go clear, waiting for the question or comment that was sure to come. She dropped her paper towel into the trash and headed for the door. No words, only the clacking of her shoes as she stepped out onto cement. The silence left behind lingered, filled only with the questions left unanswered.

Was she disgusted with me? Was she in a hurry to go somewhere? Was she going to try to get me arrested?

This was my only night of the week to be free, I reminded myself, trying to get control of my breathing again.

I put the second lash on, struggling around the tears that tried to overwhelm me.

THE HEELS WERE MY PERSONAL HELL. I DIDN'T UNDERSTAND how some women could run in them when walking was such a damn challenge. Even the tiny kitten heels I wore felt like walking on stilts. For weeks I had practiced, back and forth in my bedroom, dragging the shoes across the grungy carpet for hours on end, and slowly I'd gained my balance. I wasn't perfect, but at least I didn't have to hug the wall anymore.

I dumped my makeup back into my bag and stopped to take a final look at the mirror. I dragged my fingers through my hair, shaking out the curls of my blond wig, swaying back and forth on my heels. I pulled down my white sequined dress. The padded bra helped to finish the look.

For the first time all week, I finally looked like myself, but I felt like an impostor. I always felt like an impostor on Friday nights.

"Here we go," I whispered to my reflection. I grabbed a paper towel and dabbed at the corners of my eyes, still fighting back the threat of tears.

I took a deep breath, then plunged out into the night.

Hot air hit my face as I stepped out of the air-conditioned bathroom and onto the concrete. The humidity was worse though, and for a moment it felt like I needed to breathe deeper to get the oxygen in. I kept a confident gait as I side-stepped an older man with broad shoulders and a grim expression.

He glanced up to my face then down to my body and back up again. Did he see through me? Had I put on too much makeup? The questions tried to overwhelm me, and part of me wanted to run back into the bathroom and take everything off, but I didn't. I had practiced. I looked good, maybe even sexy. I worked hard at this. I matched his gaze and gave a small smirk, and to my surprise he smiled back. I got a little bounce in my step as I moved past him, my small flicker of confidence restored.

I breathed in the hot, humid night air. There was always a slight scent of piss near the bathrooms. In the distance, a trumpet crooned jazzy melodies into the night, and high up above the magnolia trees, the moon above was waxing and almost full. I breathed it all in, letting it fill my lungs and enter my pores.

Home. I belonged here. New Orleans was a part of my

blood, and the rich night air was invigorating. Mardi Gras was only a few days away and I could feel it in my bones.

I walked out onto the asphalt, gaining my feet, my large purse knocking into my hips with every step. Men looked me up and down, a spark in their eyes and a smile on their lips; it made me feel powerful. I checked my phone for the time. Good, I wasn't running late for once.

This wasn't the first Friday night change I had done, but it would be my last. I just didn't know it yet.

* * *

I WAS STILL SEVERAL BLOCKS FROM THE RESTAURANT, BUT I didn't mind. It gave me a chance to people watch, and the evening was a prime time for it.

I caught the scent of beignets as I passed the Cafe du Monde. They were closed this late, but somehow the smell lingered long after closing time. Across the street, a group of teens were gathered around a woman who was performing as a living statue. I only knew she wasn't a real statue because I had taken the same path each Friday night for the past five months. The woman stood so still she could pass for a mannequin. Her dress, made to look like stone, draped down to the sidewalk in perfect, still waves. Then she shifted to another position with smooth practiced poise, and one of the boys squealed in shock. I couldn't help but smile.

Passing Jackson Square, I spotted several little stands for tarot readers. An older woman swathed in scarves and skirts sat at a simple folding table beneath a purple umbrella. She was giving a reading to a young man maybe in his early twenties. His leg bounced nervously as he waited to hear his future.

There was an unmistakable energy in the air. I got the strange urge to rush over and have my fortune told too, but I didn't need that. I knew my future already. The thought made the tears threaten me again, and I took a deep breath and kept walking.

I focused on my feet, realizing I had finally perfected my stride in the heels. I grinned, the dread forgotten, and for the first time ever, I truly felt like I fit my skin. Tonight, I was Josie, a woman out for a night on the town, not Jo. In that beautiful moment, my future felt truly bright, even though I knew it wasn't.

I made my way up St. Peter to Royal Street. The crowds were far thicker. Music blared out onto the street from every bar and dance hall I could see, and laughter floated from everywhere. I was proud of myself. I had never walked so far in heels before, a full eight blocks, and I only stumbled once due to a sewer grate.

By the time I reached the entrance for Pop's Kitchen, I had broken out into a sweat, and I worried that all my carefully applied makeup had been washed away in the thick humidity, despite the spray I used that claimed otherwise. I swung the door open, and the blast of air-conditioning felt amazing. I stepped up the old familiar wooden steps, which creaked and dipped a little bit with my weight, and took in the room.

The band was taking a break—I must have caught them right in time for their lull—which was perfect. Across the busy floor of tables and chairs, I spotted Cherie, the hostess, and gave her an exaggerated wave. She waved back, with her big, beautiful grin, before returning to her table.

I leaned against a wooden beam, breathing in the scents of gumbo, seared shrimp, and sizzling fish that mingled in the air. Multicolored margaritas glinted across each of the tables like Christmas lights, and at the far end of the room I spotted the dishpan band grabbing a bite before their next song.

"Good to see you, Josie!"

I turned to see Cherie approaching the hostess stand. She had long black hair that she pinned up for a perfect messy look that I admired, and she always wore red lipstick. She was dressed in a short, black dress with little crescent moons embroidered on the bottom. They reminded me of the nearly-full moon out tonight, and I stared at them for too long.

Cherie leaned over to get my attention as I zoned out. "I saved your spot tonight! I was worried you weren't going to show." She slid a menu under her arm and grabbed some silverware.

"I got distracted people watching," I admitted. It wasn't the place to describe my near breakdown in the bathroom.

She gave me a smile and led the way across the restaurant. We had to squeeze past a large group of men who had clearly been drinking for a while. Cherie squeezed by them effortlessly, but I wasn't as small as she was. The big man stood up and pulled the seat two feet out of the way for me and my cheeks went hot.

"Allow me, my dear!" he said with an elaborate bow. I honestly wasn't sure if I should be appreciative or embarrassed, so I whispered a quiet thanks as I stepped past him. "Don't be a stranger, okay, cutie? I'll be here all night!"

The other men at the table laughed. I almost stumbled as my heel caught a hole in the wooden floor, but caught myself on the back of an empty chair, angry at myself for my clumsiness.

"You okay?" Cherie asked as I sat down at my regular table.

"Yeah, I think so. I just... wow."

"Yeah, these floors are pretty old," she said with a smile as she placed the menu down in front of me.

I stared at her for a moment, realizing she was more worried about me tripping than she was about the raucous group at the table. Maybe they weren't trying to be cruel. Maybe I was overreacting.

I ordered a swamp water and a burger with fries, not needing to look at the menu. Cherie took it away with a smirk. "I ought to know that by now!" Then she breezed away, and I had a moment to close my eyes and gather myself.

I was once again covered in a sheen of sweat despite the fan above me, and my fingers trembled on the tabletop. I dropped my hands into my lap and tried to focus on deep, calming breaths. Pop's Kitchen was one of the only places where I felt truly welcomed and appreciated. I came here every Friday night with money I barely scraped together because I wanted to support the place that accepted me, the place where I had friends.

"Alright, ladies and gentlemen," the head of the dishpan band said into his microphone with his thick Creole accent. He wore a battered top hat and, although he was shirtless, he had his metal dishpan already hooked over his shoulders in preparation. "We're coming back in two minutes. I hope you're ready to have a good time! We're going to help you shed all your worries tonight!"

I was so ready.

The crowd whooped and cheered, and I called out with them. I wanted them to help me forget myself for a little while.

Cherie brought my swamp water, a greenish brown mixture that was their house special. It was a quick way to get drunk.

"By the way." Cherie crouched down near me to keep from blocking the view of the band. "That dress looks nice on you! Is it new?"

Her eyes sparkled in the stage light and her smile lifted my soul. I nodded and giggled, so incredibly grateful that someone had noticed. Cherie smiled before climbing to her feet. "It looks really good! You should wear it more often!"

The band raked their spoons across the dishpans with a rhythm that was infectious, and the bells chimed in a perfect rowdy chorus. I swayed in my seat, soaking in the moment: the music, the drink, the delicious burger that was brought out.

In that instant it felt good to be alive.

It was a rarity.

<hr>

ADMITTEDLY I STAYED LONGER THAN I SHOULD HAVE. THE third glass of swamp water made the world just as shimmery and perfect as I wanted it to be. I knew there would be consequences later, but I just didn't care. For the first time in days, I was enjoying myself. I belonged here, more than I did at home or at work. As I cheered on the band and clapped my hands, every person in the room became family. Every person from the crowd became my friend. As Cherie came by to pick up the check and the additional tip I left for her, I downed the last of my swamp water and spilled a little down my chin. She chuckled as I wiped it up with a cloth napkin.

"Are you going to be okay going home?" she asked, the concern in her eyes pulling me down from the clouds just a little. "I mean, I know how your Pa is."

Those clouds left completely at her words, but I refused to acknowledge it. Instead I waved a hand. "No, he'll be fine. He has to get used to it sometime. I'm not changing who I am for him." It was meant to come out nonchalant, but it sounded desperate to my drunken ears.

She shook her head. "I didn't mean that. I mean... do you need a place to change?"

I drew my feet up under my chair and pushed my hand

flat on the table, curling in on myself even when I didn't mean to. Cherie was trying to be nice, I tried to remind myself. She didn't want me to get hurt. She didn't want me to show up the following Friday with a bruised jaw again. "No," I whispered. "I'll be fine."

She stared at me a long moment, the sparkle in her eyes gone and replaced with her cool, analyzing gaze. Cherie was a lovely woman, but we had never dated. She asked me out once a year ago and I turned her down, but it didn't stop us from being best friends. Cherie worried over me too much and I was a giant bucket of emotional baggage. She was definitely attractive, but I could see from across the room that Cherie had her life in order, and I was a mess. She deserved someone better than me.

Cherie put her tray of empty glassware down on the table and sat down across from me, her lips pursed.

"What are you doing? You'll get in trouble," I urged, looking around for her supervisor. She reached out and took my hand in hers, linking our fingers together. I felt my face get hot at her touch.

"Josie, listen to me a moment, will you? Just be quiet and listen."

It felt suddenly too warm in the room, and I regretted drinking so much. "I'm listening," I whispered.

"You can't keep doing this. I know you like coming here, and trust me, I appreciate that you always tip so much. But you're never going to get anywhere like this. You've got to get away from him. You have to allow yourself to live."

I stared down at the empty glasses, the chunks of ice mostly melted and leaving pools of discolored water at the base. I felt sweat trail down the back of my dress and gather in the padded bra. "I do live. I live every time I come here, and I love it."

Cherie rolled her eyes. "Coming here is an escape, it's not

living. You can't be yourself unless you get away from him. He's going to continue to hurt you again and again. There's no way you can keep on pretending forever."

"I can try," I said carefully, wrapping my lips around the words like trying on clothes.

"You've been trying. It hasn't worked. You've been living there with your dad for three years now. He's going to find out, and every night I worry about you. You can't live there with him." She squeezed my hand and her lovely, lacquered fingernails caught the harsh lights. "I want you to move in with me."

"Cherie, no..."

I shook my head, trying to keep my lip from trembling. I was too drunk for the conversation.

"Listen to me. I want you to move in with me. Your job is remote, right? I can upgrade my internet and you can move in. I don't make a whole lot and the place is going to be tight with the two of us, but I can't stand to see you doing this to yourself every week. You come here and get a glimpse of what could be, and then you go back to him and have to pretend to be Jo again. Every week you're more beaten down than the last, and I hate it."

The tears were coming, I could feel them like a balloon filled up too much with water, ready to burst. I couldn't deal with any of this. She was talking about things I couldn't even imagine. She was giving me hope where I had given up on it years ago.

"Thank you, Cherie, I really appreciate it, but I can't."

"Why not? And give me a real reason, not some fantastic reason you just thought up out of the blue."

I stared up at the lights, tears threatening to spill down at any second. "You're my best friend, you know that?" I gave a short laugh. "Maybe my only friend, I don't know." I felt her hand squeeze mine again and looked down to the table, allowing the tears to finally fall. "I'm afraid... of him. If he found out who I really was, he would be furious."

"And that's why you should move in with me," Cherie added with a smile, letting go of my hand and sitting back in her chair to look smug.

I frowned, trying to find the right words. "No, Cherie, you don't understand. If he found out what I did every Friday night, he would attack me, but if he got angry enough, I'm afraid he would kill you." I dabbed at my eyes with the napkin.

She was quiet a moment. "Me? Why would he kill me?"

"He would think you influenced me somehow," I sniffed. "He could blame you, he could blame this place, I don't know. He's just... he gets very violent, and if I had to choose..."

"No, don't you ever choose yourself like that. Don't you ever try to take it all on yourself. If he tried something, we would get a restraining order on him."

The very thought made my chest tighten. It wasn't enough, I wanted to say. It wouldn't be strong enough to stop him. All it would take is once, that was the only mistake he needed.

"No, I can't talk about this anymore, Cherie. I'm sorry, but I have to go." I got to my feet and nearly tripped over the leg of my chair. She was up in an instant.

"Look, I know it's difficult, but please consider it. You don't have to live in fear."

"Thank you. I mean it, thank you, but I don't think you understand what you're asking." I met her eyes, struggling to hold myself together, let alone stand on the damn heels. "He would find me."

THE LOOK ON CHERIE'S FACE WAS ABSOLUTE PITY AND IT hurt. If a stranger had looked at me like that, I could have handled it, but not her. I never wanted her to see me like that. She said she worried every night for my safety, and the thought of her curled up on her couch worrying for me hurt too. I walked out into the streets and the blast of cold wind pulled me out of my thoughts. My tears instantly felt freezing, and I wiped at my cheeks and eyes without caring about the makeup any longer. I was going to take it all off soon anyway. I had to if I wanted to go home.

A brief image flashed in my mind of going to Cherie's house and hanging my dress up in a little closet with my collection of heels, a smile on my lips and confidence in my step.

No, that was impossible. Damn her for even putting the thought in my mind. It would haunt me like a ghost every time Pa went for his belt.

I walked down toward Royal Street, clutching my arms around myself and trying to ignore the cold. The weatherman said it was supposed to be cold that night, but I hadn't realized it would be quite so bad. The streets that had been so filled with people were now barren. I didn't see anyone, not even parked cars or drunk stragglers wandering the street. The realization made me try to walk a bit faster, but I nearly tripped in the heels, so I had to slow my pace. *Stay focused and avoid the alleyways*, I thought to myself. Any robbers would probably be trying to find a warm place to stay out of the bitter wind.

Then I saw someone in the distance right near one of the three-story brick buildings with wrought iron detail. She came around the corner and walked toward me, only she wasn't huddled into a ball against the sharp wind; she walked confident and upright. She walked with purpose. Her long red dress trailed behind her, looking like a brilliant flag in the wind. As she drew closer, I tried to look away, not wanting to be rude, but she turned to walk directly toward me.

She couldn't be a robber, I thought to myself. There was no way she expected to escape unseen in that bright red dress. Was she drunk? Maybe that excused the fact that her arms were bare against the blasting wind. Her black hair whipped around her angled features. She wore bright red lipstick the same shade as her dress, and she was smiling. For a moment her eyes almost looked amber, and I looked up at her. I froze, unable to stop staring, she was so beautiful. She glided toward me and held her arms out. I stepped forward and allowed her to embrace me, awkwardly hugging her back.

Why was I doing this? Who was this person? I had a hard enough time hugging friends, but here I was hugging a complete stranger.

"Do I know you?" I asked as I forced myself to pull away from her warm embrace.

She laughed. "I don't think so. That's a beautiful dress though." Her voice made the tightness in my chest release just a little.

"Thank you," I whispered, giving a little curtsy.

"Can we dance?" she asked as though it was the most normal question in the world. She put a hand on my arm, slipping it down my wrist. I shivered, but not from the cold. "You're cold," she commented and cocked her head to the side.

"You're warm," I answered stupidly.

She slipped her warm hand into mine and wrapped her other arm around my waist, making my breath catch. Clearly we were dancing whether I wanted to or not, and I didn't resist her. Why would I want to? She was beautiful and she felt perfect. I wanted her to take me home with her, but that was insane. I had to get changed, see my Pa, get to work tomorrow.

"Here." Her warm breath on my ear sent a shiver down my spine. "Let me lead."

I let her.

My eyelids closed and I leaned into her. It was an old-fashioned waltz, one I had only seen in old movies. Even though I was a terrible dancer and couldn't walk in heels, I didn't fall once. She would step, and I would step in the exact mirror of hers. It was like we were connected somehow, and I couldn't stop looking at her. The curve of her cheek, her beautiful golden-brown eyes, her ruby lipstick; she was so impossibly gorgeous. Her warmth melted the cold of the wind away, and I gaped at her, afraid that if I said a single word that it would break the spell. Then she dipped me so low, I was only inches above the ground. I was gasping, not from the dance, but from her mere presence.

"You dance well," she whispered, her lips inches from mine as I hung upside down in her arms. She leaned her lips close to my throat. My heart was beating so fast I wondered if I would faint. "I wish we had more time."

The familiar panic started to build again in my chest.

"What do you mean?" I asked as she pulled me up. "Will I get to see you again?"

She leaned forward, slinking her arms around my shoulders, down my back, and around my waist, pulling me into her embrace again. This time, I pulled my arms tightly around her, feeling the silkiness of her dress, the smoothness of her skin, the tangle of her black hair. Her skin smelled impossibly like magnolia blossoms. I didn't want to let go of her; I didn't want her to leave me. I had never had anything in my life so perfect, and I didn't want to lose her.

"Please, don't leave," I urged.

She pulled away and gave me a sad smile. "If you wish to truly know me, you must know yourself, Josie. Find me again once you have." She held up a large, black card and slipped it into my hands. I took it without looking; I didn't want to look away from her.

"Please don't go, I want you to stay," I begged, wanting to sob.

She leaned in close, her lips so close to mine that if I leaned in an inch I could kiss her. Her presence was intoxicating. "It's time to shed your skin, Josie."

She put a hand on my cheek and I closed my eyes, ready for the final kiss, ready to feel her against my skin.

Instead all I felt was cold wind against my wet cheeks.

When I opened my eyes, she was gone, though I hadn't felt her hand leave my cheek. I felt at the place where her hand had been, not quite believing she had vanished in front of me. I turned around in the street, feeling colder by the second. I was alone.

What just happened?

In my opposite hand was the card she had given me, a worn, black card with a texture on the black side, but the other side was only painted a flat red. I flipped it over again and again, looking for an explanation, looking for at least a name, but there was nothing.

I DON'T KNOW HOW LONG I WALKED UP AND DOWN ROYAL Street, but I was shivering by the time I saw Cherie step out of Pop's Kitchen. She didn't see me and headed southwest on Royal, lighting a cigarette as she went. That was fine, I didn't want to talk to her, not right now at least. She would think I was crazy or maybe just drunk, which might be true. I felt drunk. Maybe it was all just an intoxicated dream?

The card though, I couldn't deny that. I held it tight in my freezing fingers as I made my way down St. Peter and passed by Jackson Square, which was completely empty. I kept hoping to see her sweeping around a corner in her brilliant red dress, or to spot her sitting at a fountain, but she was gone. I dragged myself back into the bathroom I had used earlier and took my clothes off even as tears fell. It was stupid to feel so sad; I didn't even know who she was, or if it had been real.

It's time to shed your skin, Josie.

As I changed back into my masculine clothes and pulled off my false lashes, I kept staring at the black card on the countertop. It was solid enough. That hadn't come out of my imagination or from a drunken haze.

A plan started forming. It probably wasn't a very good plan, but it got me to stop crying.

IT WAS LATE BY THE TIME I CLEANED UP AND HEADED home. The trains didn't run so late at night, but it wasn't that far of a walk. I walked up the rickety outdoor stairwell that led to the top floor of the two-story complex, hoping that Pa would be fast asleep at almost four in the morning, but I spotted the burning end of his cigarette as I crested the last step. He was sitting out on the balcony in a cheap plastic chair about ten doors down from the stairwell, watching the city sleep, wearing a sweatshirt and sweatpants with socks.

I had been drunk earlier, but I'd sobered up quickly from seeing the woman in red and the long walk in the cold. Pa, though, had started into his second six pack of beer and had a tall, stacked tower of empty beer cans on the other side of him. I slipped the black card into the pocket of my hoodie. Instinctively, I slowed my walk as I approached him, feeling the tightness in my chest and keeping my eyes down.

I went to turn the handle, hoping I could slip inside

without him commenting, but he had locked it. He turned his head to glare at me, and I froze.

"You're home late, ain't you, Jo?"

I stared at the worn door handle, at the flecked-off paint and the rust underneath. I held on to the cold metal as though it was a lifeline. It was easier if I didn't respond, if I didn't give him any ammunition that he could use against me. Maybe if he just got bored with me, he would let me pass without trying to stop me.

Pa took another swig of his beer. "What you been doing out so late? Ain't you got work in the morning?"

I swallowed down the dry patch in the back of my throat and reached into my pocket for my keys. No, that was my lipstick, they must be in the other pocket.

The chair creaked as he turned around to look at me better. "Hey, Jo! I'm talking to you. You so damn high and mighty that you're gonna ignore me in my own home?"

"Sorry," I muttered, finally getting the keys out and fumbling with them to unlock the door.

"Oh, there's your tongue, good. I'm glad you found it. Do you mind telling me what you do every Friday night that means you don't get back until the wee hours of the morning?"

"I went to a concert," I said finally. It wasn't a complete lie. "They play every Friday."

He narrowed his eyes. "Do you? Just a concert. Does that mean if I look in that bag, I'm not going to find another of your dresses hidden away?"

That made my hands shake. Thankfully the doorknob turned, and I fell more than stepped into the apartment. Without a word, I closed the door behind me, hearing Pa's words filter through.

"I thought as fucking much."

Grateful for the door being closed and the pile of beers Pa

still had to go through, I took a moment to lean against the couch, trying to catch my breath and make the tightness in my chest ease up.

He had found my dresses before. I still had the marks on my back from his belt.

Giving myself a precious few moments, I headed back to my bedroom, eager to get my bag put away and to hide my makeup and dresses. I walked a little too quickly to my bedroom and closed the door behind me, turning the lock with a sigh of relief. It didn't fix the fear entirely. If he really wanted to, Pa could kick the door in. He had done it before. But it gave me the feeling of safety and security, something I was desperate to have.

I hid the dresses in a special box under the bed labeled "comic books" and hid the makeup in a separate box labeled "kid's toys." Pa never liked either of those things, and even if he saw them, he would probably be too busy insulting me for having the boxes to actually look inside of them.

By the time I crawled into bed, I could see dawn brightening the dark skies. I knew I wouldn't be able to handle work, so I went ahead and canceled for the day. They could go without an additional vacation planner for a little while. Besides, at the moment, I just wanted to wrap myself up in a ball rather than pretend to get excited about planning a trip for somebody else.

I thought of Cherie's offer, of moving out, of living with her as who I truly was, as Josie. The tears threatened again, but I held them back. It wasn't possible. Pa would never let me leave even though he hated how I had changed. Ever since he'd driven Ma off, he'd tried so hard to turn me into the perfect son, but that wasn't who I was. It never was. He couldn't see that. He thought if he pushed enough, I would break, that this was just a phase that I would grow out of for some damn reason.

I loved him, but he was an idiot.

<hr>

I WASN'T SURE WHEN PA SHAMBLED TO BED. HE WAS supposed to be at the factory by noon, but his cursing around eleven o'clock pulled me from my sleep. I gripped my pillow and stared at the wall, listening.

The door was locked, I reminded myself. All of the makeup and dresses were hidden away. He had nothing to be mad at me about, I reminded myself, but the tightness in my chest insisted otherwise.

I jumped when he dropped a spoon on the linoleum kitchen floor. Was he drunk still? Probably. I wondered if he would get in an accident one day from drinking so much before going to work. Part of me hoped he would.

It's time to shed your skin, Josie.

It was almost noon by the time he left, and I waited ten minutes to make absolutely certain he was gone. I took a deep breath and felt the tension finally leave my chest. I felt exhausted.

I got up, showered, and poured myself some cereal before turning the television on. Ironically, they were filming on Royal Street. I stuffed food in my mouth, wondering if maybe the woman in red had been seen there, or maybe they would give some hint. Instead they were talking about the path the Krewe of Cork Parade would be taking on Mardi Gras the next couple of days. My excitement dwindled, and I started browsing on my phone.

"That's right, Grace, Mardi Gras is the time to shed your skin and become someone new!"

I looked up and stared at the television, not seeing anything they were talking about, but remembering in vivid detail the woman in red's words to me last night. What did she mean when she told me it was time to shed my skin? Did she mean it was time to shed who I was? I mean, I wanted to shed Jo and fully become Josie, but that wasn't possible for me. Was it?

I finished my food, cleaned my bowl, and turned off the television. Just as I reached for the door and slipped my hand around the rusted door handle again, I froze.

She wanted me to shed my skin, not to keep pretending. But I only pulled my dresses out for Josie on Friday nights, not in the middle of the day on a Saturday. I felt sweat break out on my face, the questions already filling my brain.

What if he came back early?

What if he saw me on the street?

With a snarl, I went back to my room, and put on a cute dress with black trees and stuffed a spare change of clothes in my bag. I picked up the card she had given me and stared at it again, confirming that yes, it was just a plain red card. Maybe it was just nonsense.

No, it meant something. I thought of the shaky plan I'd made last night and smiled. I just had to find the right person to ask.

If the scents from Cafe du Monde were difficult to resist when they were closed, it was ten times worse when they were open. I made my way to Jackson Square, disappointed that there weren't nearly as many tarot readers out so early, but there were a few. One setup I recognized: the older woman swathed in fabric set up beneath her purple umbrella. She was putting the final touches on a fold-out table. She had someone sitting with her, perhaps a friend since they were sitting beside her. I hated coming by so early, but I needed to find out more.

"Are you open?" I asked, stepping onto the large stone slabs of Jackson Square.

She looked up at me over her glasses. "Yes, yes, have a seat!"

She turned and said something in French to the person sitting beside her, an old woman with wispy white hair and a cane. Oddly enough, she had her back to the tarot reader and was staring out over the Square. It seemed really rude.

"What kind of reading would you like?" She folded back her long sleeves and pulled out a stack of cards with blue and gray cross-hatching on the back, then began expertly shuffling them, not even looking down at the table. Her blue eyes were fixed on me.

"What's the cheapest you have?" I asked with chagrin.

She smiled. "That would be a three-card reading for $20."

"That sounds fine to me." I nodded, mesmerized by the rapid shuffling of the cards. She could have said $50 or $100 and I probably would have paid it.

"Cash is fine."

"Oh, yes." I pulled out a crumpled bill and handed it over, but the woman with the cane held out her hand, not even looking at me.

The tarot reader glanced up. "Yes, it's good. Give her the money, please."

The woman with the cane took the bill and folded it twice, staring out past me instead of looking at the money. I stared at her, suddenly realizing that she was blind. I felt embarrassed for thinking she was rude.

"I'm sorry, I didn't know," I muttered.

"Don't worry about it, she's handling the money today is all," the reader said with a smile, placing her deck down on the table. "Now, let's focus on you. What did you say your name was?"

"Jo." I paused briefly before correcting myself. "Josie."

She smiled. "Ah, already I sense some confusion in you."

"Not confusion really, it's just... difficult."

"And what would you like to know, Josie?"

I moved my chair closer to the table, my back rigid as I tried to fish the words out of my overwhelmed mind. I thought of Cherie's pleading gaze at Pop's Kitchen, the scent of the woman in red and the freezing wind, and my father's coarse voice and smell of beer. I thought of the card in the pocket of my dress. Where did I even start? "I want to know what's going to happen to me. No, I want to know what happened to me, and what's going to happen next."

She laughed and readjusted her glasses. "That's a lot to pack into three cards, but let me see what I can do." She shuffled again, faster this time, and closed her eyes. Three cards were laid face down on the table.

"So, let's start with your past." She turned the rightmost card. A man wrapped in red with a long white beard stared at me. "The Emperor. This is upside down, which makes me think there's a person in your life who possibly holds a lot of control over you. Maybe they dominate you. Likely a man."

My palms went sweaty at her words. It was just a card, how could she pinpoint my life so accurately with one card? She must have seen the astonishment in my face because she asked, "You still want to continue?"

"Yes, please!" I blurted, and the words couldn't stop once they started. "That's my Pa and he gets... well, he gets angry sometimes, and you said dominate and that just perfectly describes him." I sat back and released the tension in my back. "I'm sorry, this is just already so accurate it's scary."

She smiled and flipped the middle card. I wasn't ready for the horns and wings and clear demonic imagery.

"It's upside-down," I muttered.

She shook her head. "This is the Devil. What this alludes to is that you've recently found something out about yourself, or experienced something that has changed you. It's making you see the world differently."

"Yes, that's it exactly! Only I can't really explain what even happened to me without sounding crazy."

She tapped the middle card again. "So this is where you are currently, correct?"

"Right," I said, already staring at the face-down card at the end.

"Let's see what's in store for your future." It looked like a yellow sun with a disappointed face and dogs howling from below. Only this card was right side up.

"That's good, right?"

"The Moon. Hmm, that's an odd one. So, this could mean that you're suffering from an illusion or fears, or it could mean you're following your intuition."

I reached for the card. "May I look at it?"

"Sure." She handed it over.

The moon itself resembled the images of the man in the moon. I had seen depictions of it in history books as a child. The wolves were howling at it; there were two of them, like a wolf pack. Oddly enough, it made me think of the woman in red. I gave the card back, and without even thinking, reached into my pocket for the card I'd been given the night before.

"I know this is a long shot, but I was hoping you might know what deck this came from?"

I held the card out, and the blind woman in the back shook her head vehemently, speaking in a fluid French that I couldn't understand. The only words I caught were très mauvais, which I knew meant very bad.

The reader took the card with a smile, speaking more French to her friend. But when she flipped it over and saw it was painted bright red, her smile dropped and her hand shook. "Where did you get this?" She held it out to me, as if she didn't want to touch it, and I took it back.

"There was a woman last night on Royal Street. She gave it to me, we danced..." I trailed off, realizing that neither of them was listening, as they seemed to be arguing.

The reader got to her feet and wrapped her scarves around her neck. "Do yourself a favor and burn it. Nothing good ever comes from la femme en rouge, especially this close to Mardi Gras. Burn it and never think of her again."

I got to my feet as well, realizing that I had outworn my welcome.

"I'm sorry, I didn't mean any harm."

"S'il voux plait."

I walked away, still hearing her friend still clearly frustrated. My feet couldn't move fast enough away from Jackson Square, though all I could think about was the card in my pocket. They wanted me to burn it, to erase all memory of her, to forget about her, but I couldn't do that. She had changed everything last night. She had changed me, and I had to see her again.

I had to find her.

***

I WENT DOWN TO ROYAL STREET AGAIN, THIS TIME HAVING to step around the copious people and the crush of traffic. Despite my annoyance at the tarot reader, I couldn't help but think back to the reading she had given me: the emperor, the devil, and the moon. Out of all of them, the moon struck me the most, and part of me wondered if I had any chance of finding her during the day. Perhaps she emerged only at night, like a ghost from the shadows. Maybe she worked somewhere like Cherie and didn't get out until late. Maybe she frequented the bars. Building up courage I never knew I even possessed, I stepped into bars, restaurants, and even a male strip club just to see if I could catch any sight of her. Nothing, not even a glimpse of her red skirts.

It was nearly dusk, and I was worn out and smelled of cigarette smoke. I was tired and hungry. I wanted to believe that I had maybe missed her, but I knew that wasn't true. I had searched everywhere and was no closer to finding her. I remembered her warm embrace, the feel of her hand against my back, and my eyes burned at the thought that I would never see her again. I found a patch of brick wall along Royal Street and leaned against it, staring up into the fading twilight.

The sky was clear in shades of peach and violet, and the full moon was visible just over the building lined with wrought iron across the street. It was gorgeous. Tears spilled down my cheeks, and I closed my eyes, trying to isolate myself from the noise of the street, from the music of the restaurant, from the crowd of people, from the excitement that came with Mardi Gras approaching.

The truth settled in cold and dead in my heart: I was fooling myself.

There would be no escape for me. My life would be written out in Pa's shadow and I would never truly be myself. I would never be able to embrace my true identity. I would maybe get little joys once a week at Pop's Kitchen, but little joys were all they would ever be.

The tears came harder, and I lowered myself to the ground, wrapping my arms around my knees and allowing the tears to fall. I didn't care what anyone thought of me anymore. I didn't care if Cherie or even the bartender saw me. There was a hurt inside that no amount of crying or pretending would ever be able to fix.

I sobbed into my arms, trying to be silent so I wouldn't be asked to move. I didn't care. By the time I looked up again, my eyes sore and my sleeves wet, the streetlamps had come on and the sky had turned into dark purple hues. The card, I remembered with a bolt, and reached into my pocket to pull it out.

I had forgotten about it, and now it was curved and bent from sitting on it for who knew how long. More tears threatened me, but then I spotted something like glitter on the black grid of the card. I blinked, turning it again to catch the moonlight, and I saw that instead of just a simple patterned grid embellishment, there was a silver line that connected several of them together. The line ended in a single five-pointed star. There was also a large gap in the grid that didn't make much sense.

Then I realized what it was: a map.

The gap was Jackson Square, and I traced it with my finger, muttering each of the roads. If that was Jackson Square, then that had to be Saint Louis Street, and if I followed that northwest past Bourbon and past Burgundy, that led straight to... I dropped my hand down to my side.

"Saint Louis Cemetery," I whispered to myself, blinking as though I was waking up from a dream.

Normally, going to the cemetery at night would have terrified me. Sure, they kept it locked up after dark, but that didn't mean it was very comfortable to peek through the bars, standing on the side of the road ogling tombstones. Still, I had braved walking into several places today and survived. Walking a few blocks at night was no big deal.

I got to my feet and headed to the stop lights, taking my time as the sky grew darker. As I moved past Bourbon Street, the crowds thinned, and I started to get anxious as I approached the practically empty sidewalk outside the cemetery. I held the card in my hand, and somehow that gave me the strength to continue. I needed to find her, regardless of how scared I was. She wanted me to find her. I knew that now, because I had deciphered her map. And if she wasn't there... no, I couldn't think like that. She would be there, she had to be.

———————

I SLIPPED MY HAND AROUND THE COLD BAR OF THE entrance and gave what I hoped was an inauspicious tug. It didn't budge, and I squatted down to look at the keyhole drilled into the metal gate. There was no way in. I sighed and pressed my forehead against the bars, watching the headlights of a car behind me shine light inside for a few seconds before the place went dark again.

It was hard to see inside with the cars passing constantly. Maybe I was supposed to come here during the day. Maybe I had misunderstood. But the map hadn't appeared until it was dark enough. I looked down at the card in my hand again, turning it side to side to catch the light. She wanted me to find her, she had to.

I passed by the cemetery many times when I was a kid in school. I walked by it every morning, watching the sunlight illuminate the stone within. I never dared to go near it then. The place frightened me. The thought of so many people being pushed through the aboveground ovens where they cremated bodies for centuries made my skin crawl. This time I had a purpose. This time I wasn't scared.

Walking along the edge, I dragged my fingers across the high brick wall that encased the place. It felt old. There was something about old brick that kept secrets, and the cemetery kept many secrets. I understood why the woman in red chose this place. I turned a corner down a much emptier road and continued my walk. Surely there was another way in, maybe a wall that had fallen down or a gap big enough that I could squeeze into. I turned another corner where only a single blue pickup truck parked. That's when I spotted the gap in the distance. No longer trying to pretend anymore, I jogged down to it.

Unlike the front gate, the back entrance didn't have a fancy keyhole, or even prominent spikes on top. Instead it was much plainer, with a squared off metal door and a simple chain and padlock to keep out intruders. I stuffed the card in my pocket again and, without even thinking, I hooked a foot in above one of the metal notches on the door and pulled myself up with a grunt. What I lacked in strength I made up for with determination, and I pulled myself up to the top and swung a leg over. The dress caught on the spikes, but I carefully unhooked it even as my arms shook. Then the other leg, and then it was just a matter of getting down. I was halfway there and feeling pretty good about myself. I grabbed onto one of the lower bars, but my sweaty hand slipped, and I fell hard onto my back.

Pain flared up and down my spine, and all I could do was close my eyes and wait for it to end. What if somebody saw me just lying here on the wrong side of the gate? What if the guy that owned the pickup truck walked by? Finally, after several grueling minutes, the pain began to edge off, and I opened my eyes. The full moon, bright, beautiful, and somehow calming as she lit up the world with her borrowed light. With a groan, I got to my feet and leaned against a spiked metal fence. My eyes adjusted to the brilliant white tombs all around me.

Away from the headlights and streetlamps, the moonlight lit the white stone up like beacons, and I made my way through cautiously, stepping over the broken ground in places, and walking around each of the large structures. I passed by the squat stone gravestones that lined the wall of the outer edge of the cemetery. I walked by enormous above-ground ovens that probably still held the remains of families.

After I was a good distance from the back entrance, I held up her card.

"I, um, never caught your name, ma'am, but I've come with your card." I held it up high so that the glitter of the map caught the moonlight around all the creases the card now had. I turned in circles, almost expecting her to come from the ground itself. "Lady in red? Maybe, oh, what did she call you, la femme en rouge? Is that your name?"

I walked further, brandishing the card above me like an offering. A cold wind passed, ruffling my skirt, and I shivered, once again realizing I had forgotten to bring a jacket. "You wanted me to find you, didn't you? You wanted me to come here?" I wanted her confirmation of my plea. I wanted her to prove I wasn't crazy. Only she had that power.

The place was a maze of headstones and aboveground ovens. Paths would start and end abruptly. I nearly tripped more than once from the uneven paths and winding tree roots that exploded from the soil. An owl was hidden in one of the magnolia trees, my constant companion as I searched. The cars on the road were distant now, and occasionally I caught the smell of fresh dirt, but there were no fresh graves. The side of one of the ovens was a brilliant white, but with a sharp gap on one side where red brick poked out beneath. It almost looked like an open wound.

"Come to me! Please!" I screamed into the cold night air.

The silence around me made my eyes burn all over again. I couldn't take her ignoring me; I couldn't have done all of this for nothing. She had to be there, there was no other option. The card, the reading, the map, her warm embrace... I had to have her against me again.

"Please," I whispered, my voice breaking as I slumped onto the cracked stone walkway. I dropped my hands to the ground and felt the gravel grit into my fingers. Beside me, a vine was killing a small tree, and the tendrils waved in a breeze I didn't feel. I felt numb inside, I felt like nothing mattered anymore, like I didn't matter anymore. That my future had already been determined by somebody else and that I didn't have a point. I wiped at my cheeks with the back of my hand.

"You found me."

Her voice filled my heart, and I got to my feet so fast I nearly tripped over my dress. She was standing behind the dying tree, wearing the same red gown as before. Even her crimson lipstick was the same shade as she smiled at me. "You're here!" I rushed toward her and wrapped my arms around her, nearly sobbing against her. "I've been trying all day to find you again. I thought I imagined you, and the tarot reader said I should burn your card, but I refused and—"

"Shh." She wrapped an arm around my waist and stroked my hair. "It's alright now, Josie. You've found me. The moon led you to me tonight, and that's what matters. Nothing else does. Not your father, or the tarot reader, or your work. It doesn't matter anymore."

I sniffled. "It doesn't?"

"No." She released me, but kept her arm wrapped around my waist. "Mardi Gras is nearly here." She smirked as though it was a joke.

I raised an eyebrow. "What does that have to do with it?"

"Everything. It's when you can shed your skin. Only during Lupercalia, what you call Mardi Gras, can you do so." She smiled at me and a shiver went down my spine.

"I'm not entirely sure what you mean. I want to shed Jo, I really do, but Pa would kill me."

She lifted my chin and I stared into her golden-brown eyes. "No, my dear, you're wearing a mask now. Josie is who you are, and Jo is the mask you must wear for this place. Where we're going, you'll never need to hide your true self again."

I smiled. It seemed an impossible promise. She couldn't possibly be able to fulfill that.

Then she took hold of my chin and pulled. Something... came off. It didn't hurt, but I heard it shatter as it hit the ground. It felt strangely good, like I had been closed up inside of something for too long. Only I wasn't wearing anything on my chin, my mind reminded me in a panic. I gasped and felt for what she had taken from me. I felt my cheeks, my nose, my lips... but there was a hard edge like porcelain where my skin ended and something else began.

"What is that?" I breathed.

She smiled. "Shed your skin, Josie. You don't belong in that shell."

Feeling a surge of excitement, I pulled at the edge and felt the casing around my cheek break off like the edge of a clay slab. It was exhilarating. I pulled off my nose next, and my mouth. I breathed in and realized the air had never smelled right before. I pulled away from her, overwhelmed.

"What am I doing? This feels so odd."

"Few are fortunate enough to shed their skin of humanity, Josie. Few are able to do what you can. I watched you as a child pass this place." She stepped closer with a smile. "I knew you were one of us, so fearful, so uncomfortable in your skin. I just had to wait for the right moment. I had to wait for you to be ready."

She pushed me into the wall of one of the tombs. My side cracked and I felt the shards land on my shoes. I looked down, thinking I would see my insides or something, but it didn't hurt and I wasn't bleeding. I lifted my shirt to see my skin cracked from my chest down to my torso, and there in the gap I saw thick black fur poking out.

That was me. That was who I really was. In that moment it made perfect sense and yet it didn't make any sense at all.

I pulled myself out of the shell, knocking my leg against

the edge of the tomb, shaking off the shards, and pulling off my clothes as I went. Finally I stood, feeling the breeze ruffle every part of my body, the cold of the wind no longer bothering me, and the moonlight above making the world bright and beautiful.

The woman in red smiled, and shook her head, allowing her own dark red fur to push out through her skin from head to foot. She slipped out of her dress and kicked it behind her. We were both on four legs now, and it felt right.

"Now, Josie," she whispered, her voice a dark growl that made my pulse quicken. "You serve the moon with me."

I MOUNTED THE FINAL STEP OF THE RICKETY STAIRWELL OF our apartment complex, looking for Pa, but his chair was empty. I couldn't tell if his pile of beer cans was new or old. I shivered as a cold wind blew past, bringing with it the scents of the dumpster below, of car exhaust, and of the rain in the distance. I stared up at the moon, now reaching its first quarter in the sky behind trailing clouds. I stared at my hand, ensuring that the glamour was working before taking a deep breath. Only on the full moon was it impossible to hold, but it grew easier as the moon waned.

It had been a week since I'd seen Pa, a week since I disappeared without a word or a note, a week since I shed my skin. I pulled my keys out of the pocket of my dress and unlocked the front door. I knew he was inside as soon as I pushed the door open because I caught his smell: sour alcohol mixed with sweat. I swallowed down the fear and stepped inside, closing the door behind me.

Pa was in the kitchen, and came around the corner with anger in his step and a wildness in his eyes.

"Jo!" His voice was hoarse and it was clear he hadn't been

taking care of himself. He wore the beginnings of a beard and there were dark circles under his eyes.

"Hi, Pa," I said, dropping my key on a side table beside his car keys.

"Where the hell have you been? A week gone then you come back dressed like..." he looked me up and down, his face a mixture of shock and disgust.

"I came to get my things," I said, refusing to shrink away from him. I had spent enough years doing that. I stepped past him, and he permitted it; he was clearly still in shock.

"My name isn't Jo anymore, it's Josie." I heard him follow me into my room. I ignored him as I crouched down and opened the hidden boxes under my bed. I heard him gasp as I pulled out all my beautiful skirts, dresses, padded bras, and makeup, laying them out on the bed like a sacrifice. When I dumped the last box, I got to my feet and stared at him.

"These are mine. I hid them from you because I knew you would try to destroy them."

He rushed toward me, his arm pulled back behind him. His fist collided with my jaw and I stumbled back against the wall, knocking a pile of books from my nightstand to the floor. I don't know why I let him strike me, I could have stopped it. I think I wanted to remind myself what it felt like. I wanted to remember the taste of blood in my mouth and the flare of pain that went from my jaw and spread out to cover half my face.

"Get out of that damn dress and gather all these girly things. I want you to burn them. All of them." His eyes were ablaze.

I pursed my lips, trying to refrain from crying. "No, Pa, I won't."

He gaped at me before pulling his arm back for another blow. No, I wouldn't let him hit me again. I caught his fist in midair, squeezing ever so slightly so he couldn't pull it back again.

"What?" he cried.

I put a hand on his chest and pushed him back, knocking him into the opposite wall of my room. "I said no. Please don't make me hurt you."

He watched me with wide eyes as he skittered along the wall and grabbed a beer bottle from the hallway floor. He flung it at me, but I grabbed it, used its momentum, and threw it down at his feet. He screamed and must have jumped a full foot into the air.

"I'm leaving, Pa," I said as calmly as I could, though I could feel tears threatening. "I still love you, but I don't know why."

He backed away from the doorway until he was flat against the wall in the hallway. "What happened to you? What happened to my boy?"

I grabbed my clothes and my things and began dropping them into boxes. "I never was your boy, Pa, I was your little girl. You just never wanted to accept that."

I gave him a small smile as I approached him, carrying a box of clothes. "I love you, Pa." I reached over and kissed his whiskered cheek. He didn't move, his body was rigid. I pulled away and gave him a smile. "You don't have to see me again if you don't want to."

He just stared as I moved past him and for the door. I felt tears streaming down my face as I took hold of the door handle.

"You'll still visit, won't you, Jo? I mean, Josie?"

My heart soared as I turned to him. He didn't understand, but he was trying. I gave a tentative nod. "I'd like that."

The Dirty Floor

❧

"It doesn't make any sense, you know. You could create anything you wanted in the blink of an eye, but here you are mopping floors."

Anthony sighed and crouched down to wring his mop out again. A smile played on his lips, as though this was all some big joke, but Susan wasn't about to let the subject slip.

She leaned against the cold wall, frowning when she picked up the stale odor on it. "Why waste your time mopping this dump when you could just create a clean floor instead?"

He plopped the dingy strands of his mop onto the tiles again, his movements mechanical. It was the most unwanted job in the entire prison, and each week Anthony volunteered for it. He said he didn't mind it, but as a reporter, Susan suspected there was more to it.

"Because it wouldn't be real." He paused and propped his hands on top of the handle. "Sure, I could create a cleaner floor, one that was even trimmed in gold and embedded with rubies if I wanted, but it wouldn't be real. You could try all day long to make scuff marks on it, to dirty it up, but it would remain just as I made it.

"This one has stains so old, I'm pretty sure whoever made them is long dead. I like it though. This floor may be gross, but it feels alive in a way mine never could. It shows every boot mark and every stain. Every year that passes makes the grout fade a little more. Anything I make could never do that. My floor would only ever reflect me and no one else."

Dead Man's Hill

A FLASH OF COLOR IN THE NIGHT SKY WAS THE SIGNAL, AND Stevie rushed over to the picnic blanket to get a good view. All night they had waited for this, shivering in the darkness and bundled under layers of clothes. Campfires weren't allowed of course, which meant no hot meals. Dad had brought him first thing that morning, so they had one of the best spots.

The graveyard was at the base of the hill below, and Stevie could barely contain his excitement. "Where are they?"

Dad put a hand on his shoulder and gave him a squeeze. "Calm down, I'm sure they'll show soon."

Along the edge of the hill, Stevie could see hundreds of others gathering, pushing and clustering together. Silence fell over them and the air felt heavy. Stevie could feel his heart pounding and he bounced on his toes, unable to keep still.

"I don't see anything. What's taking them so long?"

Dad crouched down next to him. "I guess it takes a while to dig out."

He hadn't thought of that. Instead of looking for shambling corpses, he started looking at the headstones instead.

Sure enough, he spotted movement next to the tallest one down there: an enormous angel statue with wings spread wide.

Stevie pointed down at it, his voice loud enough to be heard by others. "That one – it's moving!"

The ground split open even as he said it and a hand broke through the cold earth. Stevie put on his night vision goggles, barely able to contain himself. He zoomed in and watched the man dig his way out: first an arm, then another arm, and finally his head. He was rather tall and had a long mop of white hair that was now thoroughly filled with mud and grime.

"You're not scared, are you?" Dad whispered beside him.

"Uh-uh," Stevie muttered, staring transfixed as the man pulled himself out completely. His body was so decomposed that Stevie could count each rib that poked out beneath his white collared shirt. His skull was exposed, and it gleamed as it caught the moonlight.

"That's grandpa!" A little girl shrieked near him. Someone tried to quiet her, but she wouldn't listen. "My grandpa is the first!"

Stevie, who was still zoomed in on grandpa down below, was amazed to see how quickly the head spun in the little girl's direction. Then in a flash, he was darting toward the crowd, knocking himself into gravestones and stumbling before he began to make his ascent.

"Dad?" Stevie whispered, unable to keep the fear out of his voice.

His father was silent for a moment, then turned to a nearby onlooker and asked, "They going to do something?"

Grandpa was crawling up the cliffside far faster than Stevie would have expected. He didn't even need the goggles now to see him coming closer to them. Stevie reached up and tugged at his father's sleeve. The crowd was backing away, pulling their children back with them.

Dad picked Stevie up and did the same. He had taken two steps back when grandpa reached the top. Moonlight reflected in dead grandpa's eyes. Stevie was breathing so hard he was shaking. He clung to Dad's shoulder, twisting the strap of the goggles in his fingers.

Others were shouting now, screaming to kill it. Guns weren't allowed up here though, not on Dead Man's Hill. It was the same for cameras and cell phones too. They were afraid it would agitate the undead, though it seemed that shrieking little girls were just as dangerous.

Grandpa was standing directly in front of them now, turning his head slowly as though choosing a dish at a buffet. His white eyes landed on Stevie. He cocked his head to the side, making a bit of drool fall from a mouth that could no longer close, then darted forward.

"Daddy!" Stevie shouted.

There was a loud bang that reverberated across the valley and a splatter of blood splashed out from grandpa's head, streaking up the invisible wall that stood between them. Stevie stared at it with wide eyes as grandpa collapsed to his knees, then keeled over completely. Nervous laughter emerged around them and slowly the crowd moved forward again.

Dad laughed. "Aw, you weren't that scared, were you?"

Stevie shook his head, transfixed by the corpse that lay mere feet away from them.

"We can go home now if you want. Your mother said you might be too young for this. Maybe she was right."

Stevie pulled his goggles on again. "No, I want to see more zombies."

"Alright, alright," Dad sighed and put him down on the

ground again. "But if we get another runner on this side, you're not going to get picked up, okay?"

"Okay, Daddy." Stevie grinned as another zombie broke ground, this time closer to the crowd.

The little girl cried out, "Up here, Mr. Zombie!" She was standing beside him now and Stevie smiled.

"Yeah, this way!" he cried.

Pretty soon every child on the hillside was taunting it, eager to lure it up to them.

"Kids." Dad laughed and rubbed his back. "I'm glad Halloween only comes once a year."

PART II
THE BIZARRE

Cracks

IT WAS LATE ON WEDNESDAY WHEN I FIRST SAW IT.

Putting the kids to bed had taken more work than I expected when Barry put toothpaste into his little sister's hair. What was supposed to take only ten minutes took thirty instead, and as soon as little Marcy's shriek pitched, I felt another headache coming on. I've gotten them all my life. Sometimes they stay docile, a dull throbbing sensation in the back of the skull, but sometimes they get worse. It always formed as a certain pulsing rhythm in a very particular part of my head; that's how I knew it was going to turn into a full-blown migraine. I put on a smile despite my growing agitation and washed out the toothpaste without a word, pecking kisses on their cheeks before sending them to bed. Then I found a dark, quiet place to ease the roar in my head that threatened to overwhelm me.

That's why I didn't turn on any lights that night. They always made it worse.

I sank down into the leather armchair in the living room with a heavy sigh and pulled a forgotten remote out from underneath me. I closed my eyes and let my mind go calm with the stillness of the house. The children finally quieted down and I leaned back in the chair, happy that they were both asleep. The grandfather clock in the entranceway ticked away, almost apologetic for making so much noise. I was the only person awake in the whole house. So why did my skin crawl?

I opened my eyes, a crease forming between my eyebrows, and my migraine launched a new pulse of pain. That's when I saw it. Something moved in my peripheral vision. I thought it was a trick of my eyes. I turned to look at the movement, expecting it to be nothing, only it wasn't.

There in the corner of the room, down the sliver where the walls met, I saw a shadowy shape move. It was like someone had covered the edges of a scene with masking tape, blotting out everything except that singular line. I saw it watching me through the thin crack. It was the height of a person, swaying left and right as it stared at me. I didn't scream. The sound wouldn't rise out of my throat. Instead, I gazed at it while my heart pounded in my chest. With a shaky hand I reached over to turn on the lamp, my fingers not behaving as I wrapped them around the black knob.

As soon as the light flicked on, the sliver vanished. It was just a corner of our living room again, painted in cheery daffodil yellow paint that I once loved so much. I took a deep breath, rubbed my eyes, and looked again. Nothing.

"I'm just tired," I whispered to the empty room. "That's all, just tired."

All the same, I left the light on that night.

$1,200. THAT'S ALL I COULD THINK AS THE SCREEN shattered. Flecks of glass sprinkled down onto the black entertainment center as the defeated white cell phone fell to the carpet.

I winced as Jonathan continued to bellow. He used to be so careful with his devices. Back in medical school, he was horrified when he dropped his phone in the parking lot at work. He worried about how much it would cost to fix it and struggled to come up with the spare cash. Now he sang a different tune. The palm sized phones and lightweight laptops took the brunt of his rages. What perverse satisfaction did he get out of breaking something so expensive and intricate? That would be his third phone in the past year, and it wasn't even May yet.

"Please calm down," I said, careful not to get too close to him as I stepped around the glass shards that littered the carpet.

He knocked back the rest of his wine like a shot and glanced at me, deftly tapping on the edge of the empty glass. "What do you think I'm trying to do? I worked sixteen hours a day for the past four days, and they still want me to come in. Those assholes are going to have to get along without me."

I refilled his wine glass. "I'm sure they'll be fine. It's just one day."

He took a long gulp. "How are the kids?"

"Fine," I answered on reflex.

He nodded. "And Barry? Are his math scores going up?"

I looked away from him. Why was he determined to get into another rage when he was already riding a wave of it? "Barry's just not interested in math. He always wants to read instead." Jonathan shook his head and clenched his jaw, making my pulse pound in my ears. "I've tried to work with him, but he won't—"

"Jesus Christ! You don't do anything here all day. You don't clean, you don't cook, hell, all you do is doodle pictures all day."

I create, I thought to myself.

He chuckled and took a long sip of his wine.

Art is work too. I wanted to say it aloud, but my tongue wouldn't listen. My teeth clamped up like I had developed rabies.

"I figured you could at least handle tutoring your own son. At least do something more productive than dump paint on canvases all day. Math used to be your passion, and now you can't even tutor Barry?"

I looked down at the half-empty bottle of wine in my hands. It had been one year, three weeks, and a day since the nervous breakdown that forced me to quit working. The idea of going back to work to sit in a tiny cubicle and balance financial accounts made me tense up. For weeks after, I could barely talk to my friends, let alone my coworkers. Painting saved my life. It gave me a way to explain the terror that threatened every day to tear the air from my lungs.

Jonathan never understood what happened to me, and he didn't really want to. He was a surgeon, used to broken bones and gunshot wounds, not the mysterious methods of the mind. Some part of him must have thought I faked it so I could stay at home and avoid the daily grind that he was forced to endure. That breakdown cost me more than my job, it cost us our marriage. We lost our spark after that and found ourselves trapped together. He had a wife who had lost her mind, and I had a husband I couldn't leave.

He stood, took the bottle from my hands, and headed toward the stairs. His shoes crunched on the glass from his phone. "I love you, honey, but you seriously don't do shit around here." He grinned at me as though it was supposed to seep the malice out of his words. "Can you at least go by and get me a new phone tomorrow? Just tell them I dropped it again."

I closed my eyes and nodded, my brain already at work on

when I should go to avoid the crowds, what script to recite regarding the damage, and what documentation I should bring should there be any questions. I took a deep breath. He didn't care about how difficult it would be for me. It was another of his tests, another way to prove to himself that I'm really faking it all, another piece to throw into my face during our next argument, to convince me I merely lacked motivation.

He took a swig from the wine bottle, no longer even bothering with the wine glass. "Are you coming to bed?"

His flat voice made a tremor go through me, like plucking a piano string and letting the note vibrate to extinction. Years ago, that same question would be an invitation for other things. My body clearly remembered it still, but that only made the coldness of his tone all the more painful.

"In a bit," I whispered, and he left, not even commenting on why my voice broke or why I was trembling. He never asked about such things anymore. They're old habit, I suspect. In the kitchen I wrapped the leftovers I had warmed up for him and put them in the fridge. It wasn't the first time Jonathan chose wine over dinner.

I grabbed the dustpan and swept up the broken glass that had settled into the carpet. The thought of our poor maid cleaning up his broken devices made me cringe. The cost of the phone alone was probably as much as she got in a month. I swept everything up and got to my feet, wishing my hands would quit shaking. That's when I saw movement again in the corner.

Jonathan had turned on a lamp at the far end of the room, permitting plenty of shadow in the corner, and I could clearly see the shape watching me through the crack. My pulse pounded in my ears as we watched each other, both of us curious, both of us wary. It seemed closer than last time, or perhaps it was my imagination.

"Did you see all that?" I asked as I put the dustpan down on the floor. The shadow loomed closer to the crack and gave a nod.

I put down the dustpan and sat down on the floor in front of the crack. I could make out more detail when I was close. I pressed my face to the corner and shifted left and right to see. That's when I realized it was a woman. She wore a black, tattered dress. Her long hair moved in a breeze that I couldn't feel. I caught the scent of an ocean breeze and thought I could hear the distant cawing of a seagull.

"Are you trapped in there?" I asked, unable to see her face for the black veil that she wore.

I dragged my fingers along the crack and felt the gap. My brain wasn't playing tricks on me; the gap was real. I pressed my fingernails into it, and when I looked up again the woman had taken a step closer. She was so close now I could see the shiny silver buckle on her shoe. I gasped and scrambled backwards, bumping into the end table. I turned on the lamp, blotting out the crack in the wall and the woman within it.

———

"I'M SORRY, MA'AM, BUT YOUR INSURANCE WON'T COVER the phone for a third time."

I felt that nagging throbbing in the back of my skull again. The shop was too small, there were too many people, a baby was crying in the corner, and the attendant wasn't listening to me. He spoke as though I was a child instead of a fully grown adult. He didn't even meet my eyes as he clicked away on the computer.

"My husband... he drops things."

He cracked a practiced, polite smile. "Don't we all?"

My heart was climbing up my throat and the throbbing in my skull was so loud that I feared I would pass out. I glanced around quickly and spotted a tiny sign for the restroom. "Excuse me..." I managed to say even though my tongue felt thick.

The man asked something as I fled, but I didn't hear him. The bathroom was blessedly empty. I turned on the faucet with a shaking hand and washed my face with cold water, dribbling it down the back of my neck. I went into the handi-capped stall and pulled off my shirt and sat down on the toilet seat. Sweat poured off of me as I sat with my head hung forward, eyes closed, listening to the muffled voices on the sales floor. After a few minutes my pulse slowed and the pounding in my skull finally diminished. I knew the attack had faded once I started shivering.

This one wasn't as bad as the one I had experienced at work that day, but I felt crestfallen. Each time I tried to leave the house, each time I tried to live a normal life again, my body wouldn't let me. The last two times I had come to the store, I had managed to fend it off. I was proud of myself. But not this time. Maybe it was the technician giving me a hard time about the phone, or maybe it was the screaming child whom I could still hear through the thin walls, or maybe I was just broken. Maybe this was how I would always be. The tears came unexpectedly at that thought and I grabbed some toilet paper to blot at the creases of my eyes so I wouldn't ruin my makeup.

I took a deep breath and pulled on my shirt again. I turned to exit the stall, running through the script of what I would say to the technician. As soon as I put my hand on the door handle, the lights went out. Already primed for another attack, my heart leapt to my throat.

My pulse pounded in my ears as I blinked. For a brief instant I looked for a light switch before I remembered I was in a stall. If the lights were motion activated, I should have triggered them when I was moving around. Were they on a timer? My head throbbed again as I tried to remember the layout of the bathroom. That was when I realized there was still a light source in the room. It was dim, but bright enough to project my shadow onto the stall door. I turned and saw the woman in the crack staring back at me through a corner of the stall. I caught the scent of brine.

The woman bent forward as though to see me easier, but her own eyes were still shadowed.

I swallowed down the fear. Part of me was frightened to see her here, but I was also strangely comforted. She knew what I was dealing with. She saw how Jonathan treated me, and now she saw me hiding in a bathroom. Maybe she wanted to help me.

"You came," I whispered, stepping closer.

She nodded and I couldn't help but smile.

"I'm not used to having someone with me when I'm... like this. I'm not used to anyone really caring."

She cocked her shadowy head to the side as if studying me.

"I can't handle this place." I said, wiping at the tears that came once again. "I can't handle these people."

She gestured for me to come closer and I did, standing so close to the tiles of the stall that I could see the grains in the grout. She raised her chin so that light fell across her mouth, her skin so white it almost looked almost translucent. Her mouth moved, as though she was trying to say something to me, but I couldn't make it out. All I heard were seagulls in the distance, but I couldn't hear her words.

"I can't hear you."

She shook her head as though frustrated, then turned and reached out for me. Her long, shadowy fingers emerged beside me and wrapped around my wrist. I wanted to scream. Most people would have. Instead, all I could think of was how warm she felt.

I looked up into her face and felt her words echo within my mind. "Come. With. Me."

I gaped at her as I tried to make sense of any of this. Before I could respond, the bathroom door opened and the lights flared up again. The woman's shadowy hand was gone as the mother with the screaming child went to the diaper table. I stared at my arm, forcing myself to remember everything. I still felt her warmth there. I wrapped my hand around my wrist, not willing to let her heat leave me yet.

———

JONATHAN WASN'T VERY PLEASED TO HEAR THAT THE replacement for his phone would have to be paid for out of pocket. I told him what the technician had told me: that the contract stated that devices would not be replaced more than twice in a twelve-month period. Of course, he thought I had misheard or simply didn't understand it. So, he spent over an hour on the phone with his lawyer, holding the contract in his hand, being told the same thing.

When he hangs up, he hands me back my phone. "I can't believe they only replace the damn things twice a year! That's the worst insurance plan I've ever heard of." He grabs the wine bottle and picks up his laptop.

"I'm going to bed," he says, nearly tripping over the coffee table. "You won't ever come with me, so I'm bringing this instead." He adjusts his hand on his laptop and shuffles past me.

I feel the tears threaten to spill again but I wipe them away. I wait until I hear the bedroom door close upstairs, then I turn off all the lights in the living room. As soon as the last lamp goes out, I see the woman in the crack. She's sitting on the beach, her tattered, black dress stretched all around her like webbing. She's just as close as before, but this time she isn't staring at me. She's looking out at the ocean. A trio of seagulls fly by and her shadowed face follows them. I sit down beside the crack and she turns to smile at me, with only the lower half of her face visible.

"I'm sorry about earlier. You frightened me."

Her smile fades and she lowers her head as though disappointed.

"It's not your fault!" I say. "I shouldn't have been scared. You just wanted to talk to me. You did what you had to so I could hear you."

The woman turns away toward the ocean again, and I fear that she's given up on me. What if I'm the only person she can see from the beach? What if she's as desperate for companionship as I am?

"You've watched me for a while, haven't you?"

She gives a curt nod, still gazing off into the distance.

"You wanted something of me earlier... do you still want it?"

Her posture goes rigid and when she turns back to me, her mouth is ever so slightly open, betraying her surprise. There is an intensity in her that I admire and fear at the same time, a determination that makes my pulse race.

I laugh and wipe at my tears, unashamed that they have somehow sprung from my eyes. "Yes, I want to come with you."

She purses her lips, not entirely convinced I know what I'm getting into. She's right, of course, but I want so badly to escape. I'm not sure where she is or why she's trapped there, but it has to be better than living here. At least she would listen to me.

I press a hand to the crack. "Please. Take me with you."

The woman smiles before spilling forward. Her arms emerge first, reaching for me, covered in black webbing. Her rough hand caresses my cheek, warm and kind. She wipes away a tear and I tremble, though I can't tell if it's from fear or the excitement that fills me. She wraps one arm around me, then another, and another, until I feel like I'm being cocooned. She wipes away another tear from my cheek and I look up into her eyes, dark and intense. No longer is she on the seashore, but here in my living room holding me close to her.

The ocean rolls in the distance and sand starts to spill between my toes. I look back to see the crack in the wall that looks into my living room, only from this angle there is far more than a crack. The walls are translucent, like a membrane, and I watch as Jonathan stumbles down the stairs. He's oblivious at first, barking complaints about our internet, but then he spots us, wrapped together in a tangle of limbs stretched out upon the sand. I beam at him, enjoying as the horror of it falls across his face. The laptop falls from his hands and crashes to the floor. The display cracks in two and chunks of it go flying, but Jonathan barely notices.

$3,800. Only he'll have to get it repaired on his own.

Execute

It all began with a few lines of missing code. I swear if I had known what was going to happen, I never would have touched that program. I probably would have walked out of the office completely, put in my two weeks' notice, and ended my career for good.

I have a good eye for detail, and a sometimes unhealthy determination to fix things that are broken. Sometimes that leads to good things, like landing me a job as an applications developer with a small company right after getting my bachelors. Sometimes it means I lack the common sense to know when to leave something alone. I have a tendency to get obsessive over fixing code, either by writing out lengthy comments or straightening out the formatting. So, when a few lines of code went missing, I had to solve it.

I first noticed it when the program refused to compile cleanly. That means there was some typo or missing bracket that was preventing it from being readable, like forgetting an accent in Spanish class or forgetting to add conjunctions to a sentence. It happened overnight, a line cut here, a few more cut there. At first, I suspected it was due to hardware failure.

When a hard drive begins to fail, that can be a symptom, but it would normally cause file corruption that would make the file difficult to open, not remove a short piece of text. Still I emailed our systems administrator, who maintains our servers, to give it a look. He ran scans and checks, but found nothing wrong.

"All clear here." He replied back with typical terseness. "Check with Deon."

I sighed. Deon was a fellow applications developer and the only other person who had access to this code. It wasn't that I didn't want to talk to him, he and I were actually good friends. I just didn't want this to end up being my mistake and having Deon tell me so. There's a lot of unspoken pressure being the only woman in an IT group. I worked hard to appear competent even when I felt like I wasn't. I suppose it's the lingering effect of being one of the few women in my Computer Science classes in college. Still, even if the missing code was my fault somehow, Deon wouldn't give me grief over it. He would probably just laugh about it with me. I went down the hall to his office and gave a light rap on the door. Deon had a single earbud in, and gave me a smile as he leaned back in his chair.

"Morning, Imari. How are you doing?"

"Fine," I said, unable to prevent the worry from creeping into my voice. "You haven't had to work with any of my projects in the last few days, have you?"

He laughed and rocked in his chair. "Not lately. Why?"

I gave him the details and watched his relaxed expression turn to consternation. He pulled off his earbud.

"That's... strange," he said at last. "Let's take a look at the logs and see what we can find."

Despite what he was working on, Deon always had a moment to sit down and try to work out an issue with me. I always appreciated that about him. I sat down beside him as we scrolled through the logs for the week. The repository for the version control system would show who was the last person to check the code out, modify it, and check it back in again. Finally, we got to the end of the file, to one of the final revisions logged at 2:03 AM last night. My name was beside it.

Deon turned toward me, and my face flushed. Had I accidentally removed code without realizing it? That was impossible, I wasn't even awake at that hour. The lines were missing from multiple sections in the program too, so it wasn't a simple mistype.

There was no blame in Deon's voice. "Check your software. Maybe it corrupted the file on a save. From the logs it looks like a normal commit, even if it wasn't."

"Thanks. I appreciate it."

"Anytime," he said as he popped in his earbud again.

That had to be it. There really was no other explanation. Already I felt silly for even getting Deon involved.

When I sat back down at my computer again, I was glad to have gotten to the bottom of the mystery. Only when I looked at my screen, I realized that the code had been altered again. New lines had been added, but this time I knew neither of us had added them because the text was strange. It wasn't in any language I knew, and each letter faded in and out asynchronously. It looked like damage from a bad monitor, like a part of the screen had been magnetized or something, but when I scrolled up or down, the strange text scrolled too. It was like it had been burned onto the file.

My hands hovered over the keyboard as I tried to figure out what to do, my fingers trembling. As a last-ditch effort, I scoured my computer's font banks, just to see if I could find anything like the text I saw in the code, but nothing was even close. In fact, when I switched back, even more lines had been added. Hundreds of them. Scrolling through it, I could tell that it wasn't garbled junk either. There were loops, conditional statements, and what I guessed were variables.

Someone was actively modifying my code. I felt like a hostage. This was unlike any kind of hacking that I had been taught. I got to my feet, trying to decide how to tell Deon, when my mouse cursor moved up to click a small button at the top of console: COMPILE.

My mouth hung open. They weren't just hacking the program, they had taken control of my computer. Then the little cursor moved to another button and clicked.

EXECUTE.

My heart skipped a beat. The fan on my computer revved so loud it sounded like it wanted to take off. My monitor went black and strange letters started typing across the screen—the same letters I had seen in the code itself. The text quickly filled the space, and then began to scroll down so fast that my eyes couldn't keep up. That was when the electricity started to flicker.

I heard an electric pop as something in the next room blew out. The overhead lights were next. Deon poked his head into my office. He wanted to know if the power was out for me too, but my computer was whirring away. I turned to answer him, but spotted the buildings in the distance and the white flashes of light I could see in the windows that turned to darkness. What was it doing? My computer wasn't powerful enough to pull that much energy. There was no way my program, which was on a server cut off from the public network, could affect another building's power. Then came the earthquake. I suppose it was a tremor really, but the whole building shook with it.

Deon took off at that point. I don't know where he went. Down the hall I heard more electric pops as lightbulbs, monitors, and hard drives spazzed out. Soon I was all alone in my office with my PC running so hot that smoke was beginning to rise from it. I got down on my hands and knees and yanked the power plug out of the back of my PC, ignoring the arch of electricity that went with it. The machine went quiet and I sat there for a moment trying to figure out what I would say to my boss. Would they know that it was my machine that caused some sort of power surge? Would I be blamed? As I weighed the odds of being able to keep my job, I noticed a pulsing glow behind me. I had to crawl out from under my desk so that I could turn around to look, but when I saw it, my mind took a moment to make sense of it.

Most of the creature was translucent, meaning I could see my filing cabinet and bookshelf behind it. Electric blue light pulsed off its skin in waves, but was slowly dissipating. It stood tall on two long legs, and held its stumpy arms limply forward like a meerkat on its hind legs. Its eyes were a dull gray that blended with the bland colors of the office furniture. It had no nose that I could see or even a mouth, but stood perfectly still, letting the waves of blue light disappear around it. I was still on the floor, my back to my desk, and all I could do was stare at it. It was hard to see once the blue energy disappeared, and if I had left and come back, I might never have noticed it standing behind me.

Then it turned its head to look at me with its flat, gray eyes, and I noticed that the back of its skull protruded behind it about a foot. It stood so still that it reminded me of a praying mantis, especially with both its eyes sized too big for its head. I glanced to the office door, but I would have to step toward the creature to get around my L-shaped desk if I wanted to leave. I got to my feet slowly, and it followed my movements with its head. At five feet, I'm not a very tall person, but I still didn't expect to feel so small beside it. The creature stood a good two feet taller than me.

I tried to say something, I don't know what, like excuse me or something stupid, but it came out as more of a whimper. I stepped forward, hoping I could slowly make my way around it without startling it. That's when its face split in two.

It must have been its mouth, but it stretched from one side of its face to the other. The sound it made drove a shiver down my spine. It was white noise, but with crackling and electric pops like a live wire. It lifted its arms, which promptly split into three separate parts, giving it six appendages in all. They had looked rather stubby at first, but now they extended out toward me like the tentacle of an octopus.

I vaulted over the desk, something I hadn't done since I was a little girl in gymnastics class, and knocked a stack of papers and my water bottle to the floor. I didn't give a shit. I only had eyes for the door. I had almost reached it when I tripped.

I felt so stupid as I grabbed the sides of the doorway to keep from landing on my face. Then I realized that I couldn't put my left leg on the ground. Something was holding it back. My first thought was that my shoelace had gotten caught on something, but that wasn't right, I was wearing flats today.

Turning, I saw that it had grabbed my ankle with one of its limbs, but I couldn't feel it. The electric beast was lumbering toward me, shifting and wavering as it moved. I reached down to my ankle to rip the tentacle off, but my fingers went through it like it wasn't there. I pulled back my pant leg to see that it wasn't crawling up my leg, it was crawling *into* my leg. One of its electric tentacles was lodged under my skin. I could feel it moving up my calf as a buzzing feeling hummed in my leg, as though I had a vibrating phone against it.

I screamed. I yanked my leg away, trying to pull the tentacle out of my body, but I felt the slight tug as though a string was wrapped around it, keeping it from moving. Then my hand went numb.

I looked at my hand, still pressing against the doorframe, and realized another limb was buried in my forearm. That buzzing feeling was moving up my arm. Oh god, what would it do if it reached my heart?

My foot went numb. Then my fingertips. I tugged my leg back again, crying aloud as tears filled my eyes. Buzzing moved up my leg, vibrating my bones, numbing my skin in a cold emptiness. A cold, buzzing streak went through my arm, latching onto my shoulder blade, and I whimpered.

It was searching for something. Maybe my heart, maybe my brain, maybe it thought I was something completely different. I let go of the door frame, falling hard to the floor and shivering as coldness moved up my hips and down my other leg. The buzzing in my shoulder wrapped around my throat, up my jaw, toward my head.

"Please..." I whispered, barely able to speak as the buzzing spread up my stomach and into my chest. "Please don't."

Its gray eyes held no mercy.

When it finally entered my skull, my entire body went limp. The cold buzzing filled my head and drowned out any noise. Pain erupted and my vision went black. Memories flashed through my mind: my house, my family, and my pets. It didn't care about that. The pain intensified. Technology. That's what it wanted. Everything I knew about networks and highways, our wireless communications, and our satellites.

When it finally removed its tentacles from me, I couldn't move. All I could do was stare up at the ceiling of my office, up at the drop-down panels that I had never noticed were stained. My skull throbbed with the worst migraine I had felt in my entire life. My body tingled as though everything had been asleep. Breathing was difficult. The creature turned its gaze to the window. Could it see the buildings that rose up to the sky on the other side of the glass? I don't know. It stepped over me with its long legs. What did it want next? More information?

It lumbered its way out the door and slunk down the hall, making it even harder to see against the window overlooking the city. It was heading toward the server room. I tried to reach out to grab it, but my arm merely flopped on the ground.

Our uninterruptible power supply system had probably kicked in when the blackout started, so all of the servers were likely still running. It knew this because it had seen all of that in my mind.

There was no telling what it would do when it reached them.

We Summoned Monsters

My dearest sister, how I miss you these days. We may not share a blood bond, but our bond was just as true. Remember when we went into the woods and built a fort? That became our hideaway for a full week when the village blamed us for their ten dead cattle. At the first sign of disease, they blamed those with powers they didn't understand. You were always a clever builder, sister.

We went to the lake and summoned forth the monsters that slept beneath the still waters. More than just fish answered us that day, and we learned about the neighbors we never knew we had. We gave each other the strength to face those dark, shadowy creatures; we gave each other the strength not to look away. We punished our enemies that day, sister, but we should have killed them.

Together we were accepted into the sisterhood and took the marks. Every time I look at my arm, every time I feel the puffy scar across my skin, I think of you. I think of us huddled together in those woods, I think of us standing in determination before that lake, and I remember the people who took you away.

I don't know if you're still alive or not, sister, but I will find you and I will punish your captors. If they have you bound, I will free you. If they have killed you, I swear, I will find a way to bring you back. Even if I must make a foul pact with some untrustworthy wretch, you will be at my side again.

Our friendship can't be parted by death. We are a sisterhood that can't be broken. Fear not, little sister, for I am coming for you. May our enemies quake in terror.

The Mermaid's Kiss

THE COLD MIST HIT VIVIAN'S FACE AND FILLED HER LUNGS as she picked up the push broom. The rain clouds had finally passed after days of downpour. In the distance the evening sky was a deep violet. She started pushing seawater off the deck and back into the sea. Supposedly her task was to prevent the crew from slipping, but it felt pointless. The ocean would just pour more water on it later. Grady, her boss, told her they couldn't chance a broken limb out here. Broken limbs killed too many pirates, because the chance of surviving an amputation if there was an infection was low. It also made them vulnerable if a fleet from the royal navy came along, not that they had seen another ship since she came aboard. Few traveled this far north when winter was on the way, but when chased by the queen, the pirates sailed wherever they could. Most pirates would take their vessels down to the Caribbean, but those routes were swarming with navy ships these days, so they went northward.

Already her fingers were stiff and her lips stung from the chill of the salty breeze. She pushed a puddle into the sea, knowing full well that the mist would likely make her have to repeat the work in an hour.

I'm lucky to be alive, she told herself. Didn't that count for anything?

Some days she wasn't sure. The pirates had kidnapped her three months ago when she was barely eighteen. She was in the wrong place at the wrong time when the pirates raided town, and she'd been tied up and taken aboard while the other pirates ransacked the town. She had thought they were going to sell her off to the skin trade or kill her, but apparently they merely wanted someone at the bottom of the pecking order and Vivian was the unlucky winner.

After a month of fighting, she ultimately came to terms with her role on the ship. She would be given the worst tasks, the jobs nobody else wanted. She would take the beatings, the anger, and the frustration of the crew. She was there to serve them, and if they saw through her lie when she told them she was only thirteen, she feared being seen as more than a child. These pirates had some loose morals. Children were protected from sexual abuse, but women were not. Every day she bound down her breasts, even though it was painful some days and hard to breathe. Every day she saw them watching her, looking her up and down, and she wondered if they suspected that she was older than she said.

She pushed another puddle over the edge, listening to the crew members laughing below deck. They started celebrating as soon as the storms subsided, relaxing after days of pressure and plowing full speed northward; yet here she was, forced to work while they drank.

She shoved the next puddle over the edge with a grunt. She felt the frustration building up again, the helplessness, the rage, but she knew it was useless. She didn't even know where they were, let alone how she could get home. Her breath came in small puffs as she continued her work, and she promised herself that somehow she would find a way off the ship. Somehow she would find a way to escape, and in her most vivid fantasies, she found a way to kill every one of the pirates on board.

"Excuse me," a woman's voice called.

Vivian jumped and spun around with the push broom held out in front of her. It took her a moment to remember that there were no other women aboard the ship, and she froze, wondering if her mind was playing tricks on her. The mist was steady against her face, and a drip of water formed at the tip of her nose. The deck of the ship was empty except for her.

"Excuse me."

The voice was coming from the water, over the edge of the ship. Her pulse pounded in her ears. She inched closer to the edge, shuffling her black leather boots across the soaked wood, until she reached the banister. She leaned over it, expecting to see an angry crew member yelling up at her from a window below. Instead, she saw a naked woman floating in the water. Her long, black hair was spread out behind her and her arms treaded water easily. Her breasts bulged up in the water, and Vivian's eyes were drawn to them immediately. She felt a flush come to her cheeks.

The woman smiled with warmth in her eyes. "What in the world are you doing?"

Vivian held up the push broom as if it could talk for her. "I'm, um..."

She laughed, bobbing up and down in the water. "Isn't that rather silly? It's raining."

Finally words started to come back to Vivian. "What are you doing in the water? Where are your clothes?"

"Clothes? I don't wear those confining things."

She stretched and Vivian looked away from her, feeling the flush spread across her face. "It's indecent," Vivian muttered under her breath, and took a moment before looking down to her. "If the pirates saw you, they would do horrible things to you. You would be lucky if they killed you."

She shook her head. "I'm not leaving, I live here. You all are visiting my home."

"I'm... sorry," Vivian said, her words feeling crude on her lips. She was being very rude. Her parents would have been cross with her, if they were even alive still. She had no idea whether or not they had been caught in the flames that ravaged her village as the pirates left. She could still remember the smell of the smoke as they drifted away from the harbor.

"You don't belong with them," the woman in the water stated. "You're here against your will, aren't you?"

She gasped as her stomach dropped. "What? How do you know that?"

The naked woman ignored her. "What's your name?"

"Vivian."

The woman nodded. "That's a good name."

Vivian jutted her chin out. "What's yours?"

She smirked. "You wouldn't be able to pronounce my name."

Vivian swallowed down the shaky feeling in her stomach. "Where are you from? Is there an island nearby?"

She laughed. Her smile was beautiful. "Like I said, this is my home. You're floating right on top of it actually."

"Wait, you live in the water?"

The woman leaned back and lifted a shimmering, scaled fin into the air.

Tales of the deadly ocean dwellers filled her mind. Her mother said they lured men to their death and could put a curse on anyone who spoke to them. Vivian put a hand to her mouth. "You're... a mermaid?"

"I am." The mermaid dragged her fingers through her hair.

The push broom clattered to the floor as Vivian backed away. "Oh no, mermaids are bad luck! Seeing one foretells death!"

Her smile turned to a scowl. "No, we don't! Who told you that rubbish?"

In a panic, Vivian ran back to the door to the cabins and rushed down the steps, past the room where the others were celebrating, and into her own cabin. She closed the door behind her and placed her hands on the wood of the door as though the mermaid could follow her. Her heart pounded and her hands trembled. She gasped for breath, unable to get enough air into her lungs as she tried to make sense of what happened.

Sweat dripped down her back. She closed her eyes and took a deep breath.

"Why aren't you up on deck?" Grady screamed through the door. He had a harsh temper and a whip that had already left scars on her back. He also wouldn't let anyone on the ship touch her. At least, not until she was of age.

She thought of the beautiful woman in the water and closed her eyes. If she said anything to him, she knew what would happen. Spotting a mermaid meant bad luck for the crew and the boat. It was a bad omen. They could be capsized at sea from storms, wrecked on rocks, or captured.

A month back an old man with a peg leg said he saw a mermaid on the waves. He said he saw her tail glint in the evening light above the tide. The other pirates told him he was senile and seeing things, but he insisted. He didn't back down, and Vivian wondered if this was the same mermaid he saw then. The old man was forced to walk the plank because Captain Rose thought he would bring death to them all.

Vivian had not only seen one but had spoken to her! She was a fool to not know that she was a mermaid, but in Vivian's defense, she was exhausted all the time. The pirates were already mistrustful of a girl onboard, but if she admitted that she had given the mermaid her name, she would surely be keel-hauled, drowned while being torn to pieces on the barnacles under the ship. She would die a horrible death if she told the truth.

"I'm fine," she lied, trying to calm her voice, wracking her brain for an excuse, anything to keep Grady from suspecting the truth.

"Open the door."

It wasn't a request but a command. He could easily break the door and make her fix it after. She turned the knob. Grady was a tall man with a thick beard. He was missing his left eye and the left side of his face was pockmarked with smallpox scars from his youth. He scowled at her as he stepped inside, forcing Vivian to back away until her back met the foot of her bed.

"What happened? You ran down here like you saw a specter."

Vivian swallowed down her fear. "I thought I saw something out in the water, something... big."

He narrowed his eyes. "What did it look like?"

Vivian forced her mind to work. "Dark. I thought it was just the mist playing tricks at first."

"Aye." He put a hand to his beard. "And big, you say?"

She nodded.

"If there's a whale out, that means there may be fish too. You've got two good eyes, child."

She blinked. She had never heard any of her captors complement her before.

"We'll get the nets up."

IN LESS THAN AN HOUR THE FISHING NETS WERE PUT OUT. The sun dipped beyond the horizon and the stars shone above their heads in a clear sky. The air was cold enough to be felt beneath the deck, seeping into the cracks of the ship and the seams of the portholes. Vivian went on deck again armed with her push broom, only this time the deck was covered in a thin layer of ice.

She worked quickly, pushing icy water off the deck as her teeth chattered in the cold wind. The cold seeped through her rags and made her joints go stiff. The scent of fish gave her a stomachache.

Net after net was pulled up, full to the brim with fish. She remembered what the mermaid had told her, that this was her home. Was that why the fish were so numerous? Would she be angry at them for pulling fish from her ocean? Vivian watched the black waters around the ship, half expecting to see the mermaid appear, but there was nothing.

After hours of sweeping, when she could no longer feel her fingers and the deck was mostly clear of water, Vivian went back to her cabin and wrapped herself in a blanket. Her hands and feet felt like ice and she couldn't get her teeth to stop chattering. The ship rocked as another net of fish landed on the deck above. There would be more water to sweep, but she couldn't go back out. She was far too cold and feared losing fingers if she did.

The mermaid couldn't be angry. She wouldn't bless them with so many fish if she was.

Finally warmed up, she changed clothes into the only other outfit she owned, left the other hanging on a rusty nail in her room to dry, and made her way down to the mess hall.

Most of the crew were still catching fish, so she hoped to find something to warm herself up. She grabbed a wooden bowl of hot soup from the night before and sat down at one of the long tables to eat. She had only taken a spoonful when Grady stepped into the mess hall. He was sopping wet and had clearly been up on deck. He pointed at her with a wide grin.

"And they told me it was bad luck to bring you aboard!" He laughed and Vivian gave a tentative smile. "We haven't had this good of a catch for years." He came over and sat down across from her. She could hear the shouts of the men above, working to salt and place the fish into barrels. She would have so much to clean later.

"It's getting cold up there. Won't have time to catch for much longer." He knocked some ice off his arm. "Maybe you should be up in the crow's nest watching for us? You might be better than old Miles up there now."

She shook her head and looked down into her bowl of thin fish soup. The idea of climbing that high using the netting and the bare ladder terrified her.

"Not one for heights, are you?" He smiled and gave a slow nod. "We'll see. You'll try it out tomorrow. You're small, got to get you stronger if you want to survive."

She stared at him with wide eyes.

He chuckled. "Don't look like that! You'll be an expert or die trying." He pushed himself up from the table. She stared after him in horror. She would rather clean a thousand decks than climb up there.

"Wait, Grady," she pleaded, mustering up the courage to speak. "I hate heights, and I'm terrible with climbing. Please... what if I fall?"

He narrowed his eyes at her, then gave another smile. "Nonsense, kids love climbing." He turned away and started berating the hungover cook for why the night's dinner was so late. Vivian's stomach tied up in knots. She pushed her soup away.

———

LATE THAT EVENING, VIVIAN TIPTOED OUT OF HER CABIN and checked the hall. The waters had gotten choppy, and the ship rocked. No one was awake, except whoever was steering the ship. For all she knew it was Captain Rose himself. She slipped quietly down the hall and up the steps. She had to push hard against the heavy door, and as soon as it opened, the cold wind blasted her. Her whole body winced from it, but she really had to use the toilet.

She closed the door behind her and made her way across the wind-beaten deck. Icy patches were everywhere, so she took cautious steps as the boat veered and creaked. She went back to the edge of the ship where she had seen the mermaid before, but the water was black and empty.

She wouldn't come back. Why should she? They were fishing and loitering on her home. Vivian had been rude to her. She hoped she hadn't made things worse, but she couldn't shake the feeling that she had.

She went toward the beakhead and could hear the water sloshing against the sides of the ship. It was best to use the head at night when most of the crew was asleep. She hated having to hold it for so long, but she also hated being vulnerable around any of them. As she got up, she noticed red on the seat. Blood. Her eyes went wide.

She had started her bleeding again.

It had stopped once she was taken aboard the ship, and she thought herself lucky. She wanted them to forget she was a woman at all. There would be no fooling them into thinking she was a child. They wouldn't believe she was a girl to be protected, but clearly a woman who could be used for other activities when boredom or lust struck.

How could she hide the blood from the crew? They all lived on top of each other. They all knew when they ate, when they went to the heads, when they bathed. Now she had something else to worry about, and it would come every single month to curse her. There was no way she could hide bloodied rags forever. A bleeding woman was an available woman. It wouldn't matter what she said about her age, she would be a target.

Tears welled up, cooling quickly from the harsh wind. She had to figure out where she would even find rags to use that weren't used for cleaning. How would she hide them? How would she clean them?

She cried by the head for a long time, feeling her face grow cold from her tears, but unable to quell them. Grady might think she was lucky, but she was clearly the unluckiest person on the whole ship.

After a long time, her eyes were puffy, and the cold made her joints stiff and painful. She started back toward the cabin. She took her time, deciding she would have to cut up her other outfit to make rags to use. She dreaded it, but there was no other choice. She would be down to one outfit to wear, and what would happen when she was told to wash it? What excuse would she make?

The whole deck smelled like fish and her stomach turned. The black ocean surrounded her on all sides. The world was empty except for her.

Soon she would bleed heavily, and she already felt her insides twist with pain as her cramps began. It wasn't the first time she considered throwing herself overboard into the freezing waters, but this night the pull was strong. She couldn't stand living in this nightmare anymore. It kept getting worse and worse.

Tomorrow she would have to climb to the crow's nest while her insides rebelled against her. She would have to live up there, swaying back and forth all day in the cold wind, and hope she had the strength to crawl down again. Be an expert or die trying, Grady had told her. He might just get his wish.

The ocean was a welcome abyss beneath her. The water would be cold at first, but death would take that away. She put her hands on the railing and felt the ice bite into her skin, but she didn't let go. Her teeth chattered as she watched the water below lap against the ship.

A pale face appeared beneath the waters before breaking through the surface. The mermaid didn't gasp for air as she broke through like a human would. She just emerged and stared up at her.

"I'm sorry," Vivian said as her throat went tight. "I'm sorry they've been fishing in your home."

The mermaid just watched her without any expression. Her eyes were a pale blue, like a cold arctic morning. "You can't hide it from them forever. They'll discover you."

The words were like a blade to her heart and hot tears streaked down Vivian's cold cheeks again. "I can't escape. I can't do anything. I'm a prisoner here and I don't even know if I have a home to go back to." She fell to her knees beside the railing, her legs soaking through in the icy water, sobbing uncontrollably.

"Do they harm you?" the mermaid asked, her voice soothing.

"Sometimes," she sniffed, wiping at her cheeks. "But if they find out I'm not a child, it'll get much worse. "

The mermaid's blue eyes glittered. "Would you want them dead?"

The question caught her off guard, and Vivian put her hands on the railing, leaning through the gaps to see her better. "What?"

"They stole you from your home, they force you to work against your will, and you expect them to soon hurt you worse. Do you want them dead?"

"I—I don't know. If they're dead, what will happen to me?"

The mermaid grinned. Instead of human teeth, her teeth were sharp and jagged like a shark. "I would take care of you."

Vivian shivered. It might be a better fate than killing herself here. She would accept death better knowing that the pirates wouldn't find another girl to take her place, another victim to take their anger out on. "I would want them dead. I wouldn't want them to hurt anyone else."

"Good." The mermaid nodded, and then pushed herself into the air and gripped the edge of the ship just inches away from Vivian's face. Her skin was covered in tiny pale scales that shimmered pearlescent in the moonlight. She was even more alluring up close. Her black hair hung around her face and her blue eyes were striking. Her fingers were tipped with sharp claws that dug easily into the wood of the ship.

"Can I ask a favor of you then?" The woman asked, her breasts pressed against the side of the ship.

Vivian caught her breath, in awe and terror. She felt her stomach clench at the sight of her, naked and so very close. "Yes?" she squeaked.

"Will you kiss me?" the mermaid asked.

Vivian stared at her dark lips, knowing the sharp teeth hidden behind that sweet smile.

"Yes," she said without allowing her mind to talk her out of it.

The mermaid leaned in and kissed her. Her lips were soft and warm. Vivian leaned into the kiss and felt the tightness in her stomach move down. She wanted so much more than a kiss. When the mermaid finally pulled away, Vivian's face was flushed. The mermaid put a hand to her cheek as Vivian stared at her, enthralled.

"Stay safe," she said, and then dropped back into the black waters with a small splash. Her aqua tail glinted once before she disappeared deep into the darkness.

Vivian stared after her, confused and flushed.

THAT NIGHT VIVIAN BARELY SLEPT. HER WHOLE BODY WAS hot from the kiss they shared, and she could think of little else. The next day came far too early and she went to the mess hall to find it bustling. Everyone was awake and busy with their tasks.

She kept quiet as she got in line for a plate of hot trout from the previous night's haul. Of all the foods in the world, she did not want to eat fish, but she was hungry and it was the only food available. In fact, it would likely be the only food they had for months.

She sat down at the edge of one of the tables, trying to keep to herself. She had bound her chest down again, and it felt tighter than normal. She was cramping horribly too. She had only taken a few bites of trout when Grady called to her.

"Girl, are you ready to climb today?"

There was laughter at his question from the small group that sat around him. Her toil today would be a joke to him and his friends. Her body hurt and she really didn't know if she had the strength, but she had little choice.

She heard a cane strike the floorboards on the other side of the mess hall and turned to see Captain Rose enter the hall. He was a shorter man, but he had a thick mustache and cruel eyes. Vivian had only seen him a few times. While he prevented Vivian from being killed the day she was captured, he was also the one to kidnap her as part of the crew. He had also ordered her village to be burned to the ground. Of all the pirates on the entire ship, the captain was the last person she wanted to notice her.

He walked to her table and stopped opposite her, placing two hands on his cane, looking her up and down, judging her. Vivian felt the tightness of her binding with each breath, and the cramps ached in her belly.

"Grady tells me you have excellent eyesight."

She pursed her lips, choosing her words with care. "I don't know about that, sir. Anybody could have seen a whale out there."

He stamped his cane on the ground and she went silent. He studied her with hard, joyless eyes.

"When you climb the crow's nest today, don't fall."

She frowned at him.

"If you fall, I will not waste the supplies to help you. You'll be pushed overboard with the whale. Grady may find you lucky, but you've been nothing but a problem since you came aboard."

Vivian felt her heartbeat thrum in her ears.

"I'm a betting man, girl. And I bet that you're thinking about escaping, aren't you?" He snorted at her silence. "Oh yes, looking for any opportunity, possibly at the first sight of land. The nest is for those I trust, girl, and I don't trust you." He gestured to the tables around them, to the plates of food. "However, you have indeed brought us a great bounty. And Miles needs time to rest from his post sometimes, so I'm open to letting you try. If you try anything, I will have my men slit your throat without a moment's hesitation. Understand?"

Vivian shook from head to toe at his words. Was he just looking for an excuse to kill her?

He slammed his cane on the floor again and she jumped. "Understand me, girl?"

"Yes sir, I understand." Her voice trembled.

"Good." He gave a cold smile. "Then don't fall, or you'll be shark food."

She felt the blood drain from her face as he turned. He stopped to chat with Grady for a moment, but Vivian couldn't hear them. She was too shaken. Once the captain left the mess hall, the room was eerily quiet. Grady and his friends didn't make any more jokes.

Vivian dreaded what she knew she had to do.

THE DAYLIGHT WAS BLINDING AS VIVIAN STEPPED OUT onto the deck of the ship. The cold air made her pulse quicken, and she wished she hadn't been forced to wear the damp outfit from the night before. She was already shivering. Today she didn't reach for the push broom, instead she headed for the netting and the crow's nest. She stared up at it, feeling her cramps pull so painfully that she had to resist the urge to double over.

The ladder leading up to the nest was made of beams hammered into the wooden pole. They weren't even handles really, just slats of wood she would have to grip with fingers that were already cold and stiff.

"Miles!" Grady screamed.

She jumped and turned to see that Grady had come up behind her, winding a coil of rope in his hands. He also had his whip on his hip. Likely for use in case she refused.

"Already?" Miles called down excitedly. He sounded so far away up there, and she could barely see his gray hair poke out over the edge of the nest as he looked down.

"Get down here!" Grady cried again, handing off the rope to one of his friends. He was smiling, like he was excited to see her make a fool of herself.

Miles flipped himself over the edge of the nest, gripping his way down the ladder with massive arms that he looped over each other on the way down. He was scrappy with long gray hair and a scraggly beard. He had both his eyes, but hardly any teeth. He jumped off a dozen feet up and landed with a thump on the deck.

Vivian took a few steps back, eying him warily.

"Looks like you two have it then," Miles said, looking down at her with a creepy smile. "I'm off to grab some grub!"

Miles bounded away and Vivian stared at the ladder, feeling light-headed as another blast of cold wind hit. She felt a rough hand on her shoulder grab hold and shove her forward.

"Climb," Grady said with a rough voice before letting go. "Don't embarrass me in front of the captain."

Vivian nodded, and rubbed at her pained shoulder. She looked up at the ladder above her head and her stomach dropped. No, she had to focus. She had to prove that she could do this. She took hold of the thin wood of the ladder, pulling herself up with the tips of her fingers. She barely had any room for her feet on each rung. She clung to each cold, slippery beam of wood and started to climb.

Ropes went loose somewhere and something slammed against the boat. Vivian slid, and flattened herself against the ladder. She looked over to see a net of fish had been pulled up, landing hard on the deck. The boat rocked back and forth from the extra weight. The scent of raw fish overwhelmed her, and she looked away. She wasn't even a foot up and already she had nearly fallen.

"Go on, climb, girl!" Grady called again, and she heard the familiar sound of his whip being removed from his waistband. It was a cat-of-nine-tails, and the memory of the scars on her back forced Vivian to start climbing again. The ship tilted from one side to the next, as the load of fish weighed it down and they dropped more nets.

Vivian was so sick of smelling fish. She was so sick of the cold, and sick of Grady's whip. She climbed, her fingers curling in on each flat rung, her fingertips going numb as her shoes slid back and forth beneath her. Her arms started to burn then started to shake as she paused. Her whole body hurt, and she flattened herself against the ladder again trying to catch her breath. She was so far up now that Grady looked small beneath her. On the captain's deck, Captain Rose was watching her, his cane held in front of him.

Over her shoulder she saw a couple of men carry a canvas tarp over to the base of her ladder. That wasn't to catch her fall if she fell, that was to carry her body over the edge and into the water when she did. She stared at the captain's cold expression in the distance and wished with all her heart for him to suffer. She wanted to watch him die.

The boat swayed side to side and she could feel the creaking wood of the pole she clung to. She looked up to the nest. She was almost there, she just had a little ways left to go. Maybe she would make it. Maybe she would prove to all of them that she shouldn't be underestimated. She reached up for the next rung just as another load of fish landed on the deck and the boat swung to the side. Her hand slipped, then her feet, and she reached out in a panic trying to grab onto anything as she fell from almost the top of the crow's nest.

She didn't scream, she couldn't find the breath, but her panic made her suddenly aware of everything around her all at once. There were many ropes, controlling all the sails, and in her flailing, she grabbed hold of one. Her hands burned as she caught her fall, but the sail buckled backward from her weight. The ship caught a breeze and tilted to the side. Vivian hung on for her life, wrapping the rope around her arm even though it hurt.

Down below the boat kept turning to the side, and she saw the edge of the ship tilt so much that the men below had to grab hold of the rigging to keep from falling off. Fish fell off the deck and into the water. The captain hung onto the railing and was barking orders at his crew. Men were pulling ropes, readjusting sails, anything they could to keep from going sideways.

As the fish from the recent catch fell back into the ocean, Vivian saw bright aqua scales dip to the surface before going under again. Then she spotted the black-haired mermaid, smiling up at her. Vivian's heart sprang up into her throat.

Dark shapes emerged on the side of the ship closest to the water. There were dozens of them, climbing on board, onto the deck, and up to the deck where the captain stood. They looked like the mermaid, men and women with long beautiful tails behind them of pink, violet, and shimmering blue, climbing across the wood with hardly any trouble. While the pirates had a hard time holding on, the mermaids climbed up easily, dragging their scaled tails behind them across the deck of the ship.

They were all clambering up onto the boat and darting across with terrifying speed and agility. A mermaid with bright red hair leapt onto the captain. He gave a horrified scream as she bit into his throat. The crew froze in a panic as they stared up at their leader, bleeding out over the deck. The red-headed mermaid tore his throat out in a single bite and screamed into the sky. The cane fell from the captain's hand, rolled down the planks, and dropped into the water.

On the deck came more screams as the other merpeople made their way toward their prey, lunging at them with their sharp teeth and clawed hands. Vivian watched with a mixture of excitement and horror as the mermen tore through them. Vivian felt the pain building in her arm and looked to see that it had turned purple from holding all her weight with the rope wrapped around it. She couldn't stay up here, she had to get down, but she didn't know if she even could, let alone if she should. Would she be eaten too?

She slowly unwrapped her arm as the screams continued down below and held onto the rope as she began to fall, but the rope slid through, rubbing her palms raw. She fell too fast.

The blood-stained deck below rushed up to greet her, but instead of hitting it, warm arms grabbed hold of her. She was rolling across the deck, through the blood, through the icy water, until she hit something solid. Sore and dazed, she looked up to see Grady's terrified face looking at her. He was bleeding too much, and he had a horrible gash on his shoulder that had almost taken off his arm.

"Girl," he gasped, "you have to help me." He reached out to her with his good hand, pulling desperately at her sleeve. "Please!"

She pulled away from him. "My name is Vivian, not girl," she hissed.

Grady's eyes went wide. She had no pity for him or any of them.

She turned to see the beautiful black-haired mermaid beside her. She was laughing.

Vivian couldn't look away from her beautiful, icy eyes. "You saved me," she whispered.

"Yes, because you kissed me. A mermaid's kiss is never forgotten."

Tears filled Vivian's eyes. "I would kiss you every day if it meant I would never forget you."

The mermaid pushed hair out of her face. "Would you join me?"

The words were so simple and yet Vivian felt the reverberation and power of them. She looked around at the merpeople feasting on the bodies of the crew, her captors who had burned her home to the ground and probably killed her entire family. Miles from the crow's nest was the last one left, and he had two mermaids already on each of his legs. Vivian had no future in this world, she had no family, and she had no home.

"Yes," she said with a smile as tears fell.

The mermaid pulled Vivian into a deeper kiss, one that seemed to pull at her from the inside. Vivian allowed herself to be engulfed, to be lost in it, to leave behind her mortal skin, to slide out of the body she hated and to join her new family in the depths of the cold, black waters she would soon call home.

Tiny Necks

I never seem to have a big enough bag to hold them all. They struggle and spread their black wings, which makes the bag seem smaller than it is. All that cawing can cause a headache too. I have to do it quick with these clever crows. They're cleverer than most people realize. Every time I open the bag to shove another bird in, pairs of beady black eyes watch me from within, waiting to escape.

With a single motion I grab another bird out of the trap. It's best to aim for the throat. All it can do is peck and claw at my gloved hand. Crows don't try to fly away as much when there's a clamp around their throat. The black bird is all caws and feathers in my grip as I stuff it into the bag with its friends. One of them pokes a beak out, thinking it's smart, but I'm ready for it. With my other hand I cover its face like a leathery mask and shove it to the bottom of the bag, then tie up the sack.

I turn to the two birds left in the angular, wire cage and give a chuckle. "That's all for today," I say, wiping the sweat off my brow. "I guess it's your lucky day." The two birds stare back at me from the far wall of the cage, trembling as I sling the sack of thirteen crows over my shoulder. The crows in the cage don't caw, they don't fly around, they just stare at me.

Fear does strange things to birds. Most of the time they fly around in a panic, searching for an escape, but others just go silent, like the two left in the cage. They cock their heads to the side and watch as I make my way to the house. Those are the ones that always bug me, to be honest. I wish they would panic and fly around. You never know what the quiet ones are thinking. I know better than to take all of them, though. Other crows will come and see them trapped inside. Instead of being frightened away, they'll come to investigate. I always think of it as the good Samaritan trap.

The trees are less thick as I approach the house, climbing uphill and panting a bit as the sweat builds up on my skin. My eyes linger on Candace's garden. Dandelions and baby oaks cover the square plot of earth, but the railroad ties still stand on the border where I placed them. It'll take many years for them to finally rot away beneath the moss and clover that has sprung up. Each year the saplings get a little taller. I clench my hand around the sack and listen to the muffled caws within.

Candace used to spend hours in her garden, down on all fours in the dirt with her wide-brimmed straw hat and long yellow gloves. Each week when I came down to empty the crow trap, she pretended not to hear them. She never asked what I did when I took the birds down to the basement, or how her lovely vegetables were kept safe from the greedy birds. She would smile at me, her eyes drifting down to the sack in my hand, and her mouth would make a thin little line. Then she would comment on the heat or the slugs or some other trivial topic. She never said a word about the birds. The only time she even acknowledged them was when they were in her garden. They simply didn't exist unless they were in her way, and I made sure they never were. She never saw the crow trap before she died, though she had to know it was back there in the woods just out of sight.

I never kill crows near the trap. The others would get wise to it. Their invisible brethren stare down from their pulpits in the branches of the trees and watch my every move, even if I can't see them. The first time I did it, not a single bird came near the trap for months. It was like they could smell the death.

The bag is heavier than it used to be. I used to carry twenty crows to the house without breaking a sweat once, but I was younger then and Candace was alive. Somehow, she made it easier. Around the corner of the house, the basement door is nestled among tall bushes. It gives the privacy I'll need for what has to be done.

<hr>

I PULL ON A METAL CORD AND THE BARE BULB ABOVE MY head blazes to life, illuminating walls of wooden beams and cracked concrete underfoot. It smells of cut wood and earth down here, with a slight musty twinge I can never quite identify. I pin the sack's opening to the floor with a concrete block. The birds flutter and squawk inside, but they're not going anywhere. Someday I ought to organize all these boxes and put this place in order, but she's no longer here and there doesn't seem to be a reason for it now.

Candace and I had big plans when we first moved in. The unfinished basement, made of three rooms connected by a hallway, gave us all these ideas. We'd put in a second living room to act as a guest bedroom for her friends, but that was before she got sick. Now it's just a storage space, gathering mold, cobwebs, and insects, filled with boxes of Candace's things I can't throw away.

Picking my way around the piles of boxes to reach the

cluttered tool shelf on the far wall of the hall, I can't help but smile. I'm glad we never made a guest room down here because I'd never use it. Candace was the one with all the friends and family. Candace had all the visitors. The only visitors now are the ones I bring in a sack.

The sack flops in vain behind me. Their tiny claws squeak across the concrete floor, but they're quieter than they were. That happens often with the birds. I like to think it's because they can smell the death here. I'm breathing hard again as I reach the shelf and have to lean against it to wipe my brow. Some days I feel too old to be bagging crows every week. Even as I think that, though, I pull a set of black trash bags out and slip the plastic into the pocket of my jeans with two fingers. To be honest, this is one of the few things I enjoy in life, and I think Candace would approve. She would want me to be happy.

I swap out the leather gloves for longer ones that go up to my elbows. These are made for more than just yard work; these are my killing gloves. Pulling them on turns me into something more, something greater. Sure, my back still aches and my knees still protest and my breath hisses out of my throat like a leaky faucet, but I can scarcely feel any of it. I feel ten years younger as I flex my fingers in the thick, black leather. I hope the work is messy today; I hope the little bastards fight back. I turn a spigot to add water to a bucket, then toss in a few washcloths. Some days the birds struggle so much, I have to clean up afterwards. That's when I know it's been a good day.

I make my way back to the birds with more confidence, picking around the towers of boxes and mildew stains. I can almost taste their panic. They're fumbling over each other inside, scrambling over their friends. They know I'm death coming for them.

Dragging a folding chair over makes the shovel fall to the

ground beside it, bouncing with a metallic clang against the skeletal walls and pale concrete. The birds can't take that. They're cawing all over again at the sudden noise and I grin at them like a skull. I wrap leather fingers around the opening of the sack and push the concrete weight off with my foot.

Grabbing the first thing my fingers reach, I yank out a long black wing. I have to pull it quick to keep the others from escaping, and with a smooth yank I feel something tear and the crow gives a high-pitched squeal of pain. I don't hold back the chuckle. The bird comes out easily then, but still very alive. I pin the sack to the floor with the heel of my boot, then turn to the broken bird in my grip. With one hand around the bird's breast and another around its neck, all it takes is a quick turn to bring its struggles to an end. The body is warm in my hands as I drop it into a black trash bag.

Taking a moment to wipe my face again, I watch as the sack twitches and convulses on the ground. There's no question now, the tiny black birds know what's to become of them, and their fear gives me pleasure. It's beautiful to watch the understanding come to them, the panicked realization that their death will be soon. I give them a few moments to calm before I pick the sack up again. I shove another hand in, but this time the birds are too slippery and their little winged bodies evade my grasp. It must be from the brief rain shower earlier.

Then something sharp pierces through my killing gloves, pierces through that thick black material, and digs deep into the thin tissue between my thumb and forefinger. I gasp and for a moment the lip of the sack opens wide enough to let out the other birds. I'm only taken off guard for a moment though, and I close it quick and slam my boot down on the opening.

"Damn it!" I pull off the black glove to examine the damage. The wound that pierces the thin skin is throbbing as blood inks down my palm. I grab one of the washcloths out of the bucket to wrap around it and it quickly turns crimson. "Little bastards," I growl again, applying pressure on the wound. The birds seem to sense my anger. They're struggling like bottled-up hornets, and even beneath the weight of my foot, the sack is starting to slip away from me.

"Not today," I say through clenched teeth, and drag the concrete block onto the opening of the sack with my uninjured hand. I take the punctured glove over to the hanging bulb to examine it. When I bought my killing gloves, they were supposed to be able to handle barbed wire without a problem, but these are cut right through, almost as though a knife was taken to it. I'm breathing hard now, but this time out of rage. I hoped it would get messy, but I'm not supposed to be the one to bleed. Causing pain is my specialty, not theirs.

The wound throbs, and the warmth spreads across my hand. No, I won't lose control, even if I'm tempted to. I won't give in to that rage. It's a small wound compared to the ones I'll be giving. All the same, I'm trembling as I sit down. My killing gloves, my supposedly impenetrable armor, have been compromised.

THE BIRDS HAVE GONE DISTURBINGLY SILENT. THE agitation they had just a moment ago, their fear and panic, all of it's gone. Instead, the sack sits motionless beside that heavy concrete slab. I stare at the cloth, refusing to blink, looking for signs of their breathing, but the sack is still. That's not right. They have to be breathing still. I still have twelve more birds.

I feel hot suddenly. The perspiration pours down into my eyebrows and I wipe it across my arm. I've half a mind to leave that basement alone and let the birds go, but that's nonsense talking. Those birds are nothing to me. I can snap their tiny necks with a twist of my wrist. So why does this feel so strange?

I've been controlling birds for decades, ever since Candace started gardening. Each week I emptied that crow trap and killed at least a couple of crows. I know how birds behave when they're frightened. They panic, they struggle, they might claw or peck at some skin if you let them catch any, but they have trouble gaining leverage inside the sack. They're all crowded inside, one on top of the other, panicking. When they do attack, it's a desperate, blind act. This one, though, dug its beak into me like a knife. Picking up the injured glove again I feel the puncture with my bare fingers. There was no hesitation with this attack, no uncertainty at having the rubbery material in its beak; it was a bite of anger more than desperation. It was as if it knew I was inside.

I turn to the sack again, and my breath catches. The sack has fallen flat; it's as empty as an unused grocery bag, and I place my bare hand flat on top, only to feel the cool concrete on the other side. I pull the sack flat, pressing my hand all along it. Twelve birds ought to be waiting for their necks to be broken, but there's only empty air. The concrete block wasn't the problem. It hasn't moved. They couldn't have crawled out that way. I pull the sack free and feel inside it, but there are no holes.

With a heavy arm I wipe at my forehead. My arm feels like it's been dipped in a warm river. I drop the sack back to the ground and look around the dark basement. Did they get free when that bastard bit me? Did they climb loose when I went to examine the glove? I didn't hear a damn thing, and that's what makes me nervous. If they escaped, then they should be in a full panic, screaming and searching for an escape.

I climb to my feet and a caw as loud as a firecracker erupts behind me. My heart thunders in my chest and I turn in a fury to see the sack on the ground where I dropped it. Only this time something is inside. I hear the flutter of wings and the scraping of claws.

This must be what it feels like to lose your mind. The world stops making sense and things happen around you that you can't possibly understand. I don't like it. Without thinking, I pick up the fallen shovel. I haven't used it since Candace left me. Her face emerges in my mind, emotionless but approving; her gaze fuels my determination.

I heft the shovel overhead and smash it down on the thing in the bag. The metal rings against the concrete. Something inside breaks. Another slam, just to make sure. She might find my methods messy, but she never complained. She would want me to be happy, after all.

THE NOISE WOULD HAVE BEEN A NUISANCE FOR CANDACE, but she wouldn't have fussed. She'd have sat upstairs and staunchly ignored it like an obtrusive advertisement on television. She must have approved of my methods, she had to have. I'd never get a word of praise though, a word of thanks, but she never had to. I could read through the lines clearly when she said how pleased she was with the garden. She was complimenting me really, in her roundabout way, because it was by my efforts that her garden provided so much bounty. Such words didn't come often, and her smiles were practically an endangered species.

I think of her smile as I flatten the bird into the concrete.

By the time I finish, I'm wheezing with every breath and the shovel has to hold my weight for a moment. The sack has gone dark in the middle from the blood inside and I wipe my upper lip, surprised to see my trembling hand. "That was short-lived." I chuckle to the walls. "I did say I wanted a mess today, didn't I?" The dark stain spreads along the distressed sack. "I don't know what kind of Houdini bird you are, but you didn't escape me that time, did you?" I chuckle and return the shovel to the wall, then address my wounded hand.

Reaching up to steady the swaying light bulb, I hear a scratch tear across concrete that might as well tear through my chest. Slowly I turn around to face the treacherous sack, sitting exactly where I left it on the concrete. The dark stain is still there, spreading along the frayed burlap, but the two tiny black claws extending from the bottom are unmistakable. They drag a long, impossible screech against the concrete again and I back away.

"What the hell..." I whisper. "There's no way..."

As if to prove me wrong the bird caws with insistence. I hear another caw behind me, coming from the shadows of the full-sized, unfinished bathroom. I hear another set of flapping wings, this time from the larger living room ahead of me. I grab the shovel. I can see somehow missing one bird, but two? That was nearly impossible.

The crows are playing with me. I see that now. A few birds are still standing, though I still have no idea what happened to the others. There were supposed to be twelve more birds. Just thinking of that makes my stomach tighten. Maybe I miscounted them when I pulled them out of the trap? Perhaps all of this is just a hallucination. I reach down to the trash bag at my feet, and nod at the broken bird within. That one, at least, isn't going anywhere.

"You're just jumpy," I tell myself, even though my hands tremble. I'm terrified, and I'm beginning to distrust my own senses. "Don't let them get to you. Crows are clever, but they're not that damn smart."

Shouldering the shovel, I head to the hallway which

connects all three rooms together. It too is unfinished but contains the staircase to the first floor, and my cluttered tool shelf. I look into the dark bathroom. That's where I heard the first bird. The bathroom has no windows and one wall is solid concrete. It's also where I stacked most of Candace's boxes in maze-like piles. I have to navigate around the teetering piles, careful not to trip. Outside a cloud passes overhead, seeping a little bit of sunlight out of the already dark basement. I stand still for a moment for my eyes to adjust, my breath hissing in my throat.

"Typical," I whisper and the bird ahead of me caws in mockery. Crows are masters of mockery. This will be more difficult. I glance to the tool shelf, knowing there's a flashlight somewhere there, but it would make too much noise to search for it in the dark, and even if I turned it on, it might frighten the bird elsewhere. I removed the bulbs from the hanging lights ages ago with the intent to replace them, but that never happened. I could try the hanging light switch in the bathroom once I got inside, but that would definitely frighten it. No, I needed to take my time with my approach, and I'll have to remember where I've stepped before. I peer into the dark room and a pit of fear swells up in my belly. Where did that come from? When had I ever feared these fragile, breakable birds?

Step by cautious step, I pick my way around the piles of boxes, searching the darkness for any sign of movement, for a fluttering wing, for a moving beak, even for a glint of its black, empty eye. I step through the door frame, and on the second step my foot hits a box I hadn't seen. I shuffle to keep my balance, but end up groping out to catch the beams of wood to keep from hitting the concrete. The shovel slips from my fingers and clangs to the concrete floor with such a noise that my heart skips a beat.

"Shit!"

The birds chorus in their caws, and I look up just in time to spot the bird from the bathroom fly over to join its sister in the far living room. Another bird flies over to join them.

"God damn it." I wipe my mouth on my arm, panting against the hairs. My legs wobble beneath me and I lean heavily against the two wooden beams I grabbed. You would think I just finished a race instead of sneaking up on a few measly birds. I forgot about the one in the bag. I can't believe I forgot about it. I pick up the shovel and rest it against my shoulder, it feels cold and strong on my sweaty skin. "So that's how you want to play it. When I find you three, I'm going to bash your brains in."

The birds go silent. They must hear the anger in my voice. I smile, but then realize that the living room is darker than it should be. Something is covering the window. I step into the hallway to get a better look, this time using the beams to keep from toppling. The black thing is silhouetted against the bright window, and I can see long dark feathers coming off of it. I grit my teeth. They're huddled together there. They really think there's safety in numbers, when really it just gives me something to aim at. The tension leaves me a bit at that thought. If they were panicking still, that should make them easier to hit. Panicking birds make more mistakes.

I move quickly from one end of the hallway to the other, my eyes never leaving the silhouetted birds. The feathers I can see are long enough that they must be tail feathers. I'll do a sweep with the shovel, and that way I'll be sure to get all of them. If they do try to take off, I'm at least bound to hit one.

Stepping into the room, there's an obvious temperature drop. A shiver rushes through my arms. There's nothing unusual about it though; basements routinely get drafts. From this angle, the birds look bigger than I recalled. Somehow they're taking up almost half of the square window pane, and they're so still they could almost be stuffed. I grip the handle of the shovel, my heart pounding in my chest and my breath coming in wheezy pants. This room was cleared of boxes, which gives me room to take a cautious approach. I lift the shovel inch by inch, careful not to startle them this time. I brace myself for the impact, for the squawk as I break their fragile bones with the cold steel of my shovel. One of the birds flutters its wings, and I can't wait any longer. In one smooth motion I sweep the shovel around. I expected to maybe hit concrete; I hadn't expected something to grab hold.

In an instant the shovel is torn from my stinging hands and I stumble forward from the momentum. One of the birds gives a deep, unnatural caw. It's a low sound that reverberates against the concrete, that makes my teeth clench. My eyes go wide as the blood drains from my face. That was not the sound of a crow.

I back away, my heart pounding so hard that I'm shaking. With every breath, my throat makes a pathetic sound like the mewling of a kitten. I stare at what I thought was a set of crows against the window, but this time I let my eyes drift away from the window to look deep into the shadow itself. It takes a moment for my brain to pick out the parts of it, to make sense of what I'm seeing. Then I see a pair of black, glinting eyes staring back at me, and they're larger than any crow's.

"What—?" Something brushes against my ear and I flail at it, only to realize it's the string for the light switch hanging from the ceiling. The shadow figure continues to stare at me, unfazed by my jumpiness. My fingers are so shaky it takes a moment to grip the thin string, but finally I pull down on it. The room is flooded with light. As soon as I see it, as soon as I take in the figure towering before me, I know I've made a mistake. I know I've made many mistakes. There's nothing to shield me from it now, and I almost wish for the darkness to envelop it again, to wrap over it like the snow covers over a rotting corpse. I can't say it's human, and I can't say it's a bird either; yet it somehow resembles both. It stands at least seven feet high, but its human-like chest and arms are covered with black plumage.

It wears a strange cape with a collar covered in long, black feathers. That was what I had seen in the window, but that's also where the other crows now stand, all three of them. They watch from either side of the creature's head, judging me with their empty eyes. Then there's the cape itself. Staring into it, I felt like I'm looking up into a starry night sky, only it's fabric clinging to the wall behind it. Something about the cape makes me feel lightheaded and dizzy, as though I've spun around too many times. It makes the space behind my eyeballs ache.

Its face is what makes my heart thunder in my chest. At first, I hope that the head is some kind of mask. I want to say it's a bird's head, but it doesn't belong to any bird I've ever seen. The lightbulb shining from the ceiling glints bright in its enormous black eyes. The large angular beak curves downward like a buzzard. Then the creature flings its head back and lifts its crooked beak to the heavens, emitting deep caws throughout the basement. My eardrums throb and my teeth chatter at the sound.

I fall to the floor, clasping my hands over my ears, my breath wheezing in my throat. My chest hurts and breathing is difficult, as though the creature's horrible sounds thinned the air itself. The black-feathered creature just watches me, unmoved by my pain, almost intent upon it.

"What do you want?" I ask, but I can't hear my own voice. I pull my hands away from my ears and gasp at the bright red blood streaked across my palms. That's when I realize I should run. I turn and try to crawl away from it, not trusting my legs to hold me up. I can see the staircase that leads up to the house, just across the hall. If I could reach them, I could crawl up the stairs and lock the door behind me, anything to keep the crow-man as far away as possible. My hands are slippery against the cold concrete floor, covered in my sweat and blood.

The crow-man steps over me. I feel the cold breeze of its passing, and the long, black tail feathers as they graze against my balding scalp. It isn't in a hurry. In fact, it barely seems concerned with me at all. I look up to see it standing in the doorway, and seeing it against the door frame makes me realize how enormous the creature is. One of the crows on its black feathered shoulders flares out its wings. They're waiting for something, but what?

My hearing slowly comes back to me in the form of a high-pitched ringing. Beneath it, though, I can hear some rhythmic pattern that I can't quite identify. At first I think it's the sound of my own blood rushing in my ears, but as the ringing diminishes, I realize what it is. The noise rises and falls in volume, but the sound itself is unmistakable: the cawing of crows. I look over my shoulder and see their black shapes flinging themselves against the basement windows, beating their frail bodies against them in a mad frenzy. The sight fills me with more fear than I would ever have expected. When I look forward again, the crow-man is crouching in front of me, with its crooked, black beak almost in my face. I flinch backward and lift my right hand to my face reflexively. That's when the crow-man bites it off.

I stare at my hand as it dislodges from my wrist and falls to the concrete, bouncing once as it lies twitching in a widening pool of blood. Then the pain hits me. It's so intense, so sudden, so much worse than any pain I've ever experienced in my life, that I shriek. My voice echoes back to me from the skeletal walls and concrete. I stare down at the hand resting on the ground as it stops twitching, and gasp to scream again. Behind me I hear the banging intensify as the crows grow more intent. I'm on my side now, curled up in a fetal position, cradling my bleeding wrist against my chest. The crow-man is moving again. I look up with wide eyes as he approaches the basement door and puts his black feathered hand on the handle.

"No..." I whisper as tears slide from my eyes. "No, please..."

The crow-man turns his head a full ninety degrees to stare at me with its enormous black eyes. It emits a low caw, quieter than the barrage it had given earlier, then it flings the door wide. The birds fly in like a dark tornado. They sweep through the basement, all feathers and caws and glinting, black eyes. Candace's boxes fall to the floor, crashing in loud heaps. The birds swarm for only a moment before they change direction, aiming right at me. Before I can even scream, they cover me. They claw and peck and tear at me like I'm no more than roadkill. My poor maimed arm is their favorite, though. Despite my attempts to pull it against me or hide it in my shirt, they find a way to reach it. The last thing I see is the crow-man looming over me as I swat his crazed birds away. He stares at me, cocking his head to the side. It feels like his eyes pierce through me.

What does it see when it looks at me, I wonder, as my arm is getting tired and my chest feels like it's on fire and my bloodied arm reveals fresh pain with every beak that jabs into it. I wonder if any of the birds I killed all these years had felt like this just before I snapped their fragile necks. The pain is overwhelming, and I can't keep pace with the damn birds. For each one I slam away, two more take its place. A surge of regret fills me, something I never would have expected. I haven't felt so full of emotion in years, I realize as I start to sob. Not since Candace was alive.

The crow-man sees it somehow, he must know what I'm

feeling, because that's when he steps forward. In the end, the crow-man has more pity for me than I ever gave his beloved crows.

"I'm sorry," I whisper, but I don't think he cares.

He reaches down with his crooked beak and takes hold of my neck. With one final twist the deed is done.

A Slippery Customer

HE WASN'T THE MOST ATTRACTIVE MAN AT THE BAR, BUT the brand of his bulky leather jacket meant he either had money or he knew how to find it. Carolyn unbuttoned the top three eyelets of her blouse, just enough to reveal the push-up bra underneath. She flattened out her skirt that barely covered her butt and sauntered over. Jimmy glanced at her from behind the bar, his blond, scruffy hair always getting in his eyes. He smirked and nodded to her but arched an eyebrow when he saw her target.

She trailed her nails over the back of Mr. Moneybags' neck and dragged her fingertips along the leather of his shoulder. Just as she thought: real leather, none of that fake crap. "Hey sugar, you got a light?"

"Um," his breath smelled of the top shelf beer he was nursing, the foamy remnants of which still clung to his mustache and beard as he gaped at her. His eyes met her face, briefly, before descending to her chest, her legs, then back to her chest again. That confused expression slowly turned into a grin. Bingo. "Absolutely."

He fumbled at his inner breast pocket for a minute before he produced the lighter. Most probably assumed it was your typical dollar store variety, but Carolyn spotted the engraved initials at the base. She leaned in so he could light her cigarette, and spotted the billfold in his breast pocket, stuffed near to busting. There were even a few bills poking out along the top. The man was loaded. She pulled herself onto a stool beside him, blowing smoke off to the side, but studied him carefully this time. Beads of perspiration were pooled on his forehead and the hand that clung to the bar's edge was moist with sweat.

She smiled and crossed her legs so he could see just how far up the skirt went. "You don't look at all familiar. New to these parts?"

He grabbed a napkin off the table and wiped at his face. "Just passing through, really. My last job didn't pan out so well, so I decided to get away from it all."

She smiled. "Well, you nailed that then, sugar! Nobody comes around these parts on purpose. The biggest events are the Bingo competitions at the retirement home, or maybe the occasional estate sale."

He grinned. "Sounds like you're experienced."

She flashed a grin at him. "Excuse me?"

"At Bingo. Sounds like you've spent a night or two down there."

She nodded, taking a moment to pull on her cigarette. For all the nerves this guy had, he didn't shy away at her comment. Most men would have fumbled at a slip like that. Maybe laughed it off, backtracked, or at least apologized. On top of that, he was watching her a bit too closely for comfort. She'd have to watch herself around this one. The vibes he gave off reminded her of a guy into freaky sex games or worse.

He dabbed at his face again before asking, "So, you busy tonight?"

"Hmm, I don't know, sugar. I'm an expensive girl. You might not be able to afford me."

He swiveled around to face her fully, the stool squeaking under his weight. "Try me. I may be out of work, but I've got enough to spare on a sweet set like you." His eyes drifted, then settled onto her gaze fully. Carolyn had to look away.

She thought of the fat wallet stuck deep in his chest pocket, and the feel of the leather on her fingertips. "Five hundred to start."

He whistled and slurped some of his beer, his eyes only momentarily flicking away from her. "Damn, woman! You weren't joking, were you? I thought you said this place was boring?"

"All the more reason for a girl to not back down." He grinned, but Carolyn continued. "Besides, I never joke where money's involved. The best of us don't go for pocket change. Thanks for the light, anyway." She stood to leave, but he caught her wrist. She couldn't repress the shudder that went through her, even though he let go almost immediately.

"Wait, I never said I couldn't pay." He lowered his voice. "I've even got cash." His eyes were searching, desperate. Carolyn relaxed a little. Perhaps his creepy vibes were born from plain loneliness. Likely, the man hadn't had a lay in ages, on his long trip, which made him all the more insistent to take even such an expensive night.

"If you can pay," Carolyn said, "then we've got ourselves a deal."

———

SHE FETCHED THE KEYS FOR HER REGULAR ROOM FROM Jimmy, who was still smiling at her as he dropped the keys in her hand.

"It's clean this time, right?" she asked.

"As a whistle. Just be done before dawn, all right? I've got some folks who reserved it for tomorrow, so we'll need to make sure everything's clean."

"Really? Someone's actually booking your rooms?"

He grinned. "Yep, and paid up front, too."

She sighed and glanced up at the clock. Already, it was nearly midnight. "Guess I'd better get to work, then."

"Hey," he leaned over the counter. His white sleeves were rolled up around his elbows and the lamps above them revealed the red tattoos trailing upwards from his forearms. "How much did you ask for, anyway? I thought you might lose him, for a minute."

She bit her lip. "Five hundred. We'll see how much more I can get out of him."

He shook his head. "You're lucky he didn't just up and walk out." He glanced over to the man at the other end of the bar, smiling to himself and eying Carolyn, despite her distance, and lowered his voice. "He gives you any trouble, just let me know, okay?"

"I'll be fine, Jimmy. How many times have we done this, again?"

He shrugged. "You're my little sister. I think I'm entitled to worry a little about you."

Carolyn rolled her eyes and turned around. "Bye, Jimmy!"

<hr>

THE ROOM WAS HIDEOUS, EVEN BY THE BAR'S STANDARDS. IT still amazed her that anyone would want to reserve it, though she guessed the unlucky patron just hadn't looked at it in advance. The paint was peeling, and spiders had claimed almost every corner. Not that Jimmy or she did much to keep the place clean, really. It wasn't a room for relaxing with the family or for getting away from the world, or really even where a proper girl ought to take her client for time alone, but it fit her needs. Besides, if the man was drunk enough, he wouldn't give a shit.

"What's your name, anyway?" He closed the door behind him and propped his hat up on the closet doorknob.

"Rosie. And yours?" Carolyn had three different names she would alternate between. He looked like the Rosie type.

"Dylan." He unbuttoned his shirt, furrowing his eyebrows as he looked around the room. "What a dump. For this price, I ought to at least have a clean place for the night."

Maybe drink alone wasn't enough for Dylan. She sat on the edge of the bed and pulled off her top, allowing a single bra strap to slide down her shoulder. "I guess you could always cancel, if you're not happy. I'm not trying to rip you off, here."

He had been unbuckling his belt, but paused at the show as his cheeks turned red. "No, no, this is good. This is fine."

She smiled and got to her feet. "Give me a moment. A girl has to clean up, you know." She winked before slipping into the bathroom. With the door safely closed behind her, she slid off her skirt and removed the concealed dagger from her left boot. She clutched the blade in her teeth as she slid aside her discarded clothes.

"You all right, in there?" Dylan called. Did he think she was Wonder Woman? She imagined carrying that much money around in his pocket made him bossy, but that wouldn't last much longer. She removed the blade from her teeth and pulled back her hair.

"Hold your horses, sugar! I promise, I won't leave you hanging."

If Carolyn had her way, he wouldn't last the night.

———

SHE TURNED OFF THE BATHROOM LIGHT AND CREAKED OPEN the door, her dagger clutched behind her back. All she wore now was her bra and underwear, just enough to make him feel like he had a present to unwrap. "You think this is worth the money now, sweetheart?"

The bed was empty. She glanced around the room and saw Dylan's shirt and shoes tossed in a pile in the corner. Unless he was running around the bar half-naked, he couldn't have gotten far. The closet door creaked. Had that been open before? She couldn't recall. She took a deep breath but kept her smile and held the dagger firm.

She slinked over to the closet, noticing how the room felt darker than it had. Though, that could have been because she'd just left the glare of the bathroom light. Downstairs, she could hear the vague murmuring of patrons and the occasional chinking of glasses. The building was shoddily built, but there was nothing out of the ordinary, at least. "Dylan, sugar? Are you hiding from me?"

Something thumped inside the closet and Carolyn dropped the dagger down to her side. Her heart was beating hard in her chest, but she kept herself focused. Maybe Dylan was terrified of women; maybe he'd gotten cold feet and hid in the closet. Men had strange ways, sometimes.

With her free hand, she had only barely touched the doorknob, when the door was flung open. Carolyn jumped back, but the edge of the door slammed into her arm that still held the dagger tight. Something dark leaped out from within and sprinted across the room. Carolyn spun toward it, her knife outstretched before her.

Standing on the opposite side of the bed was a man she

didn't recognize. He was so tall that he would have had to hunch if he'd come in through the doorway. His face was gaunt and angular, as though he'd been without food for weeks, and his pale skin gleamed against the dim lamplight. He wore no shirt, only a pair of blue jeans that seemed far too big for his bony hips.

"Who the hell are you?" she asked.

He smiled, but it looked more like a poor imitation. "I am very sorry." His voice seemed to slither across the room in waves, as though it was traveling over water instead of air, and it took a moment for Carolyn to realize that his lips hadn't moved. Carolyn felt a shudder go down her spine. "I'm afraid that will be no good here." He pointed a bony finger at the blade in her hands, and suddenly, it grew heavy. It felt as though she was carrying an entire table instead of an 8-ounce dagger in her hand, and despite her attempt to keep it raised, her fingers couldn't take it. The dagger fell to the ground with a dull thud.

"What are you?" she whispered, her throat not working right. She backed away, wondering if this thing had been hiding in the room. This wasn't how it was supposed to work; she was the one who was supposed to be hunting. What was this thing? She thought of Dylan and asked, "What did you do with—"

"With Dylan? Oh, my dear child, please don't tell me you fell for such a farce. A talented killer like yourself should sense when she is the prey." His face shifted, melted in places, and rose in others, like a time-elapsed landscape. His body hadn't morphed, but his face now resembled the man she'd brought up here just minutes before. "I am Dylan."

She backed away, shaking her head in disbelief. "No, no, that's not possible."

"I am a shifter." His face changed back almost instantly, like a folded balloon that's been released. Carolyn felt a few hangers hit her head and realized she had backed almost into the closet. That meant the door to the room was only a few feet away. She wasn't sure if she'd be able to make it, but she had to try. "I've been traveling for quite some time, you know," Dylan said. "I knew a vicious, young woman like yourself was just the boost I needed."

She had no idea what it meant by a boost, but Carolyn had no intention of being eaten or absorbed or whatever entailed being this thing's prey. She darted for the door, her hand wrapping around the doorknob. She expected it to be locked, but the knob turned without complaint. She wrenched the door back and then felt hands clasp down on either side of her head, covering her ears. What felt like freezing ice picks jabbed into her skull, and the pain reverberated down her shoulders and spine. All she could manage was a gasp as she collapsed to her knees.

His voice seemed distant and faded by the moment. "So much energy. I promise not to waste it as you have."

***

JIMMY CLEARED AWAY A COUPLE MORE EMPTY BOTTLES FROM the countertop. His last remaining patrons were slow to leave, and he'd watched the hands tick by on the clock with increasing annoyance. The first rays of sunlight were creeping in through the grimy windows when his remaining visitors finally headed home. He wished them well and was pleased to see the generous tip one had left behind. After the door to the bar swung closed, he headed upstairs. Carolyn never took this long, unless she was having trouble. Had she offed him already, or had she fallen asleep again?

He reached the closed door and tried the handle. Locked. Now, this was just too much. He banged a fist on the door.

"Carolyn? Wake up. That room has to be cleaned, remember?"

Silence. Not even the rustle of covers or the creaking of floors.

He sighed, slightly dismayed that it was so quiet. "Carolyn? Are you all right? The bar's closed. Come on, open up, will you?"

The knob clicked and the door swung back. Carolyn's eyes were dilated, and her clothes were haphazard, hanging at odd angles. She looked heavily drugged, though that couldn't be right. Neither of them had taken drugs in years, ever since they learned that murder was far more profitable.

"What the hell? Are you on something?"

She shrugged and smiled. "Guess it's a hard habit to kick."

He sighed and flattened down a portion of her hair. "Looks like you had a rough one this time. Did he hurt you?"

She bit her lip, holding back laughter. "Nothing I couldn't handle, but I can't move him. He's too damn heavy."

"So, you were waiting for me to come take care of it, then? Damn, couldn't you have come and let me know? They sit too long and they start to smell!"

"I've got to make you feel useful somehow, right?" She put a hand on his cheek and he pulled away, feeling strangely dazed. "You don't mind, do you? I'm going to head home and get some rest."

He blinked to clear the haze. "Sure..."

"See you later, sweetie."

She must be tired, he thought. She never called him sweetie.

CAROLYN WASN'T EXAGGERATING. HIS BODY WAS HEAVIER than he had expected, and on top of that, Carolyn had made a mess with the dagger in his chest. Jimmy wrapped the body in sheets, frowning as his fingers met with the man's spongy skin. Even in death, the man felt like he sweated buckets. It took a while to drag him outside and Jimmy had to pull out a spare piece of plywood to get the man into the trunk of his car.

It was costly having to buy sheets so frequently for that room, but the money Carolyn brought in more than made up for it. The drive out to the swamp was long, with winding country dirt roads that were completely empty so early in the morning. The sun was just poking its head up over the magnolias, and as he shut the car off, a chorus of frogs and crickets filled his ears.

He went to the trunk and pulled the body out. He sure as hell wished Carolyn had stuck around to help him carry this one, especially since she was the one who picked him out. Jimmy hooked his arms under the man's underarms and dragged him across the mud until his own legs were ankle deep in the swampy marsh. He dropped the man's upper body so that his head was just barely touching the water, and went to work on the legs. He would spin the body around until it was horizontal, then he could just kick it into the green soup.

Just as Jimmy lifted the legs up, his feet slipped and he fell backwards up the slope and heard a popping sound, like a water balloon that got busted. The feet that he'd been holding suddenly shriveled down to nothing, and he looked down to see the thin skin that had been the man's feet hung in his fingertips. His eyes moved up the body: there was a large lump within the thin skin around the upper shoulders and head, making the face grotesquely large and disfigured, like a badly molded mask. The skin at the crown of the head was shredded, and must have been where the popping sound had come from. Above the head was Carolyn's sleek midsection, her breasts still cupped in an attractive pushup bra. Her eyes were wide and her skin shone pale grey beneath the thick green water.

Jimmy wouldn't remember puking, but he did remember the look of the magnolia leaves against the grey morning sky just before he passed out.

Dear, Sweet Lydia

LYDIA SMILED. HER HUSBAND HAD ALWAYS BEEN A RAT, though a mouse was probably more accurate. He was some kind of vermin at least. He would scamper away from the house in the evenings, saying he was going to the office or that someone needed his help, but Lydia knew the truth. Friends would whisper to her over coffee with the most sympathetic expressions. He was a known womanizer, though he certainly hadn't been years ago when they got married. They were young then, and she was naïve. As time passed, his interest in her changed and he grew a taste for younger flesh. She was little more than expired goods in his eyes.

Divorce was out of the question. She would be embarrassed at church and it would ruin her reputation. At her darkest, Lydia considered having children simply to help him settle down, but that was foolish. Not only was it dangerous to give birth at her age, but she couldn't bear bringing children into the world with such a weak man to call father.

The chai tea was warm and smooth, bringing heat back to her insides like a long overdue thaw. Outside the ambulance lights flashed red and blue across the snowy white lawns and the sleepy street. Occasionally the neighbors peeked out through the blinds. Lydia smiled.

The police had been questioning the young woman who lived next door for at least an hour. It was certainly a shock when her lover suffered a heart attack. Lydia wondered if rats succumbed to such things, their little hearts beating so quickly before snuffing out.

She watched the officers return to their car, point towards Lydia's house and place their hands on their hips. She imagined their long strides up the snowy driveway that her husband never shoveled and over the steppingstones that she had put in years ago against his wishes. With utmost regret they would give her the tragic news. How should she react? Disbelief was the first requirement. After that she would need to cry. If the mood struck her, she could pretend to faint and let the young officer catch her, only no, she couldn't go over the top. That would look suspicious.

But what was there to suspect?

She was just a sweet, reserved woman who had been a devoted wife for fifteen long years to a disrespectful husband. The poor thing. How could Lydia have known the cute, young neighbor Cindy was having an affair with him? Goodness, what an embarrassing way to go too! Found naked on the floor of the bathroom, the toilet still smelling of the used condom and piss he deposited.

Lydia had seen it all from the small cameras she had installed in Cindy's home. When the young woman moved in a few months back, Lydia had known her rat of a husband couldn't resist. Cindy wore the shortest skirts and always flashed a smile in his direction. Lydia wasn't sure if Cindy knew what she was doing, but it didn't matter. A fool or a conspirator: Cindy was a pawn regardless.

Cindy had been so grateful when Lydia offered to come by and help her unpack things. It took three days to go through all the boxes, but that gave her plenty of time to wire the bathroom and bedroom with the wireless cameras that recorded everything to Lydia's private server. She even had boxes to climb on to reach those pesky ceiling corners. From her cell phone Lydia could see everything, from their romps in the evening to the way her rat of a husband encouraged Cindy to drink more and more alcohol until she couldn't refuse him.

Lydia took another sip of her tea, breathing in the steam and closing her eyes. Would they bother with an autopsy, she wondered? If she claimed it was against her religious beliefs, they would likely drop it on the grounds of the extra paperwork. Better to let the man at least retain a little dignity. They wouldn't notice the alarmingly high dosage of heart medication he'd taken over the past week. Lydia had taken her time with it, taking the extra bottle of his prescription medication and slicing the pills one by one to drop their contents into his morning glass of orange juice or coffee. It wasn't quite poisoning since he was prescribed to take them daily, and he was so very forgetful. This morning had been the largest amount, with three extra pills on top of his regular dosage. He complained of chest pain all week, and had even scheduled an appointment to see his doctor. Lydia knew death would find him, but she never guessed it would turn out quite so perfectly.

She turned off her phone before Cindy could saunter her way into the bathroom to check on him. Lydia didn't want to see Cindy's terror. The woman was merely collateral damage. She would probably be moving soon, especially as the neighbors descended upon her for stealing Lydia's husband. They wouldn't know his tricks. They wouldn't understand that Cindy was a victim too, even if she didn't know it.

It was pathetic that Lydia was the woman who had to step forward and make a move, considering all his affairs and the trail of broken women that followed him. All the other women were too cowardly to do what was needed. They let the violent outbursts and bruised jaws control them, but Lydia was not so delicate. She was the only one who had the means to do it properly so that no one would suspect.

Lydia allowed herself another smile as the doorbell rang. The police had finally mustered the courage to make their visit. She finished off her tea, which had grown cooler than she liked. She wanted to move on with her life, not spend it worrying about the dead vermin next door. It was time for her final performance.

Those Terrible Golden Eyes

INTERSTATE 16 RUNS OVER A HUNDRED MILES BETWEEN THE bustling cities of Macon and Savannah, Georgia. It's also the stretch of road I dread most when driving down to visit my aunt. Composed of only two lanes and a scattering of exits, it's a perfect recipe for road rage, an inexplicable need to urinate, and a perpetual fear of running out of gas.

I've driven it before, two years ago for a house-warming party for my aunt. That was an overnight trip too. I wish I could say I got used to the black trees that stand on either side of the interstate, dark and foreboding, or to the speeders that I pray won't run me down as they pass at a hundred and fifty in the left lane. The cars travel with large gaps between each other, with maybe one or two other cars within sight, their headlights like lonely ships on a black, endless sea. Sometimes my eyes go blurry too, and it gets easier to veer into the ditch the later it gets. The drive is faster at night though, and for a broke college student eager for any vacation over spring break, cheap is essential.

To my right the trees break momentarily, revealing a house with a gravel driveway that goes straight to the edge of the interstate. It had to have been there before I-16 was built, which meant it likely was built before the 1970s. I looked it up once because I was pretty sure state laws didn't permit someone to put a house so close to enormous trucks going seventy and eighty miles an hour. I glance to the side in time to spot the squat house standing silent in the darkness, barely visible beyond the blanket of trees. A bedraggled windmill looms out of the darkness at its side, a skeletal ghost of a forgotten time. Then they disappear, enveloped again by the never-ending pines. That house is my marker, meaning I've almost reached the end of I-16. I ease back into my seat a little and relax my grip on the steering wheel.

That's when my driver's side rear tire went flat.

Flat tires don't bust out like they do in the movies. At least, not always. The only tire I ever saw blow out belonged to a semi four lanes over from mine, and it was so loud that I instinctively slammed on my brakes even though I was nowhere near it. I'm pretty sure the poor motorcyclist behind him damn near had a heart attack.

I'm good at identifying the flat tire sound on my car, at noticing the *badump-badump* of the tire lolling on the pavement, at recognizing how the dashboard doesn't sit perpendicular to the road and feeling the way the car shudders. I pull onto the shoulder and into the grass, the car bouncing with the crunch of dirt under the wheels. I'm hoping it's a false alarm despite my senses telling me otherwise. I turn on the emergency lights, bouncing yellow light off the foreboding darkness just a few feet away, revealing the true colors of the thick green foliage.

"Shit," I say, then glance to the clock to see the time. Ten o'clock. I slam my hand into the steering wheel and give a snarl, but only the insects can hear my frustration. Getting angry won't solve anything. It won't fix the flat tire, or the fact that I don't have a working spare either. A set of vehicles roar past, and I close my eyes and will myself to calm down.

Since the spare was a full-sized tire, I simply traded out tires on the first flat I got last year. At the time, I thought I was pretty clever. Then I had another flat two months back, which I only just paid off. Clearly the fates had it in for me, stranding me with a flat tire and a flat spare in the middle of nowhere. My car, my only means of escape from campus, is quickly becoming a piece of junk.

I pull out my cell phone only to see it has 30% battery left. I used to have a car charger for it, but my ex-boyfriend tore it out of the front console one night and now I can't charge anything.

With a shuddering sigh I press my head against the steering wheel. I have enough juice left to call for help, but without a spare, what can anyone do? Sure, my car could be towed to a garage, but I can't afford that. The nearest exit is ten miles or more.

I could use my last call to reach my aunt, but she would panic and rush out herself despite my protests. Since she has night blindness, that would put her in danger.

Of course, there was always the option of flagging down a car and hitching a ride to the nearest exit, but the missing persons board at Walmart was awash in young black college girls. Whoever pulled over for me might have the best of intentions or the worst.

That skeletal windmill and the squat house beside it come to mind. I stare at the battery indicator on my phone. They might at least have a landline so I wouldn't have to drain my cell. They might also have something to patch up the spare tire, too. I've heard of folks using hay to fill a tire before, and I've seen a few reality TV shows about folks in the country with crafty ways to patch a flat.

I'm surprised at how heavy the flat spare is when I yank it

out of the trunk. It'll take some time to roll it down to the house, but it couldn't be more than half a mile or so. That shouldn't take too long. I pull out the flashlight from my trunk, but the batteries are dead. I resist the urge to throw it. I pocket the keys, turn off the phone to save power, and lock up the car. With the waning moon lighting the shoulder of the interstate, and the buzz of crickets in my ears, I roll the spare along I-16, back to the squat house.

***

I'VE NEVER HAD TO ROLL A TIRE BEFORE. LET ME MAKE that perfectly clear. Doing it in the dark along the uneven dirt while cars whiz past at instant-roadkill speeds is more difficult and terrifying than I anticipated. After working up a sticky sweat, I let the tire fall onto its side and stand to stretch my aching back. My annoyance is reaching new heights. I put my hands on my hips and pant in the cool night air.

Where the hell is it? I didn't remember it being this far back. I look behind me and have to wait for another car to pass to spot the shadow of my car in the ditch. I hadn't gone very far, but damn, it felt like it. I'm warm, even with the cool breeze. A trickle of sweat rolls down my spine. Maybe I misjudged the distance. Leaving the tire in the mud, mostly because I just can't motivate myself to continue rolling it, I walk ahead.

Another car whooshes past, and afterward the sounds of crickets buzz back to their loud crescendo to fill the emptiness. I've never heard such noisy crickets before, but then again, I've never spent much time in the country. I realize with how loud the crickets are and how dark it is without any headlights around, if somebody was following me, I'd be dead. Who would be ridiculous enough to be out here alone? Other than me, of course.

I glance behind before walking faster, not willing to admit my irrational fear with an all-out run.

When I reach gravel, I relax. I must be close now and I'm eager to get away from the woods. It is strange how the trees create a wall of camouflage from this angle, the same way they do on the interstate. When I spot the windmill, standing like a pale, skeletal giant against the backdrop of pines, I stop to catch my breath. The house at its base, though, is in worse shape than I thought.

The building looks like it was pulled straight from an old 1930s snapshot of the Dust Bowl, with ramshackle planked walls and a roof that sags on one end. The gravel on its makeshift driveway is scattered throughout the dirt and overgrown grass, meaning it hasn't been replaced in some time. I rub my arms as I approach the front door. I can see at least one boarded-up window, though it was sloppily done. The screen on the front door is also bent and folded forward. It must be abandoned. No one could live in such a place. But then I spot candlelight. I blink, trying to make sure it isn't a trick of the light from the passing cars. A cool wind blows past and the light inside flickers.

Someone is home.

I knock on the frame of the door, but the battered screened door creaks open on its own. I stare at the flickering candlelight in the far room, half-expecting some psycho killer to come running out at me. But running away won't get the flat tire fixed, I remind myself. Nor will jumping at shadows. Just because they don't have electricity doesn't make them bad people.

"Hello?" I ask in a hoarse voice, stepping inside.

I feel small in here, as forgotten as the battered end table against the wall. There's something about the place that makes me move quietly, as though I might disrupt the dust. It smells like car exhaust with a tinge of mold. The floor of the hallway had once been made out of tile, but now there are only fragments. I enter what I guess must be the living room. There's a battered rocking chair in the corner, missing an arm, and a coffee table that's been pushed against the wall. That's where the yellow pillar candle rests, casting strange, distorted shadows against the beleaguered walls. I keep sensing movement out of the corner of my eyes from that damn candle, and I have to resist the urge to jump.

The wallpaper is puckered and peeling all around the room, probably from heavy rain or humidity. Bits of plaster from the falling ceiling litter the ground like confetti. The back door at the opposite end of the living room is only a frame, its screen lost long ago.

Perhaps they're outside, I think, a part of me eager to find any excuse to leave the place. As I head to the back door, I notice light. It's pouring from a room to the side that was hidden before. The door is ajar and candlelight flickers within.

"Hello, is anyone here?" I ask, but this time there's an answer.

A shrill, high-pitched cry makes me jump. My heart hammers in my chest as I get the urge to run, only I realize it's a baby's cry. Had someone left a baby here? I slowly approach the lit room, and that's when the smell hits me. It's a horrible putrid scent, like a dozen dirty diapers left to rot in the sun. I cough into my hand and try to adjust to it.

Who the hell would abandon a baby in this horrible place? Images of a fly infested infant living in their own filth wash over me, and all thoughts of my tire lying in the ditch a few yards back are tossed aside.

Steeling myself for whatever I might find, I pull the door open and step inside. It's a small bathroom. An old toilet sits near the door, with its bowl full of black water. The bowl of the sink sits on the floor beside its headless pedestal, filled with about ten candles. In the corner is a pile of foul diapers, and on the far wall is a grungy white bathtub with an old, musty shower curtain that's been pushed aside. A woman with sallow, pale skin stands in the tub dressed in a dirty dress, bouncing the crying, wrapped bundle in her arms. When her wild eyes fall upon me, I realize I've made a terrible mistake.

"Who are you?" the woman spits. "What are you doing here?"

My mind goes blank. I have too many questions on my tongue that want to be asked, but already I know this woman won't want to answer. The woman turns to me, sloshing the few inches of water around in the tub. Had she had been trying to bathe the baby? Surely not. The infant is wrapped from head to toe with a thick blanket.

Hiking up her dress, she steps barefoot out of the tub and descends on me like a hawk. "He needed a bath, is all. I wanted him to be clean!" Despite the fact that she's standing right beside me, the woman screams the words and the poor baby in her arms cries louder.

"I'm sorry," I stammer, wilting away from those wild eyes. The woman's hair stands out all around her, with bits of twigs and leaves stuck in it. "I had a flat tire and —"

"A what?" the hawkish woman shrieks. I wince at the way her voice pierces the stillness of the house. "Who are you?"

"Flora," I stammer. "My name is Flora. I had a flat tire." I back away. The baby's cries intensify, and the woman's entire demeanor flips in an instant.

"Don't worry, little one," she coos as she bounces him in her arms. "No need to cry, I'll be looking after you. Don't fret now."

Her dirtied dress leaves her forearms bare, and her skin

from the elbows down is covered with red splotches and crusty marks which I guess are needle marks. This woman is on drugs. At least that explained part of the problem. The woman's soft voice does little to soothe the bound child, and I can't blame him.

"This is private property!" she spits again with a trembling lower lip. "If you don't leave, I'll call the cops. I will! If I had a gun on me, I wouldn't hesitate, you hear me? Treating an old woman and her boy like this." Bright headlights suddenly pour into the living room from the front of the house, flooding the insides of the building with light. I wince. The crazed woman's eyes dilate to pinpricks as she looks up like a startled ostrich.

"No..." she whispers.

Outside, the rumble of an engine turns off. A car door squeals open and I hear a dog barking. "Olivia!"

Her lips tremble, and this time her voice is humble. "No, no, he shouldn't be here. How did he know?"

"Who?" I whisper, but the woman shoves the shrieking bundle into my arms.

"Take him!" she says and pushes me to the back door. "Take him and don't you dare unwrap him!" She yanks the screen door open so hard that one of the rusted hinges breaks off. I can hear the man's boots crunch on gravel as he approaches the front of the house.

"You better not have him!" the man called. "Dammit woman, get on out here!"

"Who is he?" I ask as I hold the boy against my chest.

"My husband. Now get already!"

She shoves me out the back door and I nearly lose my balance on the debris strewn across the ground.

"Hide!" she hisses. "He'll kill that boy if he finds him."

I turn around in the dark yard, my head swimming. If the man was crazy enough to kill an infant, there was no telling what he would do to me. After my eyes adjust, I spot a wood pile looming near the side of the house. The tall grass grazes my thighs as I pick my way over, and I can make out pieces of fractured building materials sticking out of the pile. It smells like wet, rotting wood.

I hear arguing from the house, almost indiscernible from the barking dog. I hunker down behind the wood pile, making sure I can still see the back door in case I need to make a run for it. Behind me, the wood pile settles. No, that's not right. That wasn't wind brushing against my ankles, that was the scattering of rodents in the darkness. I shudder and glance down to the baby against my chest, surprised that he's so quiet after his cries earlier, but perhaps just getting him out of that horrible house and away from the shrieking woman was enough to calm him. Everything is quieter out here, even the crickets.

I hear someone get slapped and I hunker down further. The dog is quiet now too, and I can hear them easily. "I know what I heard, Olivia. That was a baby crying. Now tell me where you hid it."

"You can't kill him, Steven," Olivia says. "Whatever you do, I won't let you kill him!"

"It ain't your baby! Damn, what the hell is wrong with you? It doesn't belong to you."

I look down to the bundled baby in my arms. He isn't her child. I imagine that crazy woman slinking into someone's house and climbing into a nursery like a spider, snatching the boy out of his crib. To think that she brought him back here to this horrible place that ought to be condemned, perhaps with thoughts of raising him as her own. I clutch him closer to my chest. I consider running to my car, but that would do me little good. The dog would follow me easily and even if I got there, where could I go? My car still has a flat tire. I can't even help myself, let alone a baby.

I feel a prick on my collarbone and reflexively pull the baby away. He probably grabbed some patch of skin or scratched me with his nails, but wait, isn't he wrapped up? I look down in time to see something long, black and shiny slide back into the swaddling again.

Something between a gasp and a cry escapes my lips, and the back door swings open.

The pair in the doorway are still bickering even as the dog barks at their feet, but I can barely hear them. My eyes are fixed on the bundled baby in my arms. My mouth hangs open and my throat constricts as my brain tries to make sense of what I saw. It is dark out here after all, and without light, the shadows could be playing tricks on me. All the same, my heart is pounding as a dark trickle of blood slips down from my chest and into my cleavage.

It emerges again slowly, like a snake's tongue, feeling along the cloth. Its tongue looks gelatinous somehow but forked on the end. It pierces into the fabric in different spots, again and again.

I think of the pockmarked arms on Olivia. Is it like a leech? The black, forked thing reels back into the fabric and the baby starts to cry. It's searching for me, I realize. It's trying to feed on me. I shudder.

What is this thing I'm holding? I feel a scream building inside, a pressure growing steadily within me, building until I think I might burst. My hands tremble as the baby writhes and part of me wants to drop him to the ground.

I hear a guttural clicking sound behind me, and it triggers some deep, instinctual fear that makes my mind hone in on it and grab hold. It's like the noise an alligator might make as a warning as it floats on top of a lake, a low noise that makes my stomach clench. I turn around to see a pair of yellow lights that are so close to my face that I could touch them. It's like turning around to a pair of headlights. My vision is filled by it, overwhelmed by it. Even closing my eyes doesn't remove it from my vision, and I take a step backward. A thin, translucent film shoots out from the outer edges of the lights, covers them briefly, then snaps back again. They're its eyes, I realize. The headlights are its eyes. I feel like my head is floating.

"No!" Olivia cries from the back door. "No, she can't have him! He's mine, that boy is mine." The crazed woman starts forward but Steven grabs her arm. Even though she doesn't even come up to his shoulder, he's having a hard time holding her still, and her outrage puts vigor into the dog. The black Labrador, its fur dark and shiny, bounds forward toward the monster in front of me.

"Brimstone!" The man orders, "Sit boy—Sit!"

But the dark lab is too excited to obey his master. He bares his teeth at the creature standing in front of me, and I suck in a breath, too terrified to even run. The furred thing aims its glowing eyes at the dog and gives another guttural clicking noise that makes me want to hunker down to the ground. It flaps its great leathery wings as though to take flight, but the dog only hesitates for a moment before returning to its mad barking again.

In a flash the beast is in front of the bewildered dog, and with a single swipe of its fingers, which I realize are long, black claws, it thrusts the poor dog into the wood pile behind me. Debris falls down around my legs and I feel the skittering of things crawling around my ankles, but I can't bring myself to move.

Steven pulls out a pistol and fires at the creature, only the bullets don't seem to work. In fact, every time he pulls the trigger, the creature seems to blur somehow, and I hear the bullets take chunks out of the pine trees behind it. I shake my head, unable to move as the creature is suddenly in front of them. It swipes at Steven's neck and his head topples like a broken doll to the ground. Olivia shrieks and kicks at the monster with her bare feet. I turn away and wince as her screams are cut short.

The thing in my arms starts crying again as the couples' blood pools on the dirt. It sounds just like a human baby. I hold it at a distance, not wanting to have it so close to my body, so close to my flesh, so close to my heart. I don't want it anywhere near me, especially as that forked, black feeler sticks out again. It probes around like a tentacle, but I keep my fingers away from it. Then it bursts into another cry, shriller than before. I can't drop it, I'm afraid to. If I do, that giant creature could kill me next.

It's not her baby, it's not a baby at all. I repeat the mantra in my mind, my eyes glued to the small, bundled creature in my arms. I turn the words over and over again, trying to make sense of the impossible sound emerging from its tiny throat. Nothing is real to me. Everything is distant. My hands feel cold beneath the small bundle, but that's not right, those can't be my hands. I would never hold such a thing because it could never possibly exist. Such a creature shouldn't exist. I distance myself from those limbs that are as stiff as boards beneath the bundle that sounds like a child; I ignore the wiggling creature slowly loosening its binding cloth, trying to free itself like a grotesque caterpillar.

The yellow eyes fall upon me again and I go rigid. I glance to the dog, its body just within my peripheral vision. He whimpers before lumbering toward the front of the house. He knows his masters are dead and he's running away. The dog has more sense than I do. I can't bring myself to move or even scream. My body acts like it doesn't belong to me anymore. As the monster extends its arms, glinting like a rotten tree limb, it probes with its three-fingered hands for the babe that must belong to it.

I shiver when one of its long claws drags against my

fragile skin and the coarse, matted bristles of its fur brush across my hand. Pure revulsion pulls me back to my senses. My limbs are my own again, my hands are my own, and I shove the baby toward the monster, eager to get rid of it, eager to have it as far away from me as possible. The monster emits that guttural clicking noise again and for a fraction of a second I question the logic of that impulse. What if I injured the child? What if I upset it? Mothers in the wild are notoriously protective, after all. Then three more limbs dart out from the creature to keep the baby from falling. I blink, wondering whether it grew those three limbs in an instant, or if I simply hadn't seen them. Those terrible golden eyes burn into my retinas.

With the dexterity of a raccoon, it turns the child around with its four hands and removes the cloth that binds it. Even before the cloth falls away, I know my mind is not strong enough to see it. For a moment, I'm grateful that my eyes are so burned from looking into those horrible eyes to spare me from clearly seeing the monstrous creature before me and its grotesque spawn. But despite the instinctual urge to look away, my curiosity and fascination won't let me.

I watch the tiny, shriveled form unfurl its own set of leathery wings and stretch its pairs of arms. It stares at me with its own pair of golden eyes, only they aren't as bright. The glow is faint, like the glint of a firefly. It looks at me with its open beak and stretches out its black tongue toward me. Then in a flash it retracts it in and starts babbling. It even babbles like a baby. How could it sound so much like a child despite its monstrous form? It's the perfect mimic of a human baby's babble, full of all the same intonations and affection. I have a terrible image come to mind of a baby being holed away with this beastly child, held captive for days for the sole purpose of teaching this thing how to mimic. It doesn't even need lips, it just opens its beak and the sounds come out.

My head feels loopy and dazed, and suddenly I'm on the woodpile, though I don't remember falling. The bugs and rodents scurry underneath me. The monster's headlight gaze fixes on the woodpile and I hear its footfalls approach, but I can't bring myself to move. I feel paralyzed and helpless. Then comes the familiar pricking of pain against my bare arms before darkness engulfs me.

BIRDS ARE CHIRPING AND SOMETHING WARM AND WET IS ON my hand. I squint my eyes open, unprepared for the massive headache that assails me. I sit up to see the lab licking away at my hand, his tail wagging. He's thrilled I'm alive, and so am I.

I glance to the bodies of his owners, but all that's left of them are the pools of blood and a trail that leads toward the woods. I don't intend to go looking for them.

Climbing to my feet, my head throbs in defiance and I put a shaky hand to my head. I ought to be dead like the couple, but for some reason I'm not. Maybe because I didn't attack them, they let me go. I don't have time to think about that.

As I limp my way back to the front of the house, the dog follows me, all wagging tail and happy licks on my hand. He's not the brute I thought he was last night. I feel weak and incredibly thirsty, but I don't trust the water in the tub or anything else in that damn house.

I make my way outside and spot the truck that Steven left. Careful to avoid getting my fingerprints on anything, I look through the bed and find his tools. I may be ridiculously unprepared for a flat tire, but he wasn't. Using his tools, I patch up my flat and put the spare back in my trunk.

"Well, Brimstone, you need a lift?"

He wags his tail and joins me as I hop in the car and

merge back on the interstate. I'll find a gas station some-where and clean us both up. I reach over and pet his head as he starts to doze on my passenger seat.

Somehow, together we'll find a way back to some form of normalcy.

Just Too Sweet

My mother has always had an incurable sweet tooth. Anytime she found a new type of cake, a new candy, a new cookie, she had to try it out. Some might just call her a foodie, but it was a bit more extreme than that. She had to have sweet foods in the house. My late father forgot to pick up a cheesecake once on the way home from the grocery store, and she refused to talk to him for the rest of the night. Weekends became battlegrounds when she didn't have some pastry or confectionery creation waiting for her in the kitchen. Now that I think about it, that was probably why I became a baker.

Naturally when mother's sixtieth birthday was coming up, I wanted to get her something special, something to make the drudgery of hitting sixty a little less difficult to bear. I knew I wanted to make her a red velvet cake with homemade cream cheese icing, but that simply wasn't enough. It was her favorite, sure, but there was nothing new about it. It was the same old cake I had made before for her, and I didn't want her to be reminded of the sameness of things. I wanted her to be excited about something new, something she had never tried before. So, when my friend recommended a beer that she had been told paired well with cakes, I thought I'd try it out.

Of course, it was a specialty product which was only available online. The website for it was rudimentary at best, and I couldn't even pull it up on my phone. I had to get on my laptop to even look at it, and I wasn't encouraged by the blinking text and abundance of exclamation points. The beer bottles themselves looked professional enough, though. The green glass gleamed under fluorescent lighting and the yellow label had a strange picture of a silhouetted woman dancing and wearing a mask, as though attending a masquerade. Scrawled beneath her feet in fancy black script was Chartreuse Charade.

I snorted and shook my head. I wasn't willing to buy my mother just any drink I found online, so I ordered a case for myself. I wouldn't have time to order another case before I saw her that weekend, but at least I would have something to hopefully complement the cake. With a few clicks and a sigh at having to pay for expedited shipping, the order was placed.

If I had only known then what it was, I never would have bought it.

THE BEER DIDN'T COME UNTIL FRIDAY AFTERNOON, AND I was going to see my mother on Saturday. The six-pack came in plain brown packaging, with my address handwritten in black sharpie on the outside. There was no return address, and my name was even misspelled, Imary Hamiltown instead of Imari Hamilton. I should have known then that there was something fishy about the order, but I didn't think much about it at the time. I figured it was a small mom and pop store without resources, or maybe the drink was imported and shipped out as fast as possible. I was crunched for time and promptly ignored the warning signs.

I needed to make a cake that evening; so, I didn't have time to be picky. I unwrapped the cardboard casing with the six verdant bottles poking up like bad props in an 80's movie. I picked up one and sloshed the liquid back and forth under the kitchen light, frowning as the thick sludge inside moved more like cough medicine than any beer I had ever tried.

I pulled off the cap and set the bottle on the kitchen counter as I pulled out the pans to start on Mother's red velvet cake. The Chartreuse Charade stared back at me. Sugar, flour, salt, baking powder, I tossed in all the ingredients into my mixer and turned it on. I had to give her the perfect cake. Mamma was always a critic, but this time I found the perfect cake that even she would love. This one had become my specialty at work, so I knew it would blow her away once she had a taste. Hopefully she would appreciate all the work I put into it this year. Hopefully she would notice.

I popped the cake pans into the oven. As I set the bake timer on my phone, I glanced over to the green bottle again and gave a heavy sigh. Regardless of how gross it looked I didn't want to admit that I might have wasted money. I took a quick picture with my phone and posted it to my Twitter feed, hoping to get some encouragement from friends. "Trying out a new beer. Anybody know if #ChartreuseCha-rade is any good?"

Thirty minutes of baking and I still hadn't taken a sip. I wondered if mother would be so hesitant tomorrow. I started on the icing next and dropped the blocks of cream cheese into the mixer bowl. My phone buzzed, then it buzzed again. With sticky fingers, I started up the mixer and washed my hands before checking it. The lock screen was flooded with messages, not from my friends, but from excited fans of the drink. I scrolled through them in shock. I wasn't used to getting such a quick response from my few followers, let alone getting so much attention from twenty strangers in five minutes.

I picked up the bottle and removed the lid. The liquid within was a brilliant chartreuse, a color I might normally associate with dangerous, radioactive substances in a kid's film. With a grimace, I took the tiniest of sips. As soon as the thick, green sludge touched my tongue, my heartbeat quickened. My mouth watered so much that it was almost painful and I shivered, then the sweetness kicked in. Now, growing up in my mamma's house, I was exposed to what many would consider a diverse array of sweet foods, but this topped them all. It tasted like it was produced in a lab, but my taste buds adored it. I had to cough from my body's inability to process the intense flavor. My tongue was overwhelmed, and I suddenly understood what all those tweets were raving about. I took a deeper drink, this time anticipating the euphoria, and allowed it to wash over me like a hot bath. After downing almost half the bottle, I flipped it around in my hands to read the ingredients, but found nothing terribly out of the ordinary. By the time I had finished icing the cake, the bottle was empty, and I was struggling to resist the urge to grab another.

No, I thought, I'll let Mamma have the rest. I've got a feeling she'll love it and it'll pair perfectly with the cake.

EVER SINCE MY MOTHER'S CAR ACCIDENT, SHE HAD TO USE crutches or a walker wherever she went. The doctor had told her she might need to use a wheelchair if she expected to be walking for a long period of time, but my mother was an obstinate woman. She refused to use one even at the grocery store, let alone anywhere else. All the same, I insisted she get a ground floor apartment, though she didn't think it was necessary.

Despite her determination to be independent, it was still difficult for her to take the trash bags to the front of the apartment complex each week. I'm sure she would manage it if she had to, but I didn't want her to hurt herself. Lugging a heavy bag of trash while navigating the sidewalk with a walker or crutches was bad enough, let alone doing it for three or four bags each week. So, I came by every Saturday to take out her trash and visit. Her place wasn't far from where I worked, and it was a good excuse to check up on her.

Her eyes went wide when I walked in with the red velvet cake in my hands. "Oh Imari, that is absolutely beautiful!"

"Thank you," I smiled, proud of my work, and dropped the grocery bag of beer onto the kitchen counter, struggling not to drop the cake. Mamma's home was always a bit cluttered, what she liked to call "lived-in". The coffee table was covered in piles of magazines, bills, and half-read newspapers. Books were piled in the nooks and crannies, tall enough to almost count as extra chairs. She couldn't get around as well as she used to, that's what I told myself. Last year I took a whole weekend and cleaned her living room from top to bottom, but after only a week it was back to the same mess. After that, I grew dismayed and now just tried to ignore it. Mother was set in her ways and I wasn't going to change her.

I turned to see her coming into the kitchen with her walker. She was all smiles as I gave her a peck on the cheek. "Happy Birthday, Mamma. Here, I brought you a surprise."

She arched her slim eyebrows. Despite the disrepair of her apartment, she looked fabulous in a flowery dress, pink lacquered fingernails, and freshly applied makeup. If she didn't have to use a walker, you would never be able to guess her age. "I saw the cake, honey. I'm not blind, you know."

I rolled my eyes and picked up the grocery bag. "No, this. It's to go with the cake."

She pulled on her spectacles and eyed the labels. A devious grin spread across her lips. "Lord have mercy, you got me beer."

"Sure did!" I said as I headed to the back patio to get her trash. She only had a couple of bags today, and they were easy enough to pick up.

Mamma pushed open the glass door. "Imari, stop that. Don't do that right now, you just got here."

"It won't take but a few moments," I insisted, and stepped inside again to bring the trash through.

She sighed and held her nose. "I wish you would go around instead of through the house. There's a reason I keep it outside, you know."

I ignored her protests and headed to my car to drop the bags in the trunk. It took only a couple of minutes to drive down to the dumpster near the entrance and drop them off. Mother liked to protest though. It had gotten worse since she had the walker, too; I chalked it up to her dealing with more frustration every day with getting around, but it also made her more difficult. She never liked needing help before, and she hated needing it now. She had a tendency to offload her worries onto anybody who would listen, and I was a sympathetic ear. By the time I got back, Mamma was sitting in her favorite recliner. She was already talking to me before I had even closed the door.

"Imari, where did you get this? This is simply the best beer I've ever tasted, hell, it's the best drink I've ever tasted. I've never had anything so sweet before! It's incredible."

"Mamma! You opened it already?"

She shrugged and took another sip. "I told you not to take the trash out, but you did anyway. Is that any way to treat

your mother on her birthday? You sure can be rude sometimes, Imari. I thought I taught you better than that."

I didn't answer as I stepped into the kitchen to wash my
hands. I cut slices of cake and put them out on plates for the
two of us. By the time I went back to the living room with
them, she had already opened up another bottle. "Slow down,
Mamma, it's supposed to go with the cake."

She gave a wicked smile and took another sip and closed
her eyes to appreciate it. "You don't think they put drugs in
these, do you? It tastes too divine to be legal."

I couldn't suppress a laugh as I sat down on the couch to
dive into my own slice of red velvet. When Mamma tried a
bite of her birthday cake, she grimaced.

I stared at her. "What's wrong?"

She gave a sheepish smile. "Oh it's very good honey, it's
just... the beer tastes better is all. The cake just tastes so
bland."

I felt my stomach drop. It was the very best cake I knew
how to make, I had dozens of customers praise me for it for
months, and yet here she was saying it was bland!

I glared at the green bottle in her hand as she took
another sip. "This, on the other hand, is heavenly!"

I SPENT THE FOLLOWING WEEK ANNOYED WITH HER.

Mamma always had a way of wounding my pride with just
a few words, but insulting my cakes? She had never done that
before. It was a new low for her and I just couldn't bring
myself to talk to her. Every time I thought of her foul expression when she bit into that slice of cake, my anger reared up
again.

Trying to find any excuse not to return her calls, I threw
myself into work, from arriving early to perfect the details on

a wedding cake to staying late to add an extra batch of cookies to an order. I welcomed any distraction. Mamma would rather drink beer from some seedy online company than eat the cake I made with my own hands. She didn't even like the taste of it. That was what really set my anger boiling. All the customer compliments in the world couldn't make up for that one terrible scowl she made at tasting her birthday cake. By the time Saturday morning rolled around again, I was a mess. I dreaded seeing her again, and it made me feel like a terrible daughter. But I got in the car and headed her way just like I did every Saturday, because that's what I always did.

She's my mother, I thought, shouldn't I love her despite the fact that she hardly ever had a kind word to give me? Every week I went out of my way to visit, to take out the trash, and handle any other chores she might need. I visited her every holiday, I listened to all her complaints, and I even cleaned for her. But why? Why did I do it if I didn't feel appreciated? I tried to convince myself I must enjoy the torture, or I was starved for conversation, or that I was stuck in the role of the dutiful child.

I gripped the steering wheel in my hand and had to slam on the brakes as the traffic light I had vaguely acknowledged went from yellow to red. Deep down, I knew the answer already. The cake was merely the final piece to be removed from a poorly built scaffolding. It opened my eyes to the fact that she no longer appreciated me. It was a deep-seated fear I had suspected ever since I explained to her, years ago, that I had no intention of ever getting married or having children. Her face had fallen so quickly, you would think I had some fatal disease. Her eyes welled up with tears, and her bottom lip trembled, and instantly I felt horrible for mentioning it. We went back and forth on it, her trying to convince me that I was being rash or egocentric, and me explaining that it wasn't something I wanted. When she finally accepted it, she fell into a self-loathing fit, wondering if she had raised me wrong. By the time I left late that evening, I had known that she would never see me the same way again. Mamma might never admit it, she might never even realize it herself, but that night I not only lost her respect, but I also lost her love.

Yet week after week, I tried to build it back. I guess I thought that if I could prove I was a useful child to her, somehow her affection would return. I came over and allowed the slings and arrows to pummel me with the same wry smile that I might use in dealing with a frustrated customer at work. I did chores for her, I talked with her, and we laughed over silly television shows, but anytime I mentioned my future goals or plans, she shut down. She never wanted to talk about the future with me after that. I assume because she never thought it was worth talking about. I had, after all, rejected the plans she had made for me.

I parked the car at her apartment and sat staring at her front door. Usually she had the blinds open, but today they were shut tight. I glanced at my phone, but she hadn't sent me any texts or tried to call. I took a deep breath, wiped at my eyes, and reminded myself that I was a grown-ass woman. After I took out the trash and we sat down on the sofa, I would tell her how I felt. I would open up to her and explain my version of the problem. Maybe if she saw I was speaking from the heart, she might open up, too.

The apartment door was locked, but I knocked anyway and pulled out my spare key. I checked my watch and saw that it was nearly eleven; she couldn't possibly still be asleep. The living room was dark, and near the front door was a pile of boxes that were almost as tall as me.

"Mamma, are you home?"

No response. Was she truly asleep? I headed into the

kitchen and spotted a note left on the countertop, written in her fine cursive hand:

Sorry I missed you, honey! Went out with Abe from upstairs. He's a sweet old thing — maybe if you're around when we get back, I'll introduce you to him? Also can you give me the name of a good exterminator? Lord knows I need one! Kiss-kiss, Mamma.

I couldn't repress my frustration. There was something painfully ironic about her going out on a date right when I had worked up the nerve to have a serious conversation with her. I pulled out my phone and wrote on her note the name and number of an exterminator I used at my place.

When I headed out to the back patio to get the trash can, I froze before even turning the door handle. Hovering like a mad swirl of black smoke around the patio was a cloud of insects. I let out a shaky breath and slowly slid the door open. The cloud didn't scatter as I stepped out onto the patio and closed the door behind me. The buzzing sound emanating from them was loud, like something you would expect from a hundred bumblebees. Not wanting to get too close, but still wanting to know what the hell they were, I inched closer. My first thought was that they were bees or wasps; they seemed big enough, but then one of the black bugs landed on the trashcan lid, and I saw him clearly: a large, black fly.

Now I've lived in the South most of my life, but I've never seen flies swarm in a mass that thick before. Gnats will do it plenty in the summer, but never flies, not unless there was a carcass. Based on how full the trash can was, I knew it would only be worse if I put it off until next week. Slipping back into the house, I rummaged through the pantry and found a half used can of insecticide. It didn't list that it would work against flies, but I didn't care. Now armed, I went back out to the patio again, and sprayed a stream of mist at the swarm. A few of the flies on the edges flew off at a quick pace, but most of them didn't seem to care. They just continued swarming around each other, until a few minutes later when they started to fall like fat, black raindrops to the ground. More of them were flying off at that point, and even though their tiny black corpses littered the concrete patio, I was eager to get the trash done.

I held my breath and darted towards the can. I squinted my eyes as a few of them flew at my face, but I pulled out the two stuffed trash bags and rushed back into the house. Closing the patio door behind me, I caught my breath. Sure, a few of them got inside, but they probably wouldn't last long. I hurried out to my car and dumped the bags into the trunk. My fingers were shaking as I turned the engine over. When I opened the trunk to pull out the bags again, I frowned at what was peeking out from one of the holes: a cardboard box with flies crawling all over the word *Chartreuse*.

THE FOLLOWING WEEK I TRIED MY BEST TO GET IN TOUCH with Mamma again, only this time it seemed like she was avoiding me. I tried her cell on Monday and Tuesday, and even sent a couple of texts on Wednesday. I knew they had been sent because they had a *Delivered* status on my phone. Part of me wanted to go by her house and make sure she was okay, but then I remembered that she had been on a date last weekend. Maybe she was enjoying Abe's company, and she wouldn't want her daughter poking her head in where it didn't belong. That or she was just getting back at me for ignoring her the week before. She knew how to hold a grudge, the same as I did.

I had a surprise on Friday afternoon. We had a line of customers almost to the exit of the store when she rang my phone. I had it on silent at the time, and I couldn't answer it of course, but she didn't even leave a voicemail. I sighed, wondering why she picked such a terrible time to call me back. That night I forgot to call her back. I wish I had.

Come Saturday morning, as I parked in front of her apartment, I frowned at the sight of her closed blinds in the front window. I thought of the note from last week and the mysterious Abe who lived upstairs; could my mother have been kidnapped? I told myself that if I went in and saw the same note from last Saturday untouched on the kitchen counter, I would know for sure. As I pulled out her apartment key and walked up to the door, I noticed strange black debris that had piled up about an inch in front of the foot of her door. Was that dog poop?

I crouched down and pulled a pen out to nudge it, dislodging a clear insect wing that had been merged through rain and sun with the bodies of other fallen insects. They were flies. The entire line of bodies outside the door were nothing but those ugly, black flies I had seen last weekend. I swallowed down the revulsion that filled me and got to my feet. At least they were dead. Perhaps Mamma had seen my note about the exterminator and gotten him to come out and spray at least. All the same, I was eager to check inside and quell the fear that was rising within me. The door squealed open. "Mamma?"

The darkness of the living room stunned me. Mamma had her blinds closed last time, but even then it wasn't this dark. The darkness that stood before me seemed to shift and waver, almost like I was looking in at a black sea sloshing from floor to ceiling. My eyes adjusted, and I realized it wasn't really darkness ahead of me, any more than that humming sound in my ears was some distant vehicle. The room was filled to the brim with flies. I gaped at them as they billowed and fell within the room, like a swarm of bats in the night sky. The armchair and couch bustled with life, the kitchen floor in the distance seemed to shimmer and sway, the very wallpaper moved as though it had a mind of its own, and the back door – dear God, the back door was open!

"Mamma!" The fear pitched my voice to a shriek. I heard a noise from within, a groan that could have been out of pain or exhaustion. The very thought, the very image, of my poor mother struggling along with her walker as these clouds of insects swarmed all around her filled me with a primal urgency. In sheer panic, I pulled off my cardigan and wrapped it around my mouth and nose. Keeping my eyes at a squint, I stepped inside, into the hurricane of flies.

They struck my face, they climbed around my ears; all over my body I felt their glistening wings and their delicate feet as they explored me, covered me, tried to overwhelm me. The ones around my ears were the worst though, trying to climb into my ear canals. I paused for a moment and pulled the sleeves of the cardigan up to cover my ears. In the distance, I heard the groan again, distinctively human this time. "Mamma, I'm coming! Just hold on." With the little black insects swarming all around me, I had to take my time with every step. I didn't want to fall, I didn't want to be at their mercy; I forced myself to take my time, even though the flies were finding ways to circumvent my makeshift mask. Already I could feel prodding around my lips and tickling at my nose. My eyes watered as they darted around my eyelids.

The cloud of flies was thicker as I reached the back hallway, and I spat on the ground as one found its way into my mouth. Mamma's bedroom door was just as covered as the wallpaper, but it didn't budge when I turned the knob. "Mamma!" I cried again, but the flies seemed to get excited by my presence. A large swath of them from the door flew up directly into my face as though trying to keep me out, but I shut my eyes against them and shoved my hip against the door. "Mamma!"

Tears streamed down my face as inch by inch the door opened, but it was too dark to see anything inside. I spotted the head of a ceramic gnome with its cracked hat and broken smile, lying on its back and rolling side to side as I shoved against the door. Mamma had pushed her writing desk in front of the bedroom door. I gave the door a final shove, feeling the wall indent on the other side as the desk slammed into it, and instinctively I reached for the light switch on the wall, fumbling around the dozens of flies that sat on top of it.

The overhead light switched on and I saw a massive, black shape strewn across Mamma's bed. It took some time for my mind to understand what it was. It took some time for me to believe it. I didn't want to. My mind still blocks off most of that terrible scene. I remember the groaning sound though, and the look of mother's mouth, frozen open in rictus, gaping to the heavens in horrible anguish as waves of flies swarmed in and out of her throat. I couldn't even see my mamma's face beneath all those flies. I did see the five pink fingernails that stuck out over the edge of the bed though. I know my mother's fingers almost as well as I do my own. When the coroner had me identify her body later, the fingertips were all that was left of her. Of course, when I saw her in the bedroom, she still had a full hand of fingers; the coroner only had three. Her body was pumped full of the stuff, the coroner said, full of that horrible Chartreuse Charade I had picked up on a whim. She had been too tempting, he said, she was just too sweet. The flies were merely following their instincts. To this day, I don't believe any of that. House flies don't do that. They simply don't do what they did to my mother.

In my nightmares, I still see the rest of her. In my dreams, I know what dress she was wearing, and I know the earrings too, but when I'm awake, my mind closes down. It's blocked away in some inaccessible vault, and to be honest, I'm terrified of ever looking inside. I think it was Abe who found me screaming as I ran down the street later. I don't remember how I made it outside. I don't remember how I found the strength to scream, let alone run.

Those pretty pink fingernails I'll remember forever, poking out beneath the black swarming pit that used to be my mother. Coral pink had always been her favorite color.

Payback

IT CAME SKULKING TO THE WINDOW LATE ONE NIGHT, A creature unlike any that I have seen. It was too large to be a dog, too hairy to be a wolf, and yet it crouched in a most human manner. It dragged its black claws down the length of the window, sending a shiver down my spine. We stared at each other for several moments while the wind outside beat against the walls of the house.

It stood on its hind legs, and with a howl that no creature ought to be able to make, it pushed that window down as though it was tissue paper. I stood and stumbled over my chair in my haste, wishing my cell phone was charged. I rushed to the hall, slammed the door behind me, and pressed an ear to the door.

Silence. Was I mad? Had I imagined the creature that had smashed its way into my study? Minutes passed before I built up the courage to open that door, wincing as it creaked on its hinges; I hadn't opened it an inch before the beast's claws came through. It tore down the door, as its eyes bored into mine. They were human eyes, familiar eyes.

"My God..." I grunted as the beast pushed me up against the wall. "Anna, is that you?"

It grimaced at me with pointed teeth, perhaps its own cruel smile. It glanced at my ring finger, barren of the wedding ring now that we were divorced, then snarled with renewed hatred. Of all my ex-wives, Anna was the last I would have expected to kill me. I tried to think of something to say to flatter her, but all I could remember was that she made delicious cakes.

"Honey..." I whispered. "Please don't, I lov—"

The lie died on my lips as her fangs dug into my throat.

The Impostor

I LIVE IN A TERRARIUM, PERFECTLY POSED AND DECORATED to look like a real, enjoyable place. The walls are painted bright colors, the smell of coffee and freshly brewed tea waft in from the breakfast room, and every young man or woman is dressed prim and proper with a big, bright smile.

Between me and the lush, green grass outside sits a sheet of plexiglass, smelling of fresh Windex and eternally dust-free. I watch the water on the pond lap at the shore and the birds taking turns at the bird feeder. Darlene makes a point to add more seed every other day. She says she does it just for me, but no one as clever as her would do that for an old, crotchety biddy like me. So, I know she only says that to try to please me. I don't let it work.

My fingers work on the rows of yarn, loop by loop, repetitive motions, over and over again until a blanket springs from my hands. I actually do like crochet, but I don't have anyone to make blankets for anymore. I've already given Darlene one for her husband and her adopted little girl. Mindlessly, my fingers finish a row and then start a new one. I crochet for nameless people now, for faces I'll never see. But I enjoy it, so I let my fingers work and keep my eyes on the birds, pretending the blankets get donated and aren't being thrown in the trash bin out back.

Darlene strides across the room, past the chess players and the readers and the television watchers, and kneels down to check the brakes on my wheelchair. She's a very tall girl, mid-twenties, with a short-cropped head of platinum hair. I watch her check on one wheel, then the next.

"If I were a younger woman, I would take you away from this place in an instant," I say.

She smiles, white teeth sparkling around thick Chapstick to fend off the cold. "If you were, I might just take you up on the offer."

I chuckle; this is a game we are familiar with. Darlene likes her lovers to be in college like she is. The stories she's told at times make me blush.

"What about you and Vivian?" she asks with a smirk. "You two are close, aren't you?"

"No, she's my partner in crime." I laugh. Other than Darlene, Vivian is my only other friend here. We're not close like Darlene jokes, but we're considered double trouble when we're together. She and I joke about anyone and everything, decency be damned. It ultimately got us into too much trouble. A dozen or so people with thin skins got insulted, so we've been separated for the past six months. Even though we only see each other in passing, we still try to share a few barbs. The caregivers hate it. "I suppose she has family to stay with this Christmas?" I ask, already guessing the answer.

Darlene nods. "Her family picked her up last week. I'm sure she's having a nice long holiday."

I smile but it's hard to pretend it's genuine. Darlene leans down and gives me an awkward hug, then pulls back and grins at my blush.

"Happy Christmas, Janice."

"Happy Christmas," I say. "It's hard to believe it's come again so quickly."

She goes behind me to brush my hair and pull it back for me. I could do it myself, but I enjoy the feeling of someone playing with my hair. It reminds me of my dear Daisy, and I have to put down my crochet work.

"What about you, are you having any family visit?" Darlene asks, her fingers taking hold of the loose strands and flattening them into place.

"You mean Tom? He's the only family who would."

She starts braiding my hair into fresh plaits. I recognize the familiar tugs and pulls. She sighs. "I don't know, I just thought he might drop in. He does that sometimes."

"He's spending Christmas with his in-laws an hour south of here. He doesn't have time to truck up here to visit his asshole aunt."

Darlene smacks the back of my head. I chuckle.

"Alright, his aunt who stares out the window all day, makes everyone uncomfortable, and makes blankets for the trash bin." My throat catches at the last words, and I hang my head. I hadn't expected to say it out loud, and I certainly hadn't expected the words to actually hurt.

Darlene crouches down in front of me in an instant.

"Hey! Don't talk like that. I hate when you say those things. Every one of these blankets goes to the homeless, not to a trash heap or whatever other nonsense you've invented today. Each one is loved and cherished, just like you are."

Tears dribble down my cheeks, and nobody is more surprised than I am. She pulls a tissue out of her pocket and hands it to me. I wipe at my face, keenly aware of the other eyes in the room—the silence that descends. The only noise is my sniffling and some ad on the television about useless drugs.

The old bat actually has a heart, they'll say. Who knew she even knew how to cry?

"You want me to get you something? I can grab a—"

"No, it's okay. I just want to be alone for a bit." My voice comes out high-pitched as though it's made of squeaky wet fingers on glass.

"You sure?" She studies me, her eyes roaming back and forth across my face.

I nod and she squeezes my shoulder before heading out of the room. With a concentrated effort, I ignore the stares behind me, the whispers, the many rumors I just now began. They can deal with it. We all have our weak moments. We all break down under the sheer weight of it all sometimes. I lasted a good five years without once cracking, holding in my feelings, even holding back my words. Five years is a damn long time to remain a polished stone.

I glance down to my crochet work and remember Daisy, and the tears start rolling again.

DARLENE GIVES ME A FEW MINUTES TO MYSELF, BUT SHE must see me crying still and sweeps in to take me for a bath. Despite my protests, it does help to distract myself from the memories that threaten to reemerge and overwhelm me.

One of the things I hate about getting older is losing my independence. My mind is just as sharp, but my body doesn't like to listen to me. I can stand for a while, but standing to shower or standing in line for too long is painful. I can bathe myself, but it's more exhausting than it should be. So, while I appreciate Darlene's help, I can't help but be a little resentful of her too—though I know she's trying to help.

We're quiet for most of the bath until she goes to scrub my back.

"Do you want to tell me about her?" Her voice wavers with uncertainty, and I know how difficult it is for her to ask me.

"Daisy?" I ask, already knowing that's who she means but hoping she doesn't.

"I know you loved her, but sometimes it seems like..."

I feel the hesitation in her voice and it makes my stomach clench. "Like what?" I spit the words out without meaning to and feel the sponge jerk at my response.

Darlene lets out a heavy breath. "Like you hate her sometimes too." I wince at her words as she continues. "I wasn't sure what happened to her. I know you don't want me telling anyone about her, and I haven't, but I would like to know." She sponges warm water onto my back, bubbles running gently over the scars that are just as clear despite the years that have passed. "I can tell she means a lot to you."

I consider lying. I've done it before, especially with the other women I dated after Daisy. It was easier to talk about a fake Daisy than the real one. But Darlene is my friend, despite my temper and despite how rude I can be. I feel like I owe her some truth. She deserves at least that much after putting up with my attitude for five years.

"I was driving," I admit, my gaze on the hot water of the tub. "She was always a more cautious driver than I was. Sometimes I wonder what would have happened if she drove that day. She always obeyed the speed limit, while I routinely flew past it despite her concerns. I guess I liked to show off to her, in my own stupid way."

The sponge slows down, and it takes Darlene a little longer to soak it again. "You crashed." It isn't a question, but a simple fact. I close my eyes. Fifty-three years be damned, my mind remembers everything perfectly.

Snow dusted the banks as I zoomed down a country road. I knew there was supposed to be ice, but I thought I could handle it. I couldn't. When we hit the patch of ice, the car spun, and I couldn't control the steering wheel. Then Daisy screamed. I felt her fingers grip onto my bicep.

I told her to hold on, as if that would do any good. I kept trying to hit the brakes as we left the pavement and skidded across snow and ice. A great big oak loomed over us, and I gasped just as we slammed into it.

I wince at the memory and open my eyes.

"She didn't make it, then." Her voice is soothing over the burning memories, pulling me back to the sponge against my back.

"No, she didn't," I say, recalling the red and blue lights flickering across the snow when I awoke. The man's voice in my ear asking if I could move sounded like my father. Then I looked to the passenger seat and saw Daisy skewered through with a thick tree branch. Her eyes were closed, but there was blood everywhere. Her white fur coat was covered with it. I didn't hear anything else the officer said that day—I merely screamed Daisy's name over and over again.

I splash hot water on my face to wash aside the salty tears.

"I'm sorry," Darlene whispers, moving on to soap up my hair.

"Me too."

IT'S LATE AFTERNOON WHEN DARLENE BRINGS ME BACK TO my window. The birds are mostly gone, but a squirrel is picking at the remains of the bird feeder. In the other room I can hear Christmas carols being sung around a keyboard. I frown, remembering Daisy's voice for the first time in ages. She had a lovely singing voice.

"You feel any better?" Darlene asks, pulling me from my memories. She places a hand on my shoulder.

"Actually, I do," I lie.

"Good. I have to go check on some of the others, but I'll be back in time for dinner, alright?"

"Thanks for listening to me ramble on," I add, trying to lighten the mood again. "Most folks would have fallen asleep out of boredom."

She grins. "Janice, you know me better than that!" She chuckles as she leaves me by myself. I smile after her, considering reaching for my crochet work again, but my eyes catch movement out by the bird feeder. I look, and my heart starts pounding in my chest. My hands shake, and I place a few fingers to my lips as I put words to what my mind can't accept.

"Daisy?"

She's standing in the same white fur coat that she had worn that day, only it isn't soaked in blood. Her eyes aren't closed; in fact, she's smiling down at the squirrel as it runs from the safety of the tree across the grass. She looks to be the same age as when she died—in fact, she still has the bandage around her finger where she'd gotten a papercut the night before. Her black hair isn't thick with blood, but instead flows freely in the breeze. She looks... happy. And before I know it, I'm on my feet, calling for her at the top of my lungs. I feel the assistant come over, say something to try to slow me down, to calm me, but all I see is Daisy in that beautiful coat, staring up at the trees, gazing out over the pond, looking at *anything* but me.

"Daisy, she's there! Can none of you see her? Are you blind?"

More arms wrap around me, but I'm suddenly Wonder Woman. I ignore them. I haven't felt so alive, so strong, so focused on anything in years.

"Janice, calm down." Darlene's voice pulls me back to Earth. I turn to her, my voice pleading like a child's.

"But she's right there. Don't you see her?"

Darlene shakes her head.

"There's nobody out there, I promise." She tugs on my arm, urging me back to the safety of my wheelchair. I turn back to the pond and see that Daisy is finally staring back at me. The most soul-crushing sense of loss and grief I have ever felt in my life fills me. I swallow down the dry patch in my throat, ready to urge the others to look and see her, but Daisy puts a finger to her lips and winks at me.

I narrow my brows in confusion. She doesn't want the others to know? Perhaps she doesn't want to explain yet. It must be a secret just between us.

I nod carefully so as not to let the others see that we're communicating.

"Janice, they're going to give you something to help."

"No, I'm alright now," I whisper, collapsing back into my wheelchair, feeling all the adrenaline leave me and all the pain of being tugged by so many people settle in. My body isn't what it used to be, but I don't care. My eyes are on Daisy outside. She smiles and nods back at me, and I can't refrain from smiling.

They might not be able to see her, but she can see me. I have to find a way to see her face to face. There is so much I want to say—so much I want to apologize for.

Darlene stays by my side for a good ten minutes before finally pulling away. She speaks to her supervisor a little way down the hall, but in my unique position, I can hear the conversation better than they probably want.

"What do you think triggered that? I've never seen Janice so agitated." Benny is a large, friendly man who is perhaps the nicest person in Lakeside Retreat. He has excellent bedside manners, but he rarely takes incidents seriously. I'm fortunate he's on staff today because I'm less likely to see any repercussions, especially if I start to act normal again.

"I think I got her worked up," Darlene said, her voice betraying more guilt than I had expected from her. I take a deep breath. I hadn't meant to upset her or to get her in trouble.

Out at the pond, Daisy is spinning the bird feeder to let more seed fall to the bottom. She glances up and meets my gaze, and I know in that moment that regardless of what happens to Darlene or anyone else, I must find a way to reach Daisy.

"Darlene?" I call, looking around obliviously as if I'm not sure where she is. In a moment, she's at my side, and this time I see the clear worry on her face.

"I hate to bother you, but I'm tired suddenly. Could I have my dinner early so I can retire to bed for the night?"

That familiar, cheerful smile spreads across her lips. "Sure, that's fine. It has been a long day for you." Through her smile I can see the worry in her eyes as she crouches down to remove the brakes on my wheelchair.

"It has been." I give a weak laugh, but it seems to satisfy her concern—for now.

I LISTEN TO A SNOWSTORM ROLL IN THAT EVENING WHILE I'm in bed staring at the ceiling. They expect showers all night, but we rarely get snow. It's almost a white Christmas. Footsteps move up and down the hall, and my heart flutters in my chest as I remember Daisy. I feel like a teenager, second-guessing myself and uncertain all over again. We met in college as awkward freshmen, neither of us knowing what we were doing. I was headstrong and she was timid. She was beautiful and I felt so lucky to date her. I can't help but think back to her standing by the bird feeder, watching the squirrel run with pure joy. I remember how the fur on her coat waved in the breeze, the easy smile on her lips, and the way her footsteps left impressions in the earth when she walked.

Had I hallucinated the entire scene? Had I been so distraught after the conversation with Darlene in the bath that I imagined Daisy outside? Nobody else saw her, but the rest of the world moved like she was there. Her footprints, the squirrel who had leapt from the tree as she approached, and the way she moved outside: it all pointed to her existence, even if nobody else could see her. Maybe she is for my eyes only—sent to remind me of our love, something I haven't been very good at honoring.

I close my eyes and grip the sheets, rubbing my fingertips over the scratchy fabric. My mind is filled with our secret trysts in dark closets, locked rooms, and the back seat of my car. It was so difficult coming up with lies and excuses for others while we both ached to see each other. It was a different world back then and we had to keep it secret, even though it hurt. If either of our families had known, we could have been sent off to psychiatric hospitals or, worse yet, conversion camps. Over time, the flame between us dimmed. The secrecy, the little white lies, and the difficulty of it all wore us down. Daisy wanted to end the secrecy and get into activism while I was happy to keep it silent. She wanted to tell her friends and her parents, consequences be damned, and I was terrified of her determination.

One of the nurses walks by my room pushing a rolling table, I open my eyes and watch the shadow go by beneath the door. It pulls me from my memories that threaten to swallow me whole. I want to see Daisy, I know that, but I'm also nervous. Neither one of us was ever perfect. There's so much I want to share with her and so much I need to know. What I need is a plan.

I purse my lips and focus my sleepy mind. Slowly the

pieces start to fall into place. I'll start at breakfast; fewer staff are around then after Christmas. I just have to make sure I don't slip up, otherwise I might not get to see Daisy again. I can't let that happen.

I go over my plan, step by step, from my excuse for why I don't want to eat with the others to the hand motions. It helps to quell my nerves.

I watch the first flakes of snow fall outside through the cracks between the curtains before finally falling asleep.

IN THE MORNING, DARLENE PARKS MY WHEELCHAIR BY THE windows and I take a deep breath. I clasp my hands together tight in my lap until my knuckles blanch. The urge to look outside is unbearable. All I have to do is look to my left to see through the window and peek out to the bird feeder. Daisy might be there. I won't allow it, though. I can't. If I do, it might tip Darlene off to my plan. Instead, I tap my foot to get the nervous energy out.

It doesn't help that Darlene is tired and taking her time prepping my morning schedule. She's humming Jingle Bells to herself and I can tell she's already started on her second cup of coffee. It's only 9 o'clock. She turns around with a warm smile.

"You ready for some breakfast?" Darlene's chipper voice wracks my nerves on most mornings, and I have to clench my hands together tighter to keep from spitting out the wrong words now. "You okay, Janice? You seem... anxious. "

I give a practiced shrug. "I guess I am." I stare warily at the door that leads to the dining room. As Darlene crouches down to unlock my wheelchair, I reach out and grab her wrist. Her skin feels warm against my clammy fingers.

She freezes, her brows knitting with concern. "Janice, what—?"

"Can I—" I hesitate so as not to look too practiced, willing my arm to tremble slightly. "I hate to ask anything of you after that mess yesterday."

She gives that incredible smile again and covers my hand with hers. "Hey, it's okay. What is it? Let me help you."

I stare down at the floor, building up the courage. "I don't know if I'm ready to face the others yet after the scene I made."

She takes a deep breath and nods, her hair falling slightly into her eyes. "I don't blame you. That was embarrassing, I'm sure." She studies me for a moment, and I freeze up, forgetting where to go next. Should I blurt it out? Should I wait longer? Fortunately, Darlene bridges the gap for me.

"Do you want to eat in your room?" It's a simple question. She's doing her best to be kind, and I feel bad for taking advantage of that, but I have to. For Daisy.

"It's too stuffy," I huff. "I was hoping I could eat outside. I wanted to enjoy the snow."

Her smile dims just a little, and together we turn to look through the large window beside us, as though we have both only just noticed it. The snow is a beautiful white blanket on the ground, sprinkled on the tree and bird feeder like tiny, shiny crystals gleaming in the light. A feeling of dread fills me; I don't see Daisy out there, but I have to try. I can't give up on her that easily.

"It's awfully cold out there. I don't know if they'll let you..." She turns back to me, her expression softening. "But I'll see what I can do, okay?" She gives my hand a little squeeze, and I smile—truly smile—maybe for the first time in years.

She gets to her feet and leaves me to my thoughts. I rub my hands together anxiously, glancing outside on occasion, but not daring to search for Daisy. If she isn't there, oh well, at least I tried. But if she is there, waiting for me...

THE COLD WIND NEARLY TAKES MY BREATH AWAY AS Darlene wheels me outside. A little metal table has been cleared of snow, and the concrete patio has been swept clean; the snow has been piled onto the edges of the little clearing they made for me. The air smells clean and fresh with a purity only snow can bring. Other than our little noises, it's silent. Nobody would be traveling on those treacherous roads so early in the day.

I pull the thick blanket around me and clutch the disposable hand warmers tight.

"There we go!" Darlene beams, locking my chair into place. "Wow, it is so cold out here. Want me to bring out a space heater for you?"

I want her to leave. I want to see if Daisy will approach if I'm alone, but Darlene lingers. "I'm fine, it really isn't that bad out here. I thought I was the old lady here."

She laughs and shakes her head. "There's a bowl of hot oatmeal for you and some hot tea too. I'll come check on you in fifteen minutes." She squeezes my shoulder, and I shoo her away.

"I'm fine. You have other residents to help, I'm sure."

"Fifteen minutes!" she insists, and I hear the door open and close behind her.

A stillness falls over the world. Snow falls from branches in the distance. An icicle drips behind me from a gutter. The world is muffled except for my anxious shuddering breaths and my fluttering heartbeat.

"Are you here?" I whisper, my breaths coming out in little puffs. I clutch the hand warmers in my lap, searching the empty snowy landscape: the tree and bird feeder, the little paths all obscured with snow, the thick trees in the distance, all looking like a postcard.

"Please don't tell me I'm crazy. I can't be crazy." The hope and joy are dying as I eat a few spoonfuls of my oatmeal and sip my tea. My hands are trembling. "If you were merely my imagination, you would've appeared by now. I'm not a patient person."

"I know you're not."

I freeze in mid-sip.

Stepping out from behind the tree, Daisy emerges at the far end of the path, her white fur coat gathering snow. Her smile is brilliant, and for a moment, I forget that I'm seventy-eight. For a moment, I think I'm in my twenties again.

I grin at her, feeling my heart pick up its pace in my chest. "What are you doing hiding back there? It's too cold for that nonsense."

"Is it?" she asks. Her brown eyes bore into mine, and I have trouble looking away. "I've missed you, Janice. Why didn't you come for me?"

The pleading in her voice tears at my heart. "I'm sorry—I didn't know." My eyes burn with tears. "Please forgive me."

"I waited for you. I thought you would come, but you never did."

Hot tears dribble down my cheeks and I wipe them away with the back of my cold hand.

"I don't understand what happened to you. Did you survive the accident? How come the others can't see you? Why are you so young still?" I plead for answers, and she finally glances away, wrapping one hand over her opposite shoulder. Daisy always did that when she was uncomfortable. I had forgotten that.

"I don't know if I can say. It all happened so fast." She puts a hand to her lips. How many times had I kissed those lips? How often had I traced my fingers over those perfect, pouty lips of hers? They had looked so pale when she was in that seat beside me, a large gash in her left cheek that carved down the side of her face—but now she's flawless. She's just as beautiful as ever, and it's slightly infuriating.

"I remember the crash," she whispers, and my whole body tenses. "I remember our fight."

My heart skips a beat. We had too many fights especially those last few days. Too many fights and not enough holding hands, stealing kisses, and sharing whispers. Instead I remember her glares, her anger, her frustration with me and my chest tightens. "Oh no, Daisy, don't make me think of that. I don't want to remember that!"

She continues on without the slightest hesitation. "You said I was acting childish, that I ought to grow up. You hurt me."

"I didn't mean to hurt you, surely you know that!"

She turns to look at me again, and my heart melts at her words. "You said you didn't want to date me anymore. You broke up with me."

I let out a shuddering breath and heave myself to my feet. The hand warmers hit the concrete of the patio, along with the blanket that Darlene had wrapped around my legs. I only distantly register them.

My feet are only clad in slippers that aren't really made for snow, but I don't give a damn. I have so much I want to say and do for my sweet Daisy, the woman I dared to call child-ish, the person I told to grow up but then stole her chance to ever age again.

I shuffle out onto the grass, and my feet sink down into the thick snow. Icy wet seeps into my slippers, soaking my feet. I cry out in shock, glancing down and wondering if I know what I'm doing. My teeth are beginning to chatter and my hands are shaking harder.

"Please come sit with me, babe. Just once more like we used to."

I look up at her again to see her sitting down at the base of the tree. The cardinals have flown in to feed at the bird feeder, and she's staring up at them, smiling. I had forgotten the joy she could possess on her face. I had forgotten what she looked like before the crash. The image of her broken body had eclipsed everything else somehow, and the knowledge of that loss for fifty years made me feel like such a fool. Nothing should have removed her from my mind. I watch her for a moment, emblazoning everything about her into my brain. I don't want to forget her again. I won't allow myself to forget her.

I shuffle my way through the snow to the tree, putting a hand on the trunk to steady myself and cursing my body for breaking down on me. My breaths come out in rough little clouds. Daisy laughs, and the sound lifts my heart in a way it hasn't been lifted for years.

Daisy pats the patch of snow on her other side. "Sit with me." A little prick of warning emerges from the back of my mind. Why does she want me to sit there and not here? Then I remember this is Daisy, who was always so quirky and random.

I shuffle to the other side of her and my feet sink further into the snow. I can only see my shins poking out. "It's so cold out here," I say. "Maybe we can sit on the patio instead."

Then she reaches up and clasps my hand in hers. Despite the snow and ice all around, despite the wind and the chill, her hand feels warm. It almost terrifies me—but then I meet her gaze. Her eyes are so innocent, so beautiful. Daisy always had gorgeous eyes, brown with flecks of green and gold in them when the light hit them right. In that moment, her eyes look magical.

"Please," she whispers, "sit with me."

Without a single protest, I sink down beside her on my rear. The snow soaks through my clothes almost instantly as though it isn't fully frozen. I whine a little in protest, but I can't look away from her. She is too beautiful.

The cold moves up my legs and spine. It's impossible to keep my teeth from chattering any longer.

"It's freezing," I hiss, but Daisy puts her hand up to my cheek and pulls me close. Her kiss is like fire, and the heat seems to suck the cold faster through my body. I pull away, scared because I can't move my feet. She moves to kiss me again.

"Please stop!" I cry, moving my head aside in a desperate attempt to escape her. "Why are you doing this, Daisy? I thought you loved me!"

"You left me to rot!" Daisy cries, but her voice had changed. It is too high-pitched, and her face is shifting right in front of me. "You dumped me. You killed me so no one else could have me, you monster!"

I realize too late that this isn't my Daisy. Despite every-thing—all our fights, all our disagreements, all the problems we had in our relationship, even when I dumped her, she would never have thought that. I was never possessive of her. I never tried to take her away from her friends. Our relation-ship was a secret, and I couldn't have done anything publicly to stop her from seeing anyone else. It was one of those facts that only she and I knew, one of those secrets we kept locked away close to our hearts. Even if we had broken up, we still cared for each other. At one point in my life, I had planned to take her secret with me to my grave. Even her family at her funeral only saw us as close friends, never lovers.

Now this creature has the gall to pretend to be her, to use my beautiful Daisy to draw me in. It doesn't try when I'm young enough to run away, but when I'm old and regulated to being stuck staring endlessly out that damn window.

"Darlene!" I cry, my voice little more than a whisper. Daisy laughs, showing pristine white teeth, and leans in again for another kiss. Only this time, I feel exhaustion threaten me as her lips touch mine. I groan before falling unconscious.

DARLENE'S VOICE DRAWS ME BACK. SHE'S SPEAKING IN LOW tones just out of hearing range, save for a few phrases that catch my attention.

"...blame myself...seeing things...seemed confused and scared."

As I focus in on her voice, I hear the beeping of a heart monitor, a man's deep response, too quiet for me to hear the words. Darlene sounds terrified, and I instantly feel terrible for her. I have been so focused on Daisy and on my own problems that I hadn't considered what would happen to her for bending the rules for me.

Finally building up the courage to open my eyes, I find myself in a hospital bed. Lakeside Retreat has a whole hallway dedicated to them, and it certainly isn't the first time I've been admitted there.

Darlene is talking to another assistant, a young man I don't recognize. When they realize I'm watching them, they both clam up, and Darlene turns on her smile for me.

"Hey Janice, how are you feeling?"

I try to answer, but my mouth is too dry. I lick my lips and try again. "Terrible. But I guess I wouldn't be here if I felt otherwise."

Darlene sits down on the edge of the bed: closed-off, distant, and hesitant. "Do you remember what happened?"

I don't answer right away. Instead I study her. As good a person as Darlene is, she hadn't believed me before, and even if she had seen a woman like Daisy hovering over me out there, I'm pretty sure she still wouldn't believe me.

"Not really," I lie. "It's all a little fuzzy. I remember eating oatmeal outside and enjoying the snow, then this." I lift my left wrist with the IV jabbed in. She gently pushes my arm back down as though she's afraid I'm going to yank the needle out.

"Please don't mess with it. If you do, please wait until I'm not here." Her smile flickers to one of painful anxiety.

It means: please don't do something stupid while I'm in here, I'm in enough trouble already. I frown. "Sorry for all of this. I'm not trying to be a pain."

"No, no, you're never a pain, Janice, ever. Please don't ever think that. I just..." Her leg jumps up and down. "I just worry is all. So, you don't remember sitting down in the half-frozen pond when it was twenty degrees outside?" She gives a little snicker at the end at the ridiculousness of it, but it could have been her nervousness leaking out.

I had forgotten the pond under the tree. The snow had covered it up completely. Despite staring at that tree for the last five years, the pond had slipped my mind. That was why Daisy had asked me to sit there. No, that wasn't my Daisy, that thing was an ugly impostor.

"I don't remember anything," I lie again. "I wish I did."

"The doctor thinks you had some kind of psychological break after our talk. Apparently, sometimes that happens when old, painful memories resurface. I'm so sorry, Janice. I didn't mean to hurt you."

I reach over and take her hand with my right hand, so she won't chastise me again. "It's not your fault. I'm the one who did it. You just wanted to help me."

"I know," she sighs. "You're right." I can tell from her stare that she doesn't believe me. Apparently, I'm not the only one lying.

She moves to go, but I hold onto her hand. "Before you leave, I have just one ridiculous question for you, if you'll bear with me." I lick my lips again as I built up the courage to ask. "You didn't see anyone out there with me, did you?"

There's a brief flash of something in her eyes—something like recognition or memory—before they cloud over again in confusion.

"You know, I thought I did, but it was just the shadow from the bird feeder. For like a split second, I thought someone was attacking you." She cracks a hesitant smile. "But that would have been crazy, right?"

"What do you mean?" I press, the beeping of the heart monitor betraying my nerves.

She freezes and stares pointedly away from me. "For just a moment there, I thought it was the woman in your pictures. She had the white coat and everything."

"Darlene, I don't own any pictures of Daisy."

She gives a little half smile. There's fear in her eyes, and I can't tell if it's aimed at me or at something else that she can't put to words.

"Sure you do." She gives another little laugh that doesn't remove the fear from her gaze. "There's a picture of her right by your bed. You said it was the last one you took of her. Don't you remember? You showed it to me the other day after I gave you a bath."

I put a hand to my mouth and realize that I'm shaking. "I don't remember that, not at all." I never kept anything around to remind me of Daisy. I barely felt confident enough to share her name with Darlene, let alone keep pictures of her. It's not because I don't want to, but I know I can't. I can't bear being reminded every day of what I did to her. I refused to let her be used against me by doctors and staff who didn't understand. I would never have kept her picture by my bed. Daisy was my love, my memory to cherish, not anyone else's.

Darlene's smile fades as I freeze, lost in a torrent of confusion and pain. She untangles her hand from mine, and I lay there stunned. "When they transferred you, I was asked to bring all your belongings in here. Daisy's picture was one of them."

She moves around the bed, avoiding the equipment surrounding it with practiced ease. She reaches down to the nightstand beside me. It's so low compared to my elevated bed that I hadn't even seen it there.

She picks up a small picture frame no larger than my hand and shows me Daisy. She's in the white coat she wore the day that she died. In fact, she's even sitting in the passenger seat that would later be her deathbed. I stare at it, trying to wrap my mind around what I'm seeing.

"Here, take a look." Darlene places it into my hand. Does she suspect her own memory regarding this too? Is that why she's so eager to share this false item with me?

I take it, my hands trembling. The frame is cold despite the room being a normal temperature. It's cheap and flimsy, the kind able to be picked up at any drug store. If this was one of my pictures of her—which it isn't—I never would have put her in such a drab frame. She deserved something more, maybe decked out in the fur she so loved.

I turn it over, intent on seeing if there is any clue to how it got into my room in the first place. The backing pops right off, as though it was only barely holding together.

"Cheap piece of trash," I mutter as I finally free the picture from within.

I freeze when I read the words scribbled out in my own ugly handwriting on the back: *Daisy, ready for a road trip.*

The date is noted below. That's when the world starts to spin.

It's the day she died.

———

SCHIZOPHRENIA, THE YOUNG DOCTOR TELLS ME AS HE smiles in the morning light. Probably a mild case brought on by a mixture of guilt and PTSD. I stare at him as he spouts words that sound like they come from a different language entirely.

"I'm sorry, Dr. Morsus, but that's not possible. I didn't take this photo. I didn't even own a camera back then, and Daisy wasn't that happy when we left for the drive that day. There was a foot of snow on the ground, and she was too cold to smile like this."

His cheerful expression falters slightly, though I can't really blame him. I'm sure he's thinking that the old gal is coming loose at the seams. Janice, the reliable misanthrope who always seemed angry about something, the woman who only loved her window and her crochet, had finally snapped over a girl who died half a century ago.

"Janice, I know it seems hard to believe, but given the stress you've been under for years and the secrets you've been keeping, it was only a matter of time before it became too heavy a burden to carry. There's nothing wrong with that or with you, but these episodes seem to be dangerous for you, even life-threatening. I think it would be wise to put you on some medication to see how it helps. The benefits might surprise you."

The young man is so very earnest, so clearly trying to help, that I almost feel bad for him. No amount of drugs will stop the thing pretending to be Daisy. I now know that she has the ability to look like Daisy, and even create false evidence to make me feel like I'm losing my mind. Worse yet, it's affecting my friends, people I care about. I keep thinking back to Darlene wondering if she saw someone attacking me outside when she came to check on me.

Whatever the impostor is, I refuse to give in to its lies. I refuse to let my friends be harmed, and I won't let it destroy me.

I'M MOVED BACK TO MY QUARTERS LATER THAT DAY AS THE doctor finalizes the new drugs I'll be taking. Of course, the false picture of me and Daisy is brought too—placed on my nightstand as though it belongs. I wait patiently for Darlene to leave, wait for the young doctor to finally depart, and then I get up from my bed. My body doesn't like one bit of it. Every muscle aches and complains, my feet worst of all. It feels like my slippers are full of pins and needles as I slip them on and stand. The cold left some prolonged numbness, I was told, and it will take a day or two for them to be fully back to normal.

I don't have a day or two.

I ease myself over to the window with renewed determination. The old armchair creaks under my weight, and I grip the arms, feeling the threads of the coarse fabric under my fingertips. I take my time, letting my breathing get back to normal and my heart rate calm down. I wait for the tingling in my feet to subside as I stare at the thick curtains, thinking of the young doctor's words. What if it is all in my head? What if the creature that attacked me was entirely made up by my guilt-ridden mind? I look over at the photo of Daisy sitting cheerfully on my nightstand and catching the surreal blue light reflected from the muted television. Daisy looks like she was caught in mid-laugh, a mockery of her true beautiful laugh that the creature mimicked the other day. The anger builds up in me as I stare at the crinkles in the corners of her eyes, her hand lifted partway to her mouth, to her lips.

That is not Daisy. That's an impostor pretending to be my Daisy. I'm not sure how the creature did it, but somehow it not only created that photo, but also made everyone believe that the photo always existed. I'm labeled crazy even though I know the truth. I'm put on medication even though I remember everything correctly.

I reach up with a shaky hand and push the curtain back. I hope there's nothing, just the trees covered in a beautiful layer of snow. Instead, there stands Daisy, staring right back at me through the window, a smirk on her lips.

My breath catches in my throat as my heart picks up speed like a jump-started locomotive. It takes all my determination and anger to keep from dropping the curtains back down. Instead I bite down the cry that comes to my lips and ask it the burning question.

"What are you?"

To my horror, the window lifts. It's only a couple of centimeters, but instantly I understand all that it implies. This thing could come inside whenever it wishes. Nothing keeps it in the snow and ice out there. Our domains aren't separate at all like I had assumed. Of course they aren't. How else would it have been able to put that photo on my nightstand?

I hold its gaze, waiting for it to make a move, but it just stares back at me calmly.

"I'm Daisy," it says.

"No, you're not. My Daisy was so much better than you."

She gives a pouty frown, amusement lingering in her eyes. "Are you so sure about that? According to the doctor, you don't know what's real and what isn't anymore. How do you know your Daisy ever really existed? Maybe I'm the real Daisy, and the one you remember is false?" She puts her fingers on the glass, and I involuntarily flinch. "Post-traumatic stress disorder. In other words, this could all be in your head."

"It's not, though. I know you're not her. I don't know what you did to Darlene to make her think that picture ever existed, but you and I both know it's not real."

The smile falls from her lips, and I think I can see the hint of the creature who attacked me. "Just because it isn't real doesn't mean they don't think it is." She walks along the side of the window, dragging her fingers across the glass so that it squeaks. Her fingertips leave streaks, as though she has a heat that's resistant to the cold.

I feel the threat of a sob rise up at her words, and despite my attempts to push it down, it still slips into my voice. "Why won't you leave me alone?"

"I like the taste of your sorrow, Janice. It's bitter and warm. You tried to hide Daisy's existence from these people, but why should she be forgotten? I want to remind you of her, of what you did to her. I want you to regret what you did to her again and again."

"Why?" I demand, outrage and fear collecting into one. "Why me? I don't deserve any of this."

"Sure you do," she hisses, her face becoming more like the face from before, beneath the tree. Her teeth grow sharp and her face stretches, becoming more inhuman each second. "You tried to forget her. You didn't want anyone to know how you felt about her. Even at her funeral, you tried to bury your feelings for her, to escape from her memory, to pretend like you were never close. There's no need for that now, yet still, you do it. Still you push her down, deep down into the dirt. You hide her away so no one can see her. Your feelings for her embarrass you."

My stomach drops at its words. It's true. I had tried to forget her. I remembered finding pictures of her at my old apartment years ago, when I moved out of town to escape Daisy's memory. I still remembered how the old plastic covering on the film peeled away in my fingertips. I almost kept them. I almost put them in a box to bring with me, but in the end, I threw them away like I wanted to discard Daisy's memory.

But this creature won't let me discard her. It won't let me forget and move on with my life. Daisy haunted my dreams for decades. She was the cold spot in bed between me and so many lovers. She was the unspoken name in the room every time someone mentioned my scars. She wouldn't leave me, and this creature knows it.

"I loved her," I whisper. "I still love her. You're twisting the facts around."

The creature shakes its head. "I'm simply sharing the truth that you've been avoiding for most of your life."

Tears burn in my eyes, and I drop the curtains down. I wipe at my cheeks. I don't want to remember Daisy anymore. I want to forget her forever. I don't want her memory to haunt me any longer.

Through the curtains, I see the window open up further on its own. I start to get up, to go back to my bed, maybe to hit the call button for Darlene, but the curtain is shoved aside. The creature's clawed fingers clutch at the windowsill. The creature pulls one leg through and it still looks like Daisy's leg, but instead of shoes, her feet are bare with black, frostbitten toes tipped with black nails. Daisy's beautiful white fur coat melts to its skin, transforming into sharp white bristles.

In my haste to get to my feet, I fall to the floor, crying out as the creature pulls itself fully through the window. Daisy's hair, longer than she ever kept it in life, puddles like foul water around my legs. A familiar cold sweeps up from my feet to my calves. I reach out to the leg of the bed frame, trying to drag myself away from it.

"Give me your sorrow." The creature's face is so distorted that it looks nothing like Daisy anymore. Its hair pooling around me turns green and brown, smelling like dead things forgotten in a murky swamp. "Give me your regret." It crawls over me on all fours, moving with unreal speed to clamber on top of me, I feel the bristles of its fur drag against my legs, drawing blood. "Give me your pain." It opens its mouth, dislocating its jaw more like a snake than a person, and within I see nothing but empty blackness awaiting me, no throat, nothing even resembling any animal I had ever seen. I shiver at the coldness that has now covered me from head to toe.

"But I love her still," I whimper as the creature leans forward. "I've always loved her more than anything."

It laughs with a hoarse animalistic voice and speaks to me without moving its mouth. "You lie to yourself even now. We both know the truth."

My grip goes limp on the bed post and I nod in mute acceptance. I may have once loved Daisy, but that changed. We grew apart, I resented her, and after she died, that resentment spoiled. Her death threw a shadow on my life that I wasn't ready to accept. I pushed away love because I couldn't forget her. I hated her in those cold, empty bedrooms. I hated her when I couldn't find her in anyone else I wanted to date. I hated her during every doctor's visit when I had to explain my scars. Sometimes I cried all night long because of her. In all honesty, I stopped loving my poor, sweet Daisy a long time ago.

The darkness envelopes me, and I allow it. A part of me believes I deserve it. Daisy haunted me my entire life, and here she was haunting me all the way up to the end. Part of me laughs at the insanity of it all as I fall away and lose myself in the darkness.

Down the long hallway, I hear the clipped echo of heels striking the linoleum floor. I try to place who they belong to, but names don't come to my mind as well as they used to.

The door to my room opens and Darlene steps in. It's the first time I've seen her in weeks, and although I can tell she did her best to be presentable for work, there are dark circles under her red, puffy eyes. She looks like she's cried too much and slept too little.

"Good morning, Janice." She gives me that perfect smile despite the pain she clearly carries. "I thought you might like some breakfast."

She lays the platter of food on the nightstand by my bed and notices that my television is still on. I've been watching game show reruns all morning.

"Oh wow," she exclaims with a forced laugh. "We have to change this. Now, where did the remote go?"

It had been on the table opposite my bed, but had been knocked onto the floor by a tired nurse the previous evening. I want to tell her, but I can't move my mouth to say a word. After giving up, Darlene huffs and climbs onto a chair to hit the power button on the television.

"There, isn't that better?"

I want to say yes, but all I can do is stare. My silence only seems to upset Darlene more. She gives another forced laugh, then sits down beside me and begins spoon feeding me oatmeal. I swallow down the mush whole like a plastic doll whose only job is to consume what is put to its lips.

"I know it seems a little crazy to keep talking with you." Darlene scoops up some oatmeal from my chin and lifts it to my lips. "But the doctors said they do see flickers of awareness in your brain scans. They're weak, but they're still there.

I haven't given up hope yet, but I don't think your nephew plans to come by anymore. Some people just aren't good at letting go, are they? They try to avoid it instead of just coming to terms with it. I think it's easier for me since I work here. Still hard, but a little easier."

She pops a straw into the apple juice and pushes the opposite end into my mouth. I slurp it up without any trouble. Darlene pulls the juice box away and gives a wicked smile as though sharing a secret. "I keep thinking back on what you told me, you know, the day of your attack. You mentioned the picture of Daisy on your nightstand wasn't real, and I swear ever since you collapsed, I haven't seen it anywhere. It's the weirdest thing!"

I try for the thousandth time to twitch a finger, to wiggle my nose, anything at all, but there's nothing. Daisy's impostor has taken everything from me except my life.

"I wanted to find that photo 'cause I could have sworn I saw your girlfriend the other day out by the bird feeder. She was sitting out in the snow in that white fur coat from your picture."

My heart thunders in my chest, and I urge anything to move, to shudder, to twitch. I don't care what. I can't let that thing take my only friend in the world.

"I know, it sounds crazy, but I saw it with my own two eyes." She places the bowl and drink back on the tray. "If she comes back, I'll try to talk to her. Maybe it's just a weird coincidence, right?"

I stare at her, begging with only my eyes. How I wish she could hear my thoughts! I want to tell her never to go near that thing, no matter what it looks like. I want to scream at her to go work somewhere else, somewhere safe, away from that stalking monster, but all I can muster is a tear that slides down my cheek. Darlene is too tired to notice.

"I'll come back in a couple of hours to change your

bedpan." She gives me that sweet, brilliant smile. "Don't you go anywhere now!"

The door swings closed behind her, and all I can hear is the humming of the heater in the vents. A tiny little sound escapes my lips, a cry that barely reflects the wail that tears through my soul.

Silently, I weep.

Also by Marlena Frank

The Stolen Series

Young adult, portal fantasy, faeries

Stolen

Broken

Chosen

The Wolves of Kanta Series

Young adult, dark fantasy, steampunk, werewolves

The She-Wolf of Kanta

The Blood of Kanta

The Hunters of Kanta

The Fury of Kanta

The Howl of Kanta

Standalones

Young adult, horror, sci-fi, dystopian

The Seeking

Short stories, horror, dark fantasy

The Impostor and Other Dark Tales

Ocean horror, weird, short story

Undertow

Weird western, werewolves, vampires, short story

Night Feeders

Join the Mailing List

The Blade Filled with Stars

A kingdom is under siege from a familiar enemy. Families and friends are pitted against each other without reason. Slaughter is imminent while the winged Queen Khafil soars overhead. Desperate and terrified, Anna works with her sister, Lilah, to summon aid from their mother's ancient spell book.

Determined to save their people, the sisters summon Death to help them, but Death is not easily swayed. Neither of the sisters are prepared for the consequences.

Want a peek behind the scenes?
Want to preview my books before they get released?

Get exclusive access to book goodies, giveaways, and cover reveals by joining my mailing list. Not only will you get notified of all my new releases, you'll get an exclusive copy of The Blade Filled with Stars.

Subscribe to the Mailing List
http://marlenafrank.com/mailinglist/

Acknowledgments

This collection would never have come together without the encouragement from an author friend of mine, Candace Robinson. She told me one day that I had written so much short fiction that I should publish them together. At the time I was already considering going down the self-publication route, and her words made a light bulb go off in my head. If she hadn't suggested that, these stories would still be languishing on my computer. So thank you, Candace!

Next, I must give thanks to Carla Lewis, a talented author and an incredible beta reader. She knew what these stories needed to stand out, and I'm forever grateful for her insight and guidance, even during tough times.

Vicki Greer has an incredible eye for detail and she was indispensable. I'm so grateful that she was willing to work with me on this book. Shivana Brhamadat blew me away with the cover art. When I saw what she made, I was speechless!

My sister, Kelley M. Frank, with her years of loving horror, added on the perfect touch with the lettering on the cover. Besides helping me with every step of the process, she is always my biggest supporter and motivator for all of my books. Thank you so much!

Thank you to my parents, John and Connie, for your unrelenting support throughout the pandemic and for inspiring me to pursue my passion. You've both stoked my imagination with your encouragement with horror and fantasy since I was a child. A big thank you to Aunt Charmaine, who encouraged me to continue writing on notebook paper when I was a kid. She is still a big cheerleader for me to this day, and I'm forever grateful.

A final thank you is due to my readers, mailing list subscribers, and Ko-Fi supporters. They allow me to continue to create new worlds and stories. Thank you all for your support and encouragement!

Author Notes

"Curse of Beauty"

Originally published May 2, 2016 by *Heroic Fantasy Quarterly* in their Q28 issue.

"La Femme en Rouge"

Originally published in *Masks*, a Mardi Gras anthology, on March 31, 2020 by Filles Vertes Publishing.

"Dead Man's Hill"

Originally published on my blog at MarlenaFrank.com and republished by *The Sirens Call* in their Issue #29 on October 28, 2016.

"Tiny Necks"

Originally published in *Not Your Average Monster Volume 2* published on February 29, 2016 by Bloodshot Books.

"A Slippery Customer"

Originally published in *Creepy Campfire Quarterly*, Issue #1 on January 20, 2016 by EMP Publishing.

About the Author

Marlena Frank is the author of young adult fantasy and horror novels, short stories, novellas, and book series. Many of her books have hit the bestseller charts, including her debut novel, Stolen. Her work has been praised by Readers' Favorite and featured in De Mode of Literature Magazine. Her stories have appeared in anthologies such as Emporium of Superstition, Catstruck!, Heroic Fantasy Quarterly, Georgia Gothic, and The Sirens Call ezine.

Although born in Tennessee, Marlena has spent most of her life in Georgia. She lives with her sister and two spoiled adopted cats. She serves as the Vice President of the Atlanta Chapter of the Horror Writers Association, is an active member of the Science Fiction and Fantasy Writers Association, and is an avid member of the Atlanta cosplay community.

She is also an INFJ, a tea drinker, and a wildlife enthusiast.

Support her on Ko-Fi: ko-fi.com/MarlenaFrank

facebook.com/MarlenaFrankAuthor
twitter.com/MarlenaFrank
instagram.com/authorlenafrank
goodreads.com/marlenafrank
bookbub.com/authors/marlena-frank
amazon.com/-/e/B006JPAQGS
pinterest.com/lenaf007